A Champion

Book Two

Champions Gate
A Small Town Romance Series

Kelly Abell

Cover: Select-O-Grafix, LLC.
Editor: Laura Garland

Acknowledgements

A series like this one doesn't come together without a great deal of assistance to the author.

I'd like to thank Kellie Hawkins of Brooksville, for helping me formulate the idea in the first place.

Unending gratitude to Patty Logan for being my beta reader through this entire series. You Rock!

Undying gratitude to the best editor in the world – Laura Garland. Without you I wouldn't be the writer I am today.

Many thanks to Diane Waldron for her help with knowledge on Arabian horses and the tours of Rosemont Farms. Any mistakes regarding working with these beautiful creatures are entirely my own.

I want to express my love and gratitude to my husband for all the hours he leaves me alone at the keyboard. I couldn't do it without you.

And to my readers. Without you, I couldn't bring you Characters of Passion, Power and Purpose. I'm forever blessed you buy and read my books.

Table of Contents

Chapter One

Constance Champion sat alone on the hardwood floor of the dance studio. She stretched her aching legs out in front of her as she glanced out the large windows overlooking the darkening streets of New York City. She'd left the lights low so she could watch the setting sun as she practiced the many dance moves the choreographer had thrown at her earlier in the day.

She couldn't remember ever being so sore. Even her teeth hurt. She'd left the ranch for this? Had she been sold a bill of goods by Stan, the recruiter for the USO? Singing she could do, but all this choreography? What had she gotten herself into?

She bent her knee, sliding one foot toward her. She removed her dance shoes then tenderly massaged one blistered foot, sighing in relief.

Inside her backpack, her phone bleated out the sound of a screaming goat. Wincing, she rose to her feet, hobbling to get it before it stopped. She rooted through the pocket and found her phone. Darbi…wanting to Facetime.

A wave of homesickness washed over her. As she sank to the floor, she forced a big smile then answered the call.

"Hey, Darbs. What's going on? Pardon my appearance, I just finished rehearsing."

Darbi's freckled face smiled hugely at her. Connie always envied the nanny's bright-red hair and her curls, so different from her own golden locks. Her friend's sea-green eyes all but sparkled. This woman had become her savior. Wanting to have a life of her own, Darbi had flown to Brooksville at Connie's urging, to be the girls' nanny so she could embark on this insane USO tour. She'd become one of her best friends.

"Hey, Connie." Darbi paused then her brother's face entered the picture, a stupid grin on his handsome face.

"Hey, sis."

She hadn't realized how much she'd missed her older brother Bishop—in spite of how he'd used her to take care of his triplets for almost all of her teenage years. Maybe taking care of those precious girls wasn't so hard after all. She missed them all more than she thought possible.

"Well, hey there." *What's going on? They look entirely too happy for their own good.*

Darbi thrust her hand at her computer's camera. "Look!"

Connie gaped. On the woman's hand sat a fat ruby engagement ring. "Wait…is that Mom's ring? What the—"

"I know," Bishop replied, still grinning. "I popped the question. I hope you're happy for us, Connie."

"Happy?" Her eyes welled with tears. "I'm thrilled! A little shocked, but thrilled. I never thought I'd see the day my big brother would fall in love again. And, I'm not going to say I told you so."

Bishop laughed. "I think you just did."

Unbelievable. Last I heard he was sending her packing because he'd found out who Darbi really was. I thought it was over between them. This is quite the change. Who'd have thought my big brother has a brain?

"We're so happy, Connie," Darbi's Irish lilt more pronounced with her emotion. "It took us a while to realize it, but now…I know it's soon, but when ya know, ya know."

She glanced up at Bishop with such an adoring expression, Connie's heart tripped.

"Darbi, I told you not to worry. Tell me how it happened."

Her new sister-in-law-to-be explained how she'd been just about to board a plane to go back to Ireland when Bishop and the triplets showed up. He and his ten-year-old daughters had proposed, holding a banner decorated by the girls. She relayed how everyone in the airport had cheered.

"You almost screwed up, didn't you, bro?" Connie frowned.

Her brother wrapped an arm around Darbi. "You know it." He kissed her, and she giggled.

"When's the wedding?" Another pang of homesickness wafted through her.

"We thought we'd wait until you come home at New Years," Bishop told her. "We don't want anything big, just family and a few friends. We want to get married here on the ranch."

Touched, Connie swiped a tear from her eye. "Oh, you guys, thanks. I was just sitting here feeling sorry for myself."

Bishop offered her a smug expression. "I told you this tour thing was a bad idea. Ready to come home?"

"Shut up," Connie told him, indignant. Her lifelong dream had been to sing, and when this opportunity presented itself, Connie, as her family referred to her, jumped at the chance. At the risk of angering Bishop, she'd signed the contract for a year before telling him and enduring his wrath. "The reason I'm feeling sorry for myself is this…" She placed her phone so the camera caught a shot of the huge blisters on her feet. She had blisters on top of blisters. The tips of her toes were bloody nubs.

"Ugh, gross. I could have gone my whole life without seeing that. What the heck?" Bishop leaned closer to the camera on his tablet. "Are those blisters?"

"They are, and I'm proud of them. All this dancing is something I'm not used to. I'm probably going overboard with practice, but I don't want to be the dork who holds back the troupe." She stared at her bedraggled reflection in the floor-to-ceiling mirrors, her slender body sheathed in black. A tight tank top stained with a ring of sweat from her neck to her navel covered her upper body while matching skintight leggings squeezed the rest of her. She'd piled her long honey-blonde hair on her head in a knot. Never heavy, and used to exercise, she had thought this gig would be so easy.

Wrong! I hurt in places I didn't even know I had. Plus I lack the rhythm of the other dancers. She sighed. *I'm never going to get this routine right. Stan will send me packing within the week.*

Then she remembered her first rehearsal singing on stage. She drew some courage from the memory of it, and she smiled brightly at her current exhausted self. This tour meant everything to her, and she didn't want to give it up, despite the hard work and sore body parts. "The singing I've got down cold, but the dance steps? Some days I feel like I've got two left feet."

"Aw, darlin'," Darbi sympathized. "You'll get the hang of it. You're so talented."

"Want me to call Sven to look for that loop hole?" Bishop wondered.

"Shut up. Speaking of Sven, how is he?" The family attorney had piqued her interest just before she left for New York. She struggled to keep too much interest from creeping into her expression.

Bishop raised his eyebrows. "He's fine, why?"

"He said he'd call after I got to New York, and I haven't heard from him. Has he got some big case working or something?"

"I don't think so. He was just out at the far—"

Darbi interrupted. "I'm sure he hasn't called ya because he's certain you're too busy to chat. That's what I'm guessin'."

Connie didn't miss Bishop's look of confusion, but she ignored it. "I'm sure you're right . Well, I've got a bit more rehearsing to do. Congratulations you two. I'm so happy for you. Can't wait for the wedding."

"When are you off on tour?"

"We leave in a few weeks. To Kuwait and Iraq to start for the holidays, then to Japan and England. Not sure where we go after New Year's. I can't keep up, but I'm really excited. There's a rumor some hotshot country singer is supposed to be joining the tour soon. I can't wait to find out who it is."

"I bet," Bishop scoffed.

Darbi elbowed him. "You keep us posted. Are ya happy, Connie?"

Connie summoned her brightest smile. "Ecstatic. It's really hard work, but I know, once I start performing in front of a live audience, it's going to be everything I ever dreamed it would be. Performing for our troops who work so hard to protect us gives it special meaning. Again, I'm so happy for you guys. Keep me apprised with the wedding plans, Darbi."

"I'll be talkin' to ya soon. We love ya...sis."

Connie smiled. "Love you all, too. Bye."

She punched the button to terminate the call. *So my big brother is getting married. I knew he'd fall for Darbi. She's got just the pluck to bring him around.*

A vision of Sven popped into her mind. The tall, well-dressed, well-groomed, blond Nordic god of a man had served as her family's attorney for many years. They'd all gone to school together and then worked as a team to help Bishop grow the farm from one pair of Arabians to thousands of champions he'd sold worldwide over time. Champions Gate had the strongest reputation in the horse breeding industry for producing winners. Connie remained proud of their success, and Sven had been with them every step of the way. She'd never really thought about him romantically until just before she left for this USO tour. They'd been alone one night after a family dinner where he'd supported her when Bishop had thought she'd lost her mind. He'd made a statement that night she couldn't get out of her head.

She'd accused him of flirting with Darbi, and he'd laughed. "Don't worry. There's only ever been one woman for me."

He'd stared deep into her eyes then, but said no more. One look had tripped her heart and sent her mind whirling about what a possible relationship with him might be like. She'd thought about dating him a time or two, but never took it seriously. Now that he'd expressed an interest…

"Good grief, Constance Bishop. You've lost your mind," she told her reflection. "One soul gaze doesn't mean the man wants to put a ring on it. Get yourself together."

She winced as she rose. She replaced her phone in the front pocket of her backpack and gathered the rest of her things.

The studio door banged open. Connie jumped, emitting a squeak of surprise.

"I thought I'd find you here," Wrynn, the tour's coordinator announced. "You're going to kill yourself before we ever get to Kuwait."

Connie huffed out a breath. "You scared the crap out of me. Ever thought about a subtler entrance." She continued putting her stuff in her backpack.

"I went to find you for dinner, and you were MIA." Wrynn—short for Kathryn—Rawlings, had become Connie's closest friend on the tour. The rest of the troupe had done several tours, and Wrynn had taken Connie under her wing to help her acclimate to the crazy work schedule.

Sitting on the bench, Connie removed her other dance shoe, sighing in relief.

"Oh, my God, woman. Look at your feet."

"I know. I've over done it."

"I'll say. Put on those soft boots, and we'll pick up a pizza on the way back to the dorm. I've got some salve which will fix you right up."

"That sounds wonderful." Connie slipped on a soft pair of socks followed by her boots.

Wrynn grabbed her backpack and helped her to her feet. "I've got great news," she sang.

Forgetting about her feet for a second, Connie wondered if Wrynn's news had anything to do with the country star joining them on tour. "Spill it."

Her friend paused a second, grinning.

"What? What is it?"

"Trevor Thornton is joining our tour!"

Connie sucked in a breath, her heart skipping several beats. Trevor Thornton was the hottest new country star on the circuit. His songs had broken billboard sales records for the last year. She'd become an instant fan. It didn't hurt he was easy on the eyes either.

"You're kidding!"

"I most certainly am not."

The women joined hands and hopped around in a circle, squealing.

"I love him," Connie screeched. "I can't believe I get to meet him in person."

Wrynn waggled her brows. "And you get to perform with him."

Connie felt her mouth drop open.

Her friend laughed. "You look like a fish."

"Oh wow," She performed a boogie dance. "Oh wow. I get to perform with Trevor Thornton. Oh, ow." Connie stopped dancing and limped on her sore feet.

Wrynn laughed. "You sure do. Now, let's get a pizza and go home."

Connie slipped an arm through the crook of her friend's elbow. "Agreed."

Thoughts of Sven and homesickness slipped from her mind.

Chapter Two

Sven leaned against the fence while Quinton Gates exercised the Arabian mare around the paddock on this sunny November afternoon. She was a beauty, her coat the color of mahogany and her mane and tail as black as a moonless night.

Quinton, one of his best friends, and Bishop Gates' partner, trained horses for Champions Gate. While Bishop did all the buying and selling, Quinton trained the champion racers. And Sven took care of their legal matters. He'd been their lawyer since Bishop and his first wife, Laura, started the ranch over fifteen years ago.

Sven grew up a farm boy in Brooksville, and that was where he wanted to hang his shingle when he'd graduated law school. Not wealthy by any means, but comfortable from an inheritance his farmer father left in a trust, he had the luxury to choose what he wanted to do.

He dabbled in a bit of vegetable gardening, and raised a few animals, time permitting. The horse breeders of Brooksville and the surrounding area kept him very busy.

Sven, Bishop, and Quinton had all been school chums, along with Bishop's sister, Connie, who'd tagged along, struggling to keep up with the boys. They'd played and gone on wild—and sometimes daring—adventures as kids, but they had each other's backs, and had stuck together into adulthood.

Sven adjusted his position, propping his booted foot onto the lower rail of the paddock while Quinton put the beautiful mare through her paces. Thoughts of Connie drifted through Sven's head, and he smiled. She was six years younger, but he'd loved her since she was in first grade. Why he'd never had the courage to pursue her with fervor eluded him. Oh, he'd asked for the occasional date only to be lovingly rebuffed and thought of as a brother. It had hurt at the time, but he hadn't pushed. The fact her brother was twice his size had been a bit of a deterrent as well.

I guess I always thought I wasn't good enough for her. She deserved better than a local farm boy. And now, she's off to fulfill her dream of being a singer. She won't want to settle for the likes of me; not when she can have the world at her feet.

Self-doubt wasn't his nature, but she befuddled him. He'd had a chance to stop her from going. All he'd had to do was find a flaw in her contract with the USO—and there were a few—but this opportunity meant to so much her, he couldn't bring himself to point them out. Bishop was a large enough obstacle to overcome. She'd raised his triplets from the time she was sixteen, and, as much as Sven loved Bishop like a brother, Connie had been taken advantage of. She deserved her shot. She had the voice of an angel, and the world should hear it.

Boot steps crunched on the gravel drive behind him. He glanced at his watch and sighed. *Bishop…right on time.* He tucked away thoughts of his best friend's sister, and turned. "Good afternoon."

Bishop joined him at the fence. He nodded in the direction of Quinton training the filly. "She's a beaut, isn't she?"

"She is. Got the makings of a real winner," Sven agreed.

"Connie always knows how to pick them. She'd called this one in the womb. It's like she has a sixth sense or something."

Sven laughed. "Or something." He leaned his back against the fence, facing the beautiful ranch home his friend had built for his first wife Laura. Bishop now lived there with his fiancé, Darbi, the former nanny. He grinned.

"How's your bride-to-be?"

"Feisty as ever. Her Irish blood was a boilin' this morning," Bishop attempted to imitate Darbi's Irish accent.

Sven laughed. "What did you do now?"

"Well, let's just say I didn't respect her femaleness in the bathroom."

"Left the toilet seat up again?"

Bishop chuckled. "How did you know?"

"Just a guess. Doesn't take much to get her Irish up. Have you set a date for the wedding?"

"Yeah. We're going to do it at the ranch around New Year's when Connie gets a break from the tour." Bishop pushed away from the paddock. He raised a hand in a wave at his partner. Quinton waved back. "You ready to get started? I've got a few purchase contracts for your review. They're local buyers, so it shouldn't take too long."

The two men headed for the barn where Bishop had an office in the rear of the building. Sven reached out to stroke the gorgeous horses as he passed.

"Have you heard from Connie? Does she know about you and Darbi yet?"

"We talked to her last night as a matter of fact. Smug as ever about being right about me and Darbi."

Sven laughed. "It appears that sixth sense applies to her brother as well."

"Yeah. It chaps my butt how she's always right."

"How's she doing?" Sven's gut tightened a little at asking the question. He hoped how much he cared for Connie and missed her didn't show on his face.

"She's loving life. Her feet are covered with blisters and every muscle in her body hurts from all the rehearsing, but she seems content. I still have my doubts about all this, but she deserved her chance, I guess."

"Wow, is this the same man who had me prowling through her contract looking for loopholes?" Sven chuckled.

"Darbi can be quite convincing. Oh, and thanks for throwing me under the bus on that one." Bishop strode into his office and sat behind his desk. "You were no help at all."

Sven sighed as he so often did around his friend. "She deserved her shot, bro. Her voice is too much of a gift to keep locked away in Brooksville United Methodist Church. She'll be fine."

"I guess." Bishop shuffled through some papers on his desk. He handed two folders to Sven who accepted them. On opening the first, he perused the contents of the contract. He debated on telling his friend about his upcoming plans then decided to ease into it.

"Listen, I'm going to New York in a few days. Want me to look in on Connie?"

Bishop's head lifted, and his eyebrows rose in surprise? "New York? Why?"

"Lawyer's conference," Sven lied. He really didn't have a reason to go to New York other than the pretty blonde sister of the man across the desk, but he wasn't ready to admit it yet.

"You never mentioned it before now. Don't you have to plan for stuff like that in advance?"

Sven cleared his throat. "They had a speaker drop out at the last minute and wanted me to fill in. It's a favor for a law school buddy." He shifted in the chair. "Anyway, I could look Connie up and take her to dinner. See how she's really getting along."

Bishop's eyes narrowed. "You know, it's funny but she asked about you. Wondered why she hadn't heard from you."

Sven sat back in surprise. "She did?" He fought to keep the eagerness out of his voice. Since their parting a month or so ago, he'd thought of nothing but Connie and how much he missed her. He'd dropped a hint at how much she meant to him, but never dreamed she'd picked up on it. He just figured he'd been too late…but maybe not. His heart picked up pace.

Bishop cocked his head as he studied his friend. "What's going on with you two?"

Sven feigned surprise at his normally not-so perceptive friend. "What are you talking about? She's my friend and your sister. I'm going to be in New York on business, so I'm offering to look in on her. Where's the crime?"

"No, not a crime. I just find it strange you both ask about each other all of a sudden."

"Don't be ridiculous. Do you want me to look in on her or not?"

"Sure, sure. I'll have Darbi text you her address."

Sven turned his attention back to the documents. "Thanks." He stretched out his long legs, trying to offer a nonchalant appearance to Bishop. Why it concerned him what his friend thought about his feelings for his sister, he couldn't really say. He wasn't embarrassed…maybe shy was a better word, although he'd never described himself that way. A star basketball player in high school, he'd never lacked for female attention and didn't shy away from it, but Connie had been, and still was, different. She mattered.

Bishop still watched him, but he remained focused on the contracts. "The price seems a little low on this one. Isn't Helen of Troy worth more?"

"She is, but this guy did me a solid when I needed help getting War Zone into a race, so I thought I'd cut him a break." Bishop rose and went to the mini fridge at the back of his office. "Want a beer or soda or something?"

Sven was relieved to have the subject of Connie off the table. "Yeah, I'll take a beer."

Bishop returned to the desk, a brown bottle in each hand. He twisted off the tops and tossed them in the trash can then set one in front of Sven.

"Thanks," Sven muttered as he continued to read over the agreements.

A voice rang out through the barn. "Hellooooo." Darbi came breezing into the office, her flaming curls bouncing around her pretty face.

"Oh good, you're still here, Sven. Please join us for supper. I'm fixin' the stew you like so much. And fresh bread. The girls would love to see ya."

Sven truly did love Darbi's Irish stew. Plus, he might be able to quiz her about Connie, a little more comfortably than Bishop.

He smiled at her, knowing she was the best thing to happen to Bishop in a long time.

"Thanks, Darbi. I believe I'll take you up on your offer. I skipped lunch today, and I'm starving."

She flounced around the desk, removed Bishop's Stetson, and placed a loud smacking kiss on his head. "Great. Dinner's in two hours. I trust you two can stay out of trouble till then?"

Sven loved her Irish accent. It was as delightful as she was. "We shall do our best."

"Oh, before I forget," Bishop held up a finger. "Give Sven Connie's address in New York. Apparently, he's going for a conference and wants to look in on her."

Darbi plopped on the arm of Bishop's desk chair. "Really now?"

Sven's cheeks flushed. He focused on the contracts. "It's no big deal. I just offered to check on her if you all want me to."

Darbi slapped her thighs. "I think that'd be delightful. I'm sure she'd love to see ya. I'll go get my phone and send you the address. Dinner at six. See you two then."

She hopped off the chair, gave Bishop another swift kiss, and trotted out of the office. She cooed to several of the horses on her way out of the barn.

"You are one lucky man, Bishop Champion," he remarked.

Bishop gazed after his petite Irish fiancée. "I am. I hate to admit it, but Connie knew what she was doing when she hired Darbi."

A few minutes later, Sven's phone buzzed. He pulled it from his pocket. Darbi had texted Connie's address followed by a smiley face, then the statement, "Way to go, stud."

He laughed aloud.

"What?" Bishop inquired.

"Oh nothing. Just your future wife being funny."

Kelly Abell

Chapter Three

At half-past midnight, Logan Richards wandered the empty halls of the dormitory building. His experience in the military had him used to late night patrols, but it wasn't his issue this time. He'd dreamed of Iraq again. He swiped at a trickle of sweat on his temple then wiped his hand on his jogging pants. Would these nightmares ever end? Discouraged, he sighed.

How can one incident ruin my entire military career? I'm a big boy, I should be able to control all this fear, not to mention the rage.

He reached the end of the corridor and opened the door. He'd accepted the job on the USO security force on the recommendation of a friend. He prayed his bouts with PTSD wouldn't ruin his chances at making something of himself. His counselor believed he could handle it. He'd thought so, too, but right now, he wasn't so sure. He shoved open the door and plopped on the bottom step of the stairway, sucking in deep breaths. The bang of a door closing on another floor startled him, drawing him into another flashback.

No. No. No. He grabbed the edges of the concrete step, trying to ground himself in the present. It didn't work.

The Humvee rolled past another burned out car sitting on the side of the road. He choked on the dust billowing through the window. He'd boil if he closed the window so he endured the foul air.

His uniform, slick with sweat, clung to him in the most uncomfortable places. Perspiration rolled from his scalp beneath his helmet, down the sides of his face, and into his shirt collar. Five more days and he'd be out of this infernal Iraqi desert and home on leave for two long weeks. Couldn't happen soon enough. But first, he and his team needed to deliver supplies to a strategic base established just outside of Kuwait.

Roland, the driver, focused intently on the road ahead, following the vehicle in front of them.

Logan kept his eyes glued to the shoulders of the road, flicking his gaze from one side to the other, scouring the ground for signs of buried IEDs. There, what was that?

He grabbed the radio, depressed the button…nothing happened. He looked over his shoulder to check for the power light on his com unit. Not on. Oh God. Did I not complete the charge to the radio last night? *Cardinal rule number one—always make sure your radio is fully charged.*

"Stop!"

Roland hit the brakes. Logan laid on the horn, giving three rapid blasts, the signal to stop immediately. The vehicle in front rolled on. Logan repeated the signal.

"Why isn't he stopping?" Roland stared at Logan with eyes wide. "Use your radio."

"It's dead."

"What? No—

The explosion rocked the Humvee. Fiery bits of steel, rubber, and body parts rained down on what was left of the hood of the Humvee. A shard of metal—could have been the edge of the windshield—had speared the side of Roland's head, killing him instantly. The look of sheer disbelief still frozen on what was left of his burning face.

Logan shoved at the door, trying to wrench it open before the flames reached him. Fortunately, the two guys in the back were already out and running toward the first vehicle, or what was left of it.

One of them returned, seeing nothing could be done for their comrades, and tugged at the door of the Humvee. He dragged Logan to safety just as the front end of the SUV began to flame in earnest.

"What the hell, Richards? Why didn't you use your radio?"

Logan rocked on the step, holding his head in his hands. The faces of the soldiers, his buddies, he'd seen blown to bits before his very eyes, flashed through his mind. Struggling to control his panic, he sucked in lungs full of oxygen. He tried to remember what the counselor had told him. *Focus on your grounding trigger, remember where you are. Open your eyes, look around.*

He opened his eyes. The stairwell came into focus. He tightened his grip on the edge of the stair, focusing on how the bumpy concrete rubbed against his sweaty palms. Heart hammering, he continued to rock back and forth, glancing around the stairwell, slowly bringing himself back to the present. He was better at working through the triggers, keeping most of them at bay during the day, but at night...

He rose shakily and leaned against the cold concrete wall. This security position was the best he could probably hope for in the working world of civilians. Logan was grateful for it. Here he only had one thing to focus on...keeping the performers safe. Which shouldn't be hard, really. They were only performing at secure venues like the military bases. The most diligent he would need to be would be transporting them from base to base. He had four other teammates, so should be easy peasy, right?

Tonight, he wasn't so sure. This flashback rattled him. He'd woken himself up screaming and, now, another flashback. He was grateful to be alone, his roommate on watch. A walk would do him good. He glanced up. Damn door slamming.

The melody drifted up the stairs. Solid soothing tones...a hymn...one his grandmother used to hum all the time..."Amazing Grace."

He stood stock still, his ears straining to catch each note. The voice of an angel was what Logan convinced himself he listened to. Clear, concise, rich, and melodious, the voice drifted up the stairs surrounding him like a warm blanket. His tense muscles relaxed a little, the remnants of the dream fading some. He closed his eyes as he listened to the words...

The notes of a piano followed her voice. He had to know where it came from. Dance studios and rehearsal halls were located in the dorm building, but he had no idea what floor. He rushed down the stairs and opened the door on each floor as he went. When he reached the second floor, the voice reached him, strong and clear again. Sounded like a young woman. He knew she'd have to be with the USO tour, but never had such a voice moved him so. She belonged on Broadway.

Never had he been affected by music the way he had tonight. His counselor told him to find music which soothed him, but he hadn't been able to relax to anything he'd tried. Until now. The song came through clearer, and her tone reached to his very soul. It called to the brutal parts within him, unwinding them as he listened.

Logan stopped at the door labeled *Rehearsal Hall 1*. He didn't want to scare her; after all, it was after midnight, but he had to hear more. He inched open the door. She was on the small stage, seated at the piano. There were about seven rows of seats, and he slipped in through the shadows, planting himself on the very back row.

She played and hummed, the tone remaining clear and soothing. Her petite body swayed to the rhythm of the music; her eyes closed. Her golden hair, in a loose pony tail, swung from side to side as she ran her fingers lovingly over the keys. She wore what looked like a pair of black dancer leggings and a long gray sweatshirt reaching past her thighs. He couldn't see her face clearly, but with those pipes, it didn't matter to him what she looked like. He bet her features would be gorgeous though.

Logan relaxed in the seat and stretched out his legs. A deep sigh escaped his lips, and, for the first time in hours, he totally relaxed. She began the second verse of the song, and he allowed all the nightmarish scenes of his dream to float away.

As he drifted away to the sound of an angel's voice, he slept for the first time in days.

The door's distinctive creak drew Connie's focus just as a shadowy figure slipped into the rehearsal hall. She kept playing while the person took a seat on the back row. Was it a man or woman? She couldn't tell from where she perched at the piano, but fear never entered her mind. The building was secure, and she was safe.

She continued to play and sing her favorite hymn. When she grew lonely or sad, she'd always sing "Amazing Grace."

It settled her somehow. Allowed her to focus on the tasks at hand.

Wrynn's salve had soothed her brutalized feet, but she still hadn't been able to sleep. The news of Trevor Thornton joining the tour had her heart pounding.

What if he likes the way I sound? Maybe he could recommend an agent or someone I could talk to in Nashville. Wouldn't that be so awesome?

Her thoughts drifted to her dream of becoming a country star. She pictured the Grand Ole Opry stage, gazing into the bright lights and the faces of thousands of screaming fans. She wanted to travel and see the world. Make people happy with the sound of her voice. She'd always loved the rush she got from seeing people watch her sing. Their smiles, eyes sparkling from the joy of what her singing did for them. God had granted her this gift, and she was so thrilled to finally have a chance to use it in front of people who mattered.

Connie, you should be ashamed, she chastised herself. *People at church matter. They've been blessed by your singing for years. Don't get saucy.*

She ran her fingers over the keys and a melodious string of notes. Her volume rose as she sang the last verse.

She sang the chorus one more time, and when she ended, her voice echoed through the hall. She expected the person in the back to say something, or get up and leave, but they just sat there. *Is that…snoring?. Yep, definitely snoring.*

Rising from the piano bench, she lightly descended the stairs by the stage. She tiptoed up the aisle. By the light of one of the exit signs, she could barely make out the face of a young man. He had dark hair, cut short around his ears, but full and wavy on top. His facial features were sharp and distinctive, high cheek bones and pointed nose. Very handsome in her opinion. His dark looks contrasted with the Nordic features of Sven.

Huh… Funny he should pop into my head just now. This guy could give Sven a run for his money though. He really is cute. I wonder who he is?

She took another step toward him, about to lightly touch his shoulder when he jerked awake, his entire body alert.

"What the—"

Connie took a step back, holding up her hands palms out. "Whoa there." She spoke to him much like she would to a skittish horse. "I didn't mean to startle you."

His wide eyes focused on her. She noticed they were a nice coffee-brown. He immediately relaxed. "I'm sorry. I came in to listen to you sing. I guess I fell asleep."

She smiled. "I'm not sure if that's a good thing or a bad thing."

His cheeks darkened a little. "Oh, trust me, it's a good thing. I have trouble sleeping, which is why I was roaming around." He stood and held out a hand. "I'm Logan Richards, by the way. I'm part of the security team for the tour."

She grasped his hand, and he gave her a firm handshake. Her gaze followed his strong forearm, rippling bicep, beefy shoulder, then landed on those soft-brown eyes again. Not exactly sure what she saw there…he seemed nice, definitely clicked a ten on the hot-o-meter, but his gaze held a haunted appearance.

"I'm Connie Champion. I'm one of the performers." She waved at the piano. "I sing." Then waved at her sock covered feet. "And dance, but right now, my feet hurt. I'm not used to all this rehearsing."

Logan cleared his throat. "I hope I didn't frighten you, being in here like this."

Touched he'd say so, she replied, "No. I'm used to people popping in on me, and I know I'm safe here."

"Good. I'm glad." He shifted on his feet, cleared his throat again. "Um…you have a beautiful voice. My grandmother used to sing that hymn all the time. You conjured up some nice memories for me."

"How nice of you to say. I always find it comforting when I'm a little wound up." She glanced at the clock on the wall. "I guess I better get to bed though. We start again early."

"I can walk you to your room if you'd like." He stepped into the aisle and opened the door for her.

"Thanks, but it's just up one floor. I'm good."

He pressed the elevator button for her. "It's nice to meet you, Connie. I can't wait to hear you sing some more."

The elevator door slid open, and she stepped inside. "Nice to meet you, too, Logan. I'm sure I'll see you around. Night."

The door slid shut, blocking his smiling face. She leaned against the back of the elevator and blew out a breath. "Whew. This might turn into an interesting tour indeed."

Chapter Four

Sven hailed a cab at the airport and gave the driver the address of Connie's building. His flight, delayed by a mechanical issue, had arrived a few hours later than planned. He hoped she hadn't already eaten dinner. He really wanted to surprise her and try to spend a little quality time with her. He hadn't been able to stop thinking about her since she left. Their last meeting left him feeling empty and morose. He needed to see her sunny face and tell her how he felt about her. At least she'd know. He didn't really expect anything to come from it, but he wanted her to know he had feelings for her.

You pick a fine time to tell her, you idiot, he chastised himself. Why he never mentioned his feelings eluded him. He guessed he never felt good enough for her. She was always held in such high esteem by everyone in town. Her voice held all the church goers mesmerized every Sunday. He'd been brought up Catholic, but it didn't stop him from popping in from time to time at the Methodist church to hear her sing.

The cab pulled up to the curb of a large brownstone building at the edge of the neighborhood of Chelsie.

"Here we are, buddy. That'll be fifty bucks."

Sven handed him the money. "Thanks for the ride."

"Sure thing. Here's my card if you're staying a few days in the city. I can ride you around if you needs to. Dese Uber people drive me nuts."

Sven smiled and tucked the card in his suit coat pocket. "Thanks, I'll keep it in mind. You take care."

The driver touched his cap. Sven grabbed his overnight bag from the back seat, and the cabbie drove away. He glanced up at the building then at his watch. Just a little after 6:00. He pulled out his cell phone and called Connie.

"Sven? Is that really you? I thought you'd forgotten all about me."

"Hey, Connie. Are you busy?"

"No, we just finished rehearsal, and I'm thinking about dinner. What are you doing?"

He grinned. "How about I take you to dinner?"

Stunned silence…then, "What? How are you going to do…?" The sound of her moving around the room filtered across the line, fabric rustling, then she screeched into the phone so loudly a passerby glared at him. He shrugged. "I guess she's happy I'm here."

The man walking by shook his head.

Sven glanced up at the building and on the third floor he spotted a woman in a window dancing up and down, her mouth open. Yep, it was Connie all right.

"You're here! You're really here! Hold on, I'll be right down."

He clicked off the call and waited on the front steps. Feet pounded on the stairs, and, within minutes, the front door swung open and she charged into his arms, wrapping her legs around his waist. He dropped his bag and caught her, while he steadied himself by grabbing the railing with his free hand. "Oomph," he grunted.

She planted kisses all over his face. "I'm so glad to see you."

He laughed. "Apparently." He held her against him as her legs slid down his body. "Did you miss me?"

"You, Bishop, Darbi, the triplets…everybody. I've been so homesick, and when Bishop called yesterday and told me he and Darbi were getting married, it made being homesick even worse."

He glanced down at her, brushing a strand of golden hair behind her ear. "Aren't you happy here? Bishop said you loved it."

"Oh, I do love it. I do. But I miss you all something terrible. I didn't think it would be this bad, but I've never really been away from home for any length of time before, so I guess it took me by surprise." She squeezed him against her. "Anyway, I'm so glad to see you. What brings you to New York?"

He stepped away from her. "I'm here for a conference. They needed a last minute speaker," he deftly repeated the same story he'd told Bishop. "So, how about dinner? I'm starving."

She nodded, her hazel eyes sparkling more green than brown. "Yes." Then her mouth formed a small O. She glanced down at her sweatshirt and leggings. "Oh, but I'm not fit to go anywhere right now. Can you wait for me to shower and change? You can wait in my room or the lobby of the building if you want to."

"The lobby is fine. I don't want to break any rules."

She rolled her eyes. "You're such a prude. Come on."

She grabbed his hand and led him in through the front door. He stepped across the threshold into a nicely decorated foyer. He nodded at a man seated at a large mahogany reception desk, to his right. He then entered a nice sitting room with a large fireplace where a cheery fire crackled, and took a seat in one of the twin deep-burgundy wingback chairs. He glanced at the sofa which finished off the sitting area and winced at the paisley covering with tones of tan and burgundy. Why did people think such upholstery patterns were a good idea? It made him dizzy just looking at it. At least the square glass-and-mahogany coffee table tying the arrangement together seemed classy. As were the matching floor-to-ceiling bookshelves.

"Nice digs," he commented.

"I know, right? The dorm rooms are just as elegant, and the rent is really reasonable. The USO worked out some deal with the building's owner." She waved at the man at the desk. "This is Manfred, one of the security detail. We call him Manny. Manny, this is my friend Sven from back home."

A beefy man with biceps the size of tree trunks rose and offered his hand. *This dude's a giant. He's got the paws of a grizzly. I bet he benches three hundred without even breaking a sweat..*

"Sven Christenson." He shook the man's hand.

"Manny Ortiz. Good to meet ya."

"Manny, Sven is going to wait for me down here while I get ready. Okay?"

"Sure. I'll try to keep him entertained."

"Thanks." Connie stood on tiptoe to kiss Sven's cheek. "Be back in a jiff." She dashed to the elevator, hopping from foot to foot while she waited impatiently. A door for the elevator on the right slid open. She jumped on then stuck her head out the doorway. "I won't be long." Then she popped back in. He could hear screeching again as the elevator climbed to the third floor.

Manny gestured to one of the wingback chairs. "You her boyfriend or something?"

Sven chuckled. Was he? He hoped he'd be able to say so soon. Not wanting to jinx his chances, he replied, "Just a friend from home. I think she's been a little homesick."

Manny nodded sagely then answered with his thick New York accent, "Yeah. The first timers get that way sometimes."

"Have you done this a lot? Worked with the USO?"

The big man nodded, running a hand through his thick black hair. "It's a great gig. I retired from the Corps and a friend of mine hooked me up. Been with the USO for about ten years now. It's a great job. Doesn't demand too much attention, especially when we're stateside. Even abroad it don't get too dangerous being we stick to the bases and stuff."

"Good to hear. Her family is a little concerned about her, I think."

"And what about you? You concerned?"

Sven caught his meaning. "Yeah. I'm a little concerned. I miss her, too."

The two men settled across from each other next to the fire. Sven appreciated the warmth, not used to the cold weather of the North. He held his palms out, absorbing the heat.

"Where you from? Florida? Like Connie?"

Sven nodded. "My blood's a bit thin, I'm afraid. Not used to these chilly winds."

Manny chuffed out a laugh. "Huh, you ain't seen nothin' yet. Wait till those Nor'easters start blowin' in. Freeze your you-know-whats off."

Sven chuckled. He liked Manny. It comforted him to know someone like him looked after Connie and the rest of the troupe. Part of his mission, if he admitted it to himself, was to scope out the situation. How much security the USO provided, how comfortable would Connie be, how well she seemed to be treated. First impression? Not bad at all. He glanced around the room again.

"Not too shabby."

Manny nodded. "Yeah. It's great. The man who owns the building is a vet with money. He likes to donate the space for cheap rent for the performers. Good guy, really."

"Sounds like it. A nice tax write off as well."

"You an accountant?"

Sven smiled. "Attorney."

"Ah. Shoulda guessed."

The elevator pinged, and Connie bounced out. Her blonde hair flowed out behind her as she rushed into the lobby. She wore a short black dress with matching flats. Sven's heart bumped. She'd grown even prettier in the last few weeks. Her eyes sparkled green-gold, highlighted by faint touches of makeup. He'd always liked that about her. She had such natural beauty, not needing to enhance it with a bunch of gaudy products. She held a heavy pea coat over her arm and a black knit stocking cap in her hand.

"I'm ready." She glanced at him from head to toe. "Are you going to be warm enough?" She waved at his lightweight suit.

"I have a jacket in my bag."

"Well, pull it out. It's cold up here."

Manny laughed. "Weenies." He reached for Sven's bag after he'd removed his jacket. "I'll put this behind the desk for ya. I'm on till midnight. You can pick it up when you bring her back."

Who says I'm bringing her back? The thought popped into his head before he could stop it. Of course, he'd bring her back, but spending the entire night out on the town with her was very tempting.

"Where ya stayin'?"

"I've got a reservation at the Double Tree in Times Square."

"Good choice." Manny stowed his bag behind the lobby desk. "If ya get back around midnight, I'll be glad to give ya a lift."

"Wow, that's really nice of you, Manny." Connie touched the big man's arm. "You're so sweet."

A blush crept up his neck and into his cheeks. "Ah, it's nothing. Gotta go that way anyhow."

"Well thanks, Manny. I may take you up on it. Nice to meet you, by the way."

"Same here. You two have fun now."

Sven pulled on his jacket then helped Connie with her coat. She tugged the hat down over her ears. They stepped out into the brisk fall air. Wind whipped between the buildings, making the temperature feel slightly colder than it truly was. Sven was grateful he'd brought the jacket. This weather was a far cry from the balmy seventy-nine in Florida.

Connie slipped her hand through the crook of his elbow. "I'm so glad to see you. What a fantastic surprise."

"Yeah, I wanted to surprise you. You said you've been a little homesick?"

"Yes. It's my first time so far away and for so long. I didn't think it would hit me like it did. Don't get me wrong, I love what I'm doing here, and everyone is so nice. I've made some wonderful friends already."

They walked down the steps and stopped on the sidewalk. Connie glanced up at him. "Thank you for supporting this, Sven. I know Bishop can be intimidating at times, and he really wanted you to find a way out for me. I'm thankful you stood behind me."

His heart melted. All through his teenage years, he'd wanted her to look at him with those doe eyes full of gratitude. All he'd ever wanted to do was please her. She deserved so much after what she'd been through with Bishop and the triplets. She'd sacrificed so much. This was her shot.

"You needed this chance, Connie. You might find it isn't at all what you expected and want to come home, but my guess is you'll be hugely successful. Plus, singing for those who fight for our country is a way to give back. I know you enjoy that, too."

She smiled warmly. "You always did seem to understand me, Sven." She squeezed his arm. "Now, what kind of food are you in the mood for? I don't know too much about the restaurants in the city. I haven't gotten out too much. I know there's an awesome pizza place right up the street, but we could catch a cab and go somewhere more famous if you want."

"Whatever you'd like to do. I want you to enjoy yourself tonight. What time do you have to be back?"

She sighed. "We have rehearsal pretty early in the morning. At seven. But I don't care if I'm tired. I want to enjoy every minute I can with you. How long are you here?"

He reached into his coat pocket for the cab driver's card, then his phone. "A few days. I didn't know how much time you'd have free, but, hopefully, we can work in a bit of sightseeing while I'm here."

"Fantastic. Let's see, today's Thursday and I have Saturday off so perfect. Wrynn and I were going to do some shopping, but I'm sure she'll understand."

"Wrynn?" He punched the cab driver's number into his phone.

"She's my new bestie. Kathryn Rawlings, but we call her Wrynn for short. She's the tour organizer. I can't wait for you to meet her."

Sven nodded and held up a finger when the cab driver answered. He ordered the cab. While they waited, they strolled up and down the sidewalk in front of the building.

"We could go back inside until he gets here," Sven suggested.

"No. I like the cold air. So different from back home."

He wrapped an arm around her shoulders. "You always were a little weird."

Her jaw dropped. "Ah. I beg your pardon. You were the weird one, always wanting to build something instead of playing or riding with us. I'm surprised you didn't become a general contractor instead of a lawyer."

"Dad said I was too smart to just build things. He pushed me to go to law school. I didn't mind too much, I guess. I mean, I like being an attorney, but it's not as satisfying as creating something with your hands."

"And you look a lot sexier in a tool belt with no shirt than you do in a suit," Connie teased.

His heart flipped at the compliment. Did she really think he was sexy? He certainly thought she oozed sex appeal. Every man in Brooksville wanted a chance to go out with her. She'd broken a lot of hearts in town when she chose to leave.

The cab pulled up to the curb. He opened the door for Connie then slid in beside her.

"Where to?" the cabbie asked.

"The best Italian place in the city." Sven glanced at Connie. "You got me craving it after you mentioned pizza."

"Price range?"

"Sky's the limit." Sven smiled. "But we don't have reservations, so I guess somewhere we can walk in."

"I know jus' da place," the cabbie replied, pulling away from the curb.

After navigating rush hour traffic for more time than Sven had patience for, the cabbie pulled up in front of a place called Zia Maria's.

"My brother-in-law works here. Best Italian food in Manhattan. And at this hour you should be able to find a table. If not, tell 'em Gino sent ya. That'll get ya in."

Sven thanked Gino and tipped him well. "I'll call you when we're ready to go back. What time to you end for the day?"

"For yous two? Wheneva'."

"Probably just dinner tonight, but we may need your services on Saturday for a tourist day." Sven grinned down at Connie.

"Sure, sure. Just give me a call."

"Okay, Gino. Thanks. See you soon."

Sven climbed out and offered Connie his hand. They stood on the corner, breathing in the enticing aromas of rich Italian cuisine.

"Let's go do some damage, eh?" He waggled his brows at her.

Connie hesitated. "I don't know, Sven. This place looks pricey."

"Didn't you hear me tell the cab driver the sky's the limit? Stop worrying. How often do I get to spend the evening in Manhattan with a beautiful woman? Besides, what do I have to spend my money on anyway?"

Connie actually giggled. "Okay, but I warn you, I can pack away a lot of pasta."

"Let's go see how much."

Chapter Five

Using Gino's name worked like a charm. The place was packed, but the hostess took them straight to a table by the bar. Not the most romantic setting Sven would have chosen, but he was grateful to be seated at all. Aromas of cheese, tomato sauce, garlic, and fresh bread wafted from the kitchen. His stomach growled.

"Teresa will be your server," the hostess told them, handing them menus. "Our special tonight is chicken marsala. I'm gonna tell you, you've never had chicken marsala like this. I highly recommend it."

Sven smiled. "We'll keep it in mind. Thank you."

The hostess dipped her head in a slight bow and left.

"This is a really nice place, Sven. I swear, I'm impressed. You haven't been in New York for two hours and you've already secured a private driver and found one of the best places in town to eat."

He tapped a finger to his temple. "I'm smart."

She laughed. How he loved the sound of her laugh. He'd really missed her, yet pride swelled in him. He knew how hard it'd been for her to stand up to Bishop and strike out on her own. She'd so cleverly arranged for a fascinating nanny to come from Ireland. One who happened to be the daughter of Bishop's prime competitor in the Arabian breeding circuit. Darbi had just the right personality to capture Bishop's heart. Connie had handled her brother brilliantly.

He glanced across the table at her and held out a hand. Her small warm palm slid against his, sending tingles of electricity up his arm. He gripped her fingers.

"I've missed you, Connie."

Her expression softened, her eyes deepening into more emerald than gold. "You have?"

He nodded. "I've…"

Teresa, their waitress arrived at the table. "Good evening, welcome to Zia Maria's. I hear you're friends of Gino's."

Sven chuckled. "Does he own this place?"

"He thinks so, but no, his brother-in-law is the chef. However, he's our best advertising."

"It worked for us," Connie commented. "The place smells wonderful."

"What can I start you off with? We have an amazing wine list."

"Do you have any recommendations?" Sven wondered.

"I have to say, our house Merlot is extraordinary, but we have all the big names if you're inclined to go with them."

He glanced at Connie, and she nodded.

"Excellent. We'll have a bottle of the house Merlot."

"Certainly. I'll put it in."

She told them about the specials then left them alone to peruse the menu.

"Anyway," Connie peered over the top of the menu. "You were saying how much you missed me?"

He smiled. Again, he wondered why he'd waited so long to tell her how he felt. Now, she was about to embark on what could be a promising singing career, and she may never return to Brooksville. His stomach clinched. He wasn't sure he could handle it. But he'd kick himself for sure if he didn't say what was on his mind. He took a deep breath…

The waitress returned the with wine. Sven exhaled, fighting to control his frustration. He went through the cork and tasting ritual, conscious of Connie's wide eyes and expression of wonder.

When Teresa left them again, Connie leaned closer to him. "Where did you all the wine tasting stuff?"

"I'm not a total hick. I get around. You'd be surprised at the places I go with some of my clients."

She blushed, which he found adorable. "I'm sorry, I didn't mean to offend. I just never really knew this side of you."

He grinned, patted her hand. "I'm not offended, you goof. But there is something I'd like to say." He cast an annoyed glance at the kitchen. "Before Teresa returns for our orders."

Connie smiled. "It's fine." She placed the menu face down on the table then held his gaze. "I know what I want."

Was there an underlying meaning to her words, or wishful thinking on his part? He couldn't tell. He took another deep breath.

"I miss you, Connie." He reached for her hand.

"You do?" Her eyes grew slightly misty. "I miss you, too."

"No, I mean, I *really* miss you. More than I thought I ever could. You know we've been great friends for years, but what you don't know is I've carried a secret crush on you since you were in grade school."

Her hazel eyes sparked gold under the amber light in the restaurant. A smile grew on her face, accenting the adorable blush in her cheeks. "Really?"

He nodded, the heat creeping into his own cheeks.

"Why did you wait so long to say anything." She waved her hands around. "And now when I'm about to leave the country."

He sighed. "I don't know. I guess I always felt somewhat inferior. You had Bishop for a brother who is a world-renowned horse trader. You have a stellar reputation as his partner, in case you didn't know. You're beautiful, smart, you're talented beyond belief. I'm just a farmer's son. Until a few years ago, I really had nothing to offer."

Her expression softened, and she squeezed his hand. "I really hope you're kidding about all this inferiority crap. You are one of the most brilliant men I know. Your brain has cleverly crafted all the deals which made Champions Gate what it is today. We would be nothing without you, Sven. Bishop and I both know this. We depend on you."

Sven dipped his head and cleared his throat. He'd just opened his mouth to speak when Teresa popped up at the table again. "Can I take your order?"

Sven bit his lip to hold in his frustrated retort. He probably should have planned this discussion for a private picnic. Connie ordered the lobster ravioli, and he chose seafood risotto. Teresa dropped off a basket of fresh bread with olive oil and herbs for dipping.

Once he felt the attentive waitress would be scarce for a while, he continued.

"I know I have no right to tell you what I'm about to tell you. My timing couldn't be worse. You're about to embark on an adventure you so deserve. I hope what I say won't change how you feel, but I need to say this." He paused, gazing at her expectant expression.

"Well?" she commented impatiently. "Out with it."

"I have romantic feelings toward you, Connie. Like I said, I know the timing sucks, and I don't want to hold you back from anything coming your way, but I wanted you to know how I feel. I think I've always loved you."

Her eyebrows rose.

"Oh crap, I've scared you. I don't expect you to feel the same way right now. I know all this is a complete surprise."

She shook her head. "Not completely. I picked up on something the night we had dinner and told Bishop about my plans. I have to say, I'm a bit frustrated you waited so long. You're a catch, Sven. I just never looked at you that way, never anticipating you felt the way you do about me." She glanced down at the uneaten roll on her bread plate. She cleared her throat.

He waited, fully expecting a gentle rejection.

"Since that night, I've begun to think of you differently. I've looked at you in a more romantic light other than where I'd always forced my mind to go. I think you're sexy as a Nordic god. You remind me so much of the actor who played Eric Northman on *True Blood.*"

Sven nearly spewed his wine. "Are you serious?" He wiped his lips with his napkin, checking his tie for spill over.

Connie laughed. "I don't know why you're so surprised. The girls at school talked about you all the time. About half of them would have committed murder to go to the prom with you."

"And you? Would you have gone to the prom if I'd asked?"

She paused. She'd probably never considered him as dating material then. And there was the age difference.

"Are you kidding? I'd have said yes in a minute. Why did you never ask? Now, I'm mad. The only choice I had left was Robbie Torqueson, and I ended up having the most miserable night of my life. He jerked me around the dance floor so hard, he ripped the sleeve out of my dress. I was mortified."

Sven laughed so hard he nearly doubled over. He had to wipe his eyes with his napkin.

Teresa arrived with their meals. "I'm glad to see you're enjoying yourselves. Are you two married?"

Sven's expression froze.

Connie answered for him. "No, we're just very close friends." She cast a sideways glance at him. "About to see where this might go."

Teresa grinned. "I'm so happy for you. There's nothing like falling in love with a best friend. Enjoy your dinner and your time together."

Sven wiped his sweaty palms on the napkin draped over his lap. Talk about taking the express train to the subject.

Connie laughed. "You look like you just ate a bad clam. Are you okay?"

He swallowed. "I hadn't meant to spring this on you in such a direct way. I thought I'd be a little smoother."

"You've always gotten straight to the point. It's one of the things I've always admired about you." She took a bite of her pasta. "Oh Lord, this is sinful. Try yours."

He did and their playful conversation continued through the meal. After the plates were cleared and a second wine bottle emptied, Sven held both her hands across the table.

"Connie, I'm sorry I never told you how I felt before. I really don't want to rush you into feeling the same way. You're about to embark on what I hope will be a wonderful adventure. I just wanted you to know how I felt before you headed off to parts unknown."

She squeezed his fingers, her hazel eyes alight with those gold flecks he loved so much. "I'm glad you told me. I have to be honest…it has taken me by surprise, but pleasantly so. After I left Florida, you were all I thought about. The last zinger you left me with had me going crazy wondering what you meant by it."

"I know. I wish I'd been braver back then."

"You're anything but a coward, Sven. But I do want to take this slow. See how it develops. If we can grow a relationship long distance, then we might have a shot at it lasting for the long haul. I have to be truthful, though."

Uh-oh. Here it comes. She's about to squash my heart. He braced for her next statement.

Connie squeezed his hands again. "I want more than anything to be a singer. I want to perform in the spotlight. It's been my dream since I knew I had a voice. Whomever I choose to love will have to be okay with my choice, and it's a lot to ask."

She spoke the truth. A singer was who she was, what she was born to be. Honestly, he wasn't sure how he'd feel if she made it big.

"I know." He sighed. "Let's take it one day at a time and see where this goes. Yeah?"

A beautiful smile brightened her face. "Yeah."

Kelly Abell

Chapter Six

Darbi sat with Dusty at the kitchen table, surrounded by bridal magazines and catalogues. The wedding was in a few months, and she'd barely gotten started on what she wanted for the ceremony. She smoothed the pages of the catalogue in front of her. Dusty had arrived at lunch to talk to Quinton and stayed for a bite with Darbi. Glancing at the barely touched sandwich, she didn't have much of an appetite.

"Um, Dusty? When ya come back from wherever it is your mind traveled, can ya help me decide on the flowers?"

Her friend stirred her iced tea with a long skinny spoon. The ice rattled against the glass. She didn't respond.

"Hey." Darbi snapped her fingers.

Dusty jumped. "What?" A pink stain flooded her face. "Oh, I'm sorry. I've got a lot on my mind. You were saying something about flowers."

"What's eatin' ya? You've barely touched your lunch, and you've had this lost-in-a-fog look on your face for the last ten minutes."

Dusty sighed, played with the edge of the bread. "I've got a case weighing pretty heavy on me. I'm not really sure what to do or where to turn."

"Tell me about it. Maybe I can help."

In response, Dusty blew a raspberry. "I doubt it. Unless you want to take in a pregnant teenage girl until the baby comes and she graduates from high school."

"Wow. How old is this girl? Such a heavy load for a youngin."

Dusty smiled. "Your vernacular makes me laugh. Plus, I just love the Irish accent. Never lose it. Don't become too Americanized."

Darbi raised her eyebrows. "Americanized is it? Well, I'll tell ya what my da used to say. You can take the girl outta Ireland, but you'll never take the Irish outta the girl."

"Good." Dusty popped a chip in her mouth. "I like you just the way you are."

"So, you're having trouble placing the young thing because she's preggers?"

Dusty shifted in her seat, scooting the plate away from her. "I'm sorry. The sandwich is great, but I'm not hungry. Just the thought of food makes me nauseous."

Darbi rose and took the plates, dumped the remaining food in the trash can, then went to the kitchen sink. She ran water over the dishes then dried her hands on a towel. She joined her friend again at the table.

"You're not expecting yourself, are ya?"

Dusty nearly spit out her tea. She swallowed quickly then grabbed a napkin from the holder in front of her. "Good grief, no. You have to spend time with a man before that happens."

Darbi chuckled. "I see the way Quinton looks at ya. I thought for sure there was somethin' romantic there."

"I wish. I think I'll have to practically march into his house totally naked with a sign around my neck saying, 'I want to spend the rest of my life with you, Quinton Gates,' before he'd even get a hint of how I feel about him."

The picture of the scene and the startled look on Quinton's face nearly had her doubled over in laughter. "I'm sorry" She struggled to regain control. "That's so funny to picture. He's a little on the thick side, isn't he?"

Dusty rolled her eyes. "I'll say. Maybe I should hit him with a brick instead."

Darbi shook her head. "No, no, I think the naked thing with the sign would do the trick."

The two women giggled over the joke. When they settled down, Darbi noticed Dusty still seemed troubled. "What's on your mind, friend?"

"I'm so exasperated at Mia. I had such a good thing going for her at the Spencers', and then she goes and gets herself pregnant. Mrs. Spencer won't have such a sinful girl in her home around her children, so I'm going to have to place Mia elsewhere. But to be honest, no one wants a pregnant teen in this town."

"Sinful is it? People make mistakes. Why can't Mrs. Spencer just love the girl through her troubles instead of makin' them worse?"

"A good question. I don't know what I'm going to do. Mia is a nice girl. I just think this guy, who is leaving for college next year, wanted a quick roll in the hay. He's not taking any responsibility for the baby. He's claiming she sleeps around, so who knows who the father is."

"A simple DNA test would solve it, wouldn't it?"

"Both parties have to agree. It's not something I can force either of them to do. She's devastated. She thought he loved her. Same old story. Young vulnerable girl falls for a cad."

Darbi noticed a tear at the corner of her friend's eye. She handed her a tissue. "This case really has you upset, doesn't it?"

Dusty dabbed at her eyes. "Mia doesn't deserve the life handed to her, is all. I partially blame her for getting pregnant because she knew how to prevent it, but I also know how it is to be hopelessly in love. Enough to do anything to get the guy's affection."

"Love is truly blind sometimes," Darbi agreed. "Was she forced into it, maybe?"

Dusty shook her head. "That's what Quinton asked, but I don't think so. She's not showing any signs of that type of trauma. Just a broken heart because Todd's used her up like an old dish rag."

"When do you have to place her?"

"Mrs. Spencer wants her out by the end of the week."

Darbi whistled. "Doesn't give ya much time. Can she stay with you until you find something?"

"No, unfortunately. We can't get personally involved. Best I could do is pay for a motel room for a few days."

Darbi tapped her fingers on the table. She glanced around the large farmhouse kitchen with its enormous attached family room. She thought about the vast number of guest rooms on the second floor. There was a truly nice room in the wing she stayed in. An idea formed in her mind.

"What?" Dusty watched her.

"I'm thinkin' on somethin'. I'll need to talk to Bishop and the girls first, but I'm wonderin' why she couldn't come here. We could foster her until the baby comes or she graduates or both. She could earn her keep by helpin' with the horses. Until it becomes too dangerous."

Dusty's mouth dropped open. "Are you serious?"

"I am, yes. But I have to talk to Bishop about it first. I probably shouldn't have said anythin' to ya. He can be a stubborn eejit." She turned a page in the floral catalogue, then sighed.

A tear slipped down Dusty's cheek. "Darbi, you are the best. Even if it were just for a week or so, until I can work out something else. It would be so helpful. I'll talk to Bishop."

"No, no. I'm the one to do that. I'll get him all silly with a few beers then spring it on him after dinner. You're sure this girl wouldn't be a bad influence on our triplets?"

"I'm sure." Dusty had every faith Mia wouldn't let her down. "She gets good grades and wants to go on to college. Not sure how it will work now, but she'll figure something out. She'd love working with the horses. I can't think of a better solution."

She threw her arms around Darbi's neck.

Darbi patted her back. "Now, don't go gettin' all excited. I have to run it by Mr. Stone Face. Sometimes, he's got about as much compassion as a fence post."

Dusty swiped the catalogue from Darbi's hands. She turned a few pages then sucked in a breath. She tapped a finger on the page. "White roses and calla lilies. That's what you want for flowers." She reached for a bridal magazine. She turned a few pages, gasped again. "And here's your dress. God, this would look wonderful on you."

Darbi wrinkled her nose. "It's pink." She grabbed a strand of her hair and thrust it toward the woman across from her. "Ginger hair and pink do not go together."

Dusty grinned. "It's not pink; it's called blush. And I bet you could get the same dress in white, although I think the redheads-can't-wear-pink thing is a myth. You'd be stunning in this dress. Bishop would faint at the altar."

"I'm afraid I'll have to buy somethin' off-the-rack. There's just not time to have it altered."

"Nonsense. Order this in white. I know a seamstress who can fix this right up. She owes me a favor."

Darbi eyed the gown then glanced at Dusty who nodded in encouragement. She really didn't have a great deal of time to look around. They'd decided to have the wedding at the ranch over New Year's so Connie could join them.

"I miss Connie."

"I know you do. I do, too. She'd probably be better at this than I am."

Darbi's cheeks burned. "Oh Dusty, darlin', I didn't mean it that way. In less than two minutes, you've found the dress and the flowers. I'll just turn the whole thing over to ya. You're way better at it than I am." She sighed and glanced at her engagement ring, a lovely ruby which once belonged to Bishop's mother. "I hope he knows what he's doing."

Dusty grabbed her hand. "I've never seen Bishop this happy. He loves you and so do the girls. Their so excited they can't stop talking about the wedding."

Darbi smiled, touched beyond measure. She'd been so well received in Florida, despite her and Connie's deception at how she got here. She still couldn't believe her good fortune.

Dusty grabbed her laptop and booted it up. "Let's find dresses for the girls next."

Darbi scooted her chair over so she could see the screen. She thought again about Quinton and what an idiot he was not realize what a treasure he had right in front of his face. An idea began to form in her mind. She'd find a way to get those two together. By God, she would.

Chapter Seven

Later in the afternoon, after she'd settled Scarlet, Ivory, and Violet to work on their homework, Darbi wandered down to the barn. She'd promised Dusty she'd have an answer to her about Mia as soon as she could.

What in the world possessed you, Darbi girl? The last thing you need right now is to take on a pregnant homeless teenager. You've got a weddin' comin' up and three girls to look after.

She sighed. The poor girl had no one. She glanced over her shoulder at the farmhouse, nice and snug in the November sunshine. She'd been blessed all her life, never having to imagine what it might be like to live without. Oh, they'd stretched a budget tight enough, but they always had plenty. She couldn't imagine not having family to lean on. Poor little Mia had no one. She built her argument in her mind as she stepped into the back of the barn.

A few horses nickered at her. She took a moment to rub the head of her favorite, Heaven's Star, mother of the colt named Brennan's Miracle, after her. She and Scarlet had led Heaven through a very difficult breech birth not too long ago. Reflecting on the moment, she believed that had been the turning point for Bishop falling in love with her. This horse, even though she'd belonged to his first wife, Laura, was the catalyst for her present happiness. For that, she'd be forever grateful. The beautiful Arabian nudged her hip.

"Oh, you're a sly one, aren't ya, girl?" Darbi reached into her jeans pocket and pulled out a carrot. She fed it to the horse. "Always seemin' to know what I'm about."

She patted Heaven's neck then headed toward Bishop's office. He sat in his oversized chair, his back to the large window overlooking the south pasture. Several Arabians wandered and grazed. She spotted Quinton in the training ring working with a seal-brown mare.

"Hello, darlin'." She waved as she stepped into the room. "Who's Quinton got in the ring there?"

"Hmm?" Bishop glanced up from his laptop, then followed her pointed finger. "Oh. Morning Glory. She's finally about the right age to begin her training."

"She's got a promising gait. I can see it from here."

Bishop nodded and reached for his fiancée. Darbi settled on his lap, planting a kiss on his forehead.

"Not as much promise as our life together." He kissed her lips.

She punched his shoulder lightly. "You're ever the charmer, aren't ya?"

He smiled. "I try. So…what brings you down here this afternoon?"

Darbi rose from his lap. "I've somethin' I need to talk to ya about. And it's serious. So, I'll need your full attention."

She seated herself in one of the chairs on the other side of the desk. She held out a hand. "Come join me over here so we've not got this huge barrier between us."

Bishop's face grew pale. He slowly rose to join her. "You're not sick, are you? Oh God, don't tell me you've got cancer or something."

Touched, she smiled. "No, honey, my love, I'm not sick."

"Thank God." He plopped into the other chair. "You just scared ten years off my life. But wait…" He sat up straighter. "The girls…"

"Are fine." Darbi laughed. "You worry too much."

He blew out a breath. "Whew. Okay. I think I can handle anything else."

I don't know Bishop darlin'. But here goes.

"You know Dusty came by for lunch today."

"Yeah."

"She's got a problem I think we can help her with. You know what she does for a livin', right? With child services and all?"

"Yes," he replied, his expression wary.

Darbi took a deep breath and plunged forward. "She's got a case she's particularly upset about, and I think we can help out."

"How?" He dragged the word out.

"Now, Bishop Champion, you hear me out before you go a judgin'. We aren't perfect people either."

He held up a palm. "I'm listening. What kind of scheme is forming in that mind of yours?"

Darbi told him about Mia and her predicament. She then told him about her idea. To his credit, he didn't immediately respond she'd lost her mind. He sat for a moment, elbows propped on the arms of the chair, his chin resting on one fist.

After several seconds, he spoke. "I'm not sure you've thought this all the way through. It'd be like taking on another child. A much older teenager. We already have our hands full with the triplets, and now you want to add a hormonal pregnant teenage girl to the mix? Sounds like a recipe for disaster to me."

"I'm not a complete eejit. I know there'll be problems, but Dusty says she's a good girl, makes good grades, wants to please. She made a mistake, and no one else in this town seems to want to forgive her. The boy isn't taking responsibility for his actions, and I find it reprehensible, but what are you going to do?"

"Who's the father?"

"Some boy named Todd Wheeler."

"Chip Wheeler's son?"

Darbi sat back. "You know this boy?"

"I know his dad. And I must say, I'm not surprised. Chip's not really known for his integrity. Looks like the apple didn't fall too far from the tree. Besides, Todd's got a scholarship to University of Florida to play football after he graduates. A baby would certainly screw that up. I can see why he'd deny being the father."

"Bishop! You condone what this boy has done?"

He held up both hands, palms out. "Easy, babe. I'm not condoning anything. I'm just sayin' I'm not surprised by his actions. He should step up to the plate though. I can see why Mia would be heartbroken."

"Heartbroken, embarrassed, hurt, angry…all of the above. Her mother's a drug addict and nowhere to be found. Mrs. Spencer doesn't want her in her home because she's a bad influence on her other children." She rose and paced the small office. "Honestly, where is the charity in this town? Can you imagine how the poor girl must feel?" She waved her arms. "And we have so much. This lovely ranch, the lovely house with all those bedrooms. Three girls to keep her company. And we could use an extra hand around the barn. I wanted to start those riding lessons. She could help. If she can't work with the horses, she can keep the schedule."

Bishop rose and put his large hands on her shoulders. "We're getting married in less than two months. Taking on a pregnant teen now is a lot to deal with."

"I ran a household with five children all under the age of seventeen. I think I can manage to plan a wedding and look after our family including a teenage pregnant girl. Let's try it, Bishop. We could make sure she knows it's temporary. At least until Dusty can find her something permanent. That way, no one is brokenhearted if she needs to go to another home. Let's do this for Dusty. She really seems to have a special place in her heart for this girl."

Bishop held his future wife close. She snuggled her face into his T-shirt. He always had a manly scent of horse and hay about him. She loved it.

"I know it's a lot to ask. To take on, but I feel so bad for this child."

He stroked her mass of ginger curls. "Let's at least meet her first. Have her out to the farm for a meal. See how she gets along with the triplets. Then we can decide. Fair enough?"

Darbi knew she'd asked a lot of him, and, frankly, she'd been prepared for more resistance. She supposed it only made sense. Mia may not like them. She may prefer to live on her own than with them. Darbi couldn't imagine why, but she'd witnessed stranger things in her day.

She nodded. "Okay. Fair enough. I'll go let Dusty know. But she only has till the end of the week, so not far away."

Bishop chuckled. "Since today is Thursday, I'd say you're right. I'm inclined to try it, but I just want to meet her first. Get a first impression. I love Dusty, and she's no bleeding heart, but she can get too involved in her cases sometimes. Quinton says he doesn't know how she doesn't go nuts."

"I agree. It's a tough job, but I'm glad we've got someone like Dusty doing it. She's Heaven's angel as far as

I'm concerned. She helped me pick out the flowers, my dress, and dresses for the girls."

"Wow, all in one afternoon?"

"She's amazin'. I miss Connie and wish she were here to help, but Dusty is filling her shoes nicely."

"Speaking of Connie, have you heard from Sven?"

"No." Darbi headed toward the door. "Obviously, you haven't either. Did ya expect to?"

Bishop walked around to his desk chair and sat. "He said he would check on Connie. I thought we might have heard from him by now."

"Give him a break. Let them enjoy themselves."

Bishop stared up at her. "What do you mean?"

"Oh nothing." She turned and left him wearing a puzzled expression. "Eejit," she muttered through a smile.

Darbi wasted no time calling Dusty. She told her of the temporary arrangement if all went well at dinner. She still had about two hours to prepare a meal, so she suggested Dusty bring Mia that very night.

She then called down to the barn and told Bishop he'd be grilling steaks and to invite Quinton for supper. She laughed at the worried tone in his voice.

"Darlin', let's just see how we get on. This child needs a home, and we have a perfect one. Now, end your day so we can get dinner started. I told Dusty to be here at six."

She pulled the triplets together into the kitchen, sat them in a row at the bar.

"Girls, I've somethin' serious to tell ya, and I'll need your thoughts and support."

All three chests puffed up, and the girls sat up straighter in their chairs. "What is it?" they said in unison.

Darbi still had trouble believing they could all be so in sync. She smiled.

"You all know the kind of work Dusty does, right?

"Child welfare or something?" Violet said.

"Right." Darbi folded a dish towel and slid it down the bar. "She has a particularly difficult case, and I think we can help her." She glanced at three expectant faces.

"What can we do? Are we getting a baby to take care of? Oh, it would be pretty cool to have a baby in the house." Scarlett clapped her hands.

Darbi smiled. "Not exactly. There's this girl named Mia, and she's expecting a baby."

"Uh-oh," Ivory chimed in. "That doesn't sound good."

"Always the practical one, aren't you, my Ivory." Darbi ruffled the girl's blonde locks. "She's made a mistake. Trusted a boy to be there for her, and he let her down. Plus, she doesn't have a real home. Her mother is addicted to drugs, and no one knows where she is."

"What about her father?" Violet asked.

"I don't believe she even knows who he is," Darbi replied.

"How terrible," Scarlet added.

"It is, yes. So…the current foster home is kicking her out because the mother feels she'll be a bad influence on her children. Dusty is having a hard time placing her elsewhere."

"Bring her here," they all three agreed.

Emotion choked Darbi's throat, and tears stung her eyes. Her heart swelled with pride at the generosity of these girls. They had suffered a great deal on their own, losing their mother at birth and having a father who'd remained distant and unable to cope with them until recently. She walked around the bar and hugged each one in turn.

"I'm so proud of ya, girls. That's exactly what I was going to propose. In fact, she's coming to dinner tonight to meet us all. I'm sure she'll be nervous, so I want us all on our best behavior."

The practical Ivory spoke up. "What did Dad say? How hard was it for you to talk him into it?"

"Not as hard as ya might think. He wants to do it on a trial basis, but I've a good feelin' about this. I think it's going to work out just fine.

Violet slapped a palm on the bar. "Let's get ready for Operation Mia."

They all laughed.

Dusty arrived with Mia at exactly six. Bishop was out by the grill with Quinton, monitoring the steaks. The girls helped with chopping vegetables for the salad. Darbi had just taken the potatoes out of the oven when Dusty and Mia stepped into the kitchen.

"Hey girls." Dusty greeted them with a smile.

All three clambered over to her, wrapping her in a hug.

A petite strawberry blonde stood at the doorway to the kitchen. She wore jeans and a brightly colored tank. Her face was clean of makeup, her complexion smooth as porcelain. Darbi could see why Todd had been attracted to her.

What a pretty little thing. And she looks so lost. Well... Darbi wiped her hands on a dish towel. *We'll take care of that straight away.*

She stepped around Dusty and held out a hand. "You must be Mia. Welcome to our home."

Mia shyly accepted her hand, giving it an awkward shake.

"I'm Darbi, and this is Ivory, Scarlet, and Violet. I had them each wear a T-shirt the color of their name so you could tell them apart."

Mia smiled. "Hello. It's nice to meet you. And thanks for that." She glanced at the triplets. "It really would be hard to tell you apart."

"Oh, you'll get used to it. It's easy once you get to know us. I'm the drama queen, Ivory is the smart one, and Scarlet loves animals and always smells like a horse," Violet informed her.

"Hey," Scarlet retorted. She offered Mia an embarrassed smile. "I don't *always* smell like a horse. Do you like them? Horses, I mean?"

Mia nodded. "I don't really know much about them, but I love to watch them."

"We'll take you out to the barn after supper," Scarlet said, enthusiastically. "You can meet Brent, our new colt. I helped bring him into the world."

Ivory rolled her eyes. "Here we go. We get to hear this story for the one hundredth time."

Darbi intervened, for she truly had heard the story about that many times. "You girls go get washed up. I'll finish the salad. Show Mia around the place, would you? But save the barn for later. Dinner is almost ready."

Violet took Mia by the hand. "Come on. We'll show you our rooms."

Mia offered Dusty an unsure gaze, to which she nodded. "Go on," she mouthed. "It'll be fine."

Mia nodded and allowed herself to be led back into the hall and up the stairs. All three girls chattered along the way.

"Wow," Dusty said. "I never dreamed she'd get this kind of reception from the triplets. It was awesome."

Darbi nodded. "They're great girls. Connie's been an awesome mother figure to them. I hope I do as well."

"Oh, you are, Darbi. You're the one who brought Bishop back into their lives. They'll be forever grateful, I think."

"Maybe so." She handed Dusty a knife. "Want to help me finish up the salad?"

"Sure thing."

Dusty chopped tomatoes, onion, and cucumber while Darbi handled the lettuce and mixed the dressing.

"I hope she'll be comfortable here." Darbi tossed the ingredients into the large wooden salad bowl.

"Are you kidding? I think she's going to love it. And you're the perfect female to get her through this crisis. She's terrified about being pregnant. She knows how people make fun of girls like her at school."

"Doesn't Florida have a program where kids can study at home? Virtual or some such? I thought I heard one of the mothers from the school mention it."

Dusty nodded. "They do, but I'm not sure we should encourage it right away. She needs to adjust to what's she's done. There is some responsibility on her part in this. But it is an option if things get too difficult for her."

"We'll just see how it goes. Ah…here come the boys."

The back door opened, and Quinton and Bishop entered followed by the enticing aroma of grilled steak.

"Meat's done," Bishop announced. "Where's the guest of honor?"

Darbi placed the salad on the table, followed by Dusty who had the potatoes on a baking tray. "The girls are upstairs showing her around."

Bishop's look grew doubtful, but then he smiled. Darbi knew he felt they'd rushed this, but she grew more confident by the minute it was the right decision.

"Bishop, thanks for this. I know it's hard bringing a stranger into your home, but I promise you, I wouldn't allow this at all if I thought for one minute there'd be major trouble. I wouldn't put the triplets in harm's way for anything in the world." Dusty hugged him.

He wrapped an arm around her shoulders. "I know you wouldn't. We can try it for a while to see how it goes. I'm just worried about the stress with the wedding coming up and all." He spoke in a low tone only those in the immediate vicinity could hear. "Darbi can be a little unstable."

Dusty slapped him on the chest.

"I heard that, Bishop Champion," Darbi called from the dining room.

"I think this is a great idea," Quinton chimed in. "It's the perfect solution for Mia. I have a good feeling about this."

Darbi caught Dusty's loving look at Quinton. She smiled.

"Thanks, Quint. That means a lot." Dusty stepped from Bishop's embrace and gave the big man a hug. She held on just a little longer than friendship warranted, but Quinton didn't seem to notice.

Eejit. I'm goin' to have to have a talk with the stupid brute.

Darbi called the girls. When they entered the dining room, Mia offered her a shy smile.

"This house is amazing. I've never seen anything like it."

"Hi, Mia." Bishop extended his hand, a warm smile on his face. "Thank you for the compliment. I built it."

Her eyes grew wide. "You did?"

Bishop held up his hands. "With these."

"Sure enough, he had help though," Darbi chimed in. "He's just wantin' ya to think he's some kind of superhero."

Bishop frowned, and they all laughed.

"Sit down now, before it all gets cold. Those steaks look fabulous. Thanks, hon."

Bishop nodded toward Darbi. "My pleasure, my soon-to-be wife."

Darbi passed around the food, making sure everyone had plenty to eat, then she sat and filled her own plate.

The conversation grew animated as the triplets entertained Mia with their antics. Darbi caught Bishop's eye a few times during the meal. He gave her a slight nod at their last exchange. It warmed her heart. It could work, and that was all she needed for now.

She went to the kitchen to get the apple pie she'd taken out of the freezer and put in the oven before everyone arrived. When she'd sliced and served, she looked at Mia.

"So, I hear you'll be needin' a place to stay for a while."

Mia paused mid bite, doubt and anxiety showing in her expression. "Um…yes, ma'am."

"Oh Lord, you'll have to stop the ma'am stuff with me." Darbi waved a hand. "Makes me feel like me grandma. But I will expect ya to use it with others."

Mia ducked her head and nodded.

"Mia." The girl glanced up holding, Darbi's gaze.

"We'd like you to stay with us for a while. For as long as it suits both parties. Sort of a trial period if you'd like. You may find all this chaos is just too much to handle."

Mia smiled. "Oh, no, ma'am…I mean, no. I love it. And I can help out. Clean, cook, watch the triplets if you need to go out."

"Hey!" The triplets echoed each other.

Bishop shot them a look, and they settled back to eating their pie.

"We've practically got an army around here for the cookin' and cleanin', but I could use you with the horses. I'm thinkin' about starting some ridin' lessons, and I'll need help. If you're comfortable with that, I mean."

"I don't know how to work with horses, but I could learn." Then she glanced down at her middle. "As long as it's safe, I guess."

Darbi grinned. "We won't put ya in any danger. I promise ya. So, you'll move in on the morrow?"

"Huh?" Mia asked, confused.

"She means tomorrow," Violet offered. "You'll need to get used to her accent. She says some really funny stuff sometimes."

The other two agreed.

After dinner, the triplets led Mia to the barn to introduce her to some of the horses. Dusty helped Darbi do the dishes while the men stepped outside to clean the grill.

"Couldn't have gone better," Dusty commented, hugging Darbi. "Thank you. I can't believe you're being so generous."

"She seems like a sweet girl who's made a bad choice. It happens. Does she plan to keep the baby, then?"

Dusty shrugged. "I don't think she's gotten that far in the decision process."

Quinton and Bishop stepped back inside.

"Quinton, why don't you drive Dusty and Mia back to town," Darbi suggested.

"I've got my car, Darbi. That's not necessary."

"Yeah, she has her car. What would we do in the morning?"

"Mia will need the truck to move her stuff over in the mornin'. You can go get them both and bring her here."

Quinton scratched his head, not quite comprehending Darbi's plan. "Don't she have school tomorrow?"

Darbi smiled at Dusty. "I think she can miss school one day, can't she?"

Dusty frowned, as confused as Quinton. "I guess. I'd planned to bring her over tomorrow afternoon, but…"

"Perfect. It's settled, then. Scoot. I'll finish up here."

When the trio had left, Bishop cornered Darbi in the kitchen. "What was that all about?"

She smiled. "You'll soon see, my love."

Chapter Eight

Connie sat on the rooftop of her building. The chilly wind blew around her, but she remained warm wrapped in a heavy blanket. She sipped a cup of hot cocoa, glancing up at the night sky. A few stars shone through the glow of the city lights. She listened to the traffic honking and grinding in the streets below. She loved New York. Her legs ached from all the walking she and Sven had done, but she'd loved every minute of it.

They'd ridden the ferry to Staten Island, gone up to the top of the Empire State Building, visited the memorial for the twin towers, shopped, and eaten some of the most glorious food. Her stomach and her heart were full.

Getting to know Sven in a romantic way had been strange at first. They'd shared so many childhood experiences as "buddies" being with him female to male had seemed awkward. She hadn't really been sure how to behave. Holding his hand meant something entirely different to her. Having his arm around her shoulders warmed her more than it did when they were kids. Why hadn't she seen how he felt about her before? The gazes he offered her were full of longing and affection. Had they been there all along?

Frustration crept its way into her mind. *Why did you wait so long, Sven? Why now? When I'm about to leave the country for parts far away. When I won't see you for months. How can this possibly work?*

He'd apologized about ten times for bringing his feelings up to her.

"I'm sorry, Connie. I know my timing stinks, but I just couldn't let you go so far away without knowing how I feel about you. I've always loved you, I think. From that time when you were in second grade and I was in fourth. I saw you fall off the jungle gym and was the first one to get to you."

"I remember." She smiled at the memory. "You were so sweet. Mean old Arlin Jacobs pushed me off."

"I never told you this, but I punched him after school. Went straight to his house and socked him in the nose."

Connie's jaw dropped. "What? You didn't."

"I did. Got grounded for a month for it, but it was worth it. He never bothered you again, did he?"

She laughed. "No...he didn't." She'd laid her head on his shoulder as they gazed out at the view from atop the Empire State Building. "My hero."

"I'd like to be," he murmured.

She'd glanced up into those blue-green eyes. He was so handsome. Surprise had filled her when he bent his head and kissed her gently on the lips. She touched them now, remembering the tingle which had coursed through her entire body.

Wow, he can kiss. Why did he have to wait so long? I might not have left the farm if he'd been a little more up front about how he felt.

Really? Would she have turned down this wonderful opportunity with the USO if she'd had a man in her life? Maybe, but it was too late to lament over it. A tinge of fear tickled her spine. What if she began to develop strong feelings for Sven and he decided he couldn't handle the distance? She had signed a one-year contract with option to renew if the show went well. How could any man cope?

"Dang it, Sven, why now?"

"Who are you talking to?" Wrynn's voice came out of the dark.

Connie jumped, nearly dropping her cup of cocoa. "You scared me to death."

Wrynn laughed. "I'm sorry. I thought you'd hear the door slam. What are you doing out here? It's freezing."

"Oh, just thinking."

Wrynn joined her, plopping down in the lawn chair next to her. She wore a heavy down coat over a hoodie and thick sweat pants. "This is nuts." She flipped her mahogany pony tail behind her.

"I like the cold air. It helps me think."

"Yeah, okay. What do you need to think so hard about? You're doing great in rehearsal, and I swear, I've never heard a voice like yours. I'm amazed some talent scout didn't scoop you up before."

Connie laughed. "You don't get too many talent scouts in Brooksville, Florida."

"Manny told me you had a visitor."

Connie glanced at her friend's mischievous smile and raised eyebrows. "Manny's got a big mouth."

Wrynn laughed. "He does. So tell me, who's the mystery man?"

She sighed. "He's a friend from back home. He's the attorney for our ranch. He and my brother grew up together. He's been a friend of the family all our lives." Once she started, the words just flowed. She didn't realize how much she needed to share this craziness with someone.

"Right before I left for this tour, he made a casual comment about me being the woman for him. *All our lives,*

Wrynn. We've been friends all this time, and he's *never* mentioned it until I leave town for a one-year commitment. *Why?"* Connie could hear the frustration of her own words.

Wrynn sighed, settling more comfortably in the chair, pulling her coat around her. "Men just aren't bright sometimes. They don't know what they've got until they lose it."

Connie glanced at her friend's silhouetted profile. "Sounds like you're speaking from personal experience."

"A story for another time. So," Wrynn said, scooting her chair around to face her friend, "spill it. How did the day go?"

Connie wanted to hear more about Wrynn's love life, but she let the subject go. She wanted a girlfriend's take on what Sven could be up to.

"We had a fantastic day. It started off a little weird because I'd never really seen him in a romantic light before. Every touch, gaze, word meant something in a different context. But as the day progressed, it got easier. He's so handsome, and about the most considerate man I've ever met."

"Got pictures?"

Connie pulled her phone from her coat pocket and pulled up the photos.

Wrynn swiped through the shots of the day. "Holy crap, girl! He's a god."

Connie grinned. "I know, right? I've always thought he was handsome, but now it's like"—she smacked her forehead—"bam!"

"I came up here all excited to tell you about the new security guy, Logan Richards, but whew. With this hunk of man love, who needs him?"

Connie reached over and grabbed her arm. "I met him."

"What? Logan?"

"Yes. And you're right. He is dreamy."

"When did you meet him? I was going to introduce you today."

"A few nights ago. Probably Wednesday or early Thursday morning. I couldn't sleep and was playing in the rehearsal hall. He snuck in to hear me sing. He seemed to be a very troubled guy. He said my singing helped him relax."

"Music soothes the savage beast, eh?"

Connie laughed. "If you say so."

"What did you think of him?" Wrynn grabbed Connie's mug and sipped her cocoa.

"Help yourself."

"Mm, this is good."

Connie rolled her eyes. "As far as what I thought of him? He's adorable. Those eyes and the chiseled face? Yummy. But I didn't really get to know him at all. I'll look forward to it."

"Well, you're probably not interested, what with the Viking god Sven in your future."

Connie snorted. "We shall see. I'm not sure where it will go. Long distance relationships don't tend to work out very well. He may not be able to cope with all the weird hours, time zones, not being able to see each other. This is all so new. I'm not sure where I want it to go yet, but I am thinking about him a lot."

"Lord, who wouldn't? He's gorgeous. If you decide you don't want him, I'll step in."

Again she rolled her eyes, not sure her friend could see her gesture in the dark. "I'll have to watch my back around you. Were you a boyfriend stealer in high school?"

This time Wrynn laughed. "I wish. I had braces, stringy hair, and glasses in high school. Plus I weighed about fifty pounds more than I do now."

"Those guys better watch out at your reunion. You're going to steal the show."

"Ha! That'll be the day. Seriously though, you don't know about Sven?"

Connie sighed. "It's all so sudden and new. My brother will faint when he hears about Sven's feelings toward me. He just won't believe it. I'm not sure I do either. Why all of a sudden?"

"Did you ask him?"

Connie shrugged. "Not in so many words. He said he wished he'd told me years ago, but he never felt worthy. He would have had to battle his way through a throng of admirers and he wasn't sure I'd have even recognized him."

"Wow, lack of self-confidence much?"

"You had to know how Sven grew up. His father was a domineering man. Strict on all his kids. We weren't different economically speaking, but his dad forced their humility and humbleness. I think that's where some of it comes from."

"Ah." Wrynn nodded. "I guess it makes sense. So he has brothers?"

Her hopeful tone tickled Connie. "Yes, he does. I think they're both married though."

"Well, damn."

They sat in silence for a few minutes. Finally, Wrynn rose. She handed the empty mug back to Connie.

"It's freezing out here. I'm going in."

"Okay. I'm not far behind you."

"Are you going to see Sven again tomorrow?"

"No. We said our goodbyes tonight. He has an early flight. I'll miss him. It was really good to see him."

"Long distance can work, ya know."

Connie gazed out over the rooftop. "I guess we'll find out."

Chapter Nine

Sven balanced on the ladder, stretching to reach the last shingle on the end of the roof. He swung his hammer, banging the nails in place. Straightening, he smiled. Finally, the building was watertight and he could move his horses from his brother's barn to his own. Working on this old dilapidated property gave him purpose. He'd always enjoyed working with his hands and building things.

He carefully climbed down the tall ladder, peering into the barn on his way down. He paused about six feet off the ground, staring into the dark musty space. There was still a great deal of work to be done on the stalls and the tack room. He may even add some sleeping quarters on the other side of the tack room, just in case he ever decided to own more than the five horses he already had and needed a live in caretaker.

Working with the wood, screws, nails, and paint gave him time to reflect on his weekend with Connie. It had been exactly seven days since he'd left New York and he missed her dreadfully. They'd enjoyed their time together, talking and getting to know each other on a new level. He mentally kicked himself for not making his move more than a year ago when it finally occurred to him he was worthy of the Champion princess.

That was the way he'd always thought of her while they were growing up. He laughed. As a young girl, she'd resembled a princess about as much as his dog Myrtle resembled a swan. His father always said Connie was full of spit and vinegar. She could throw a baseball harder than all the boys. She sat a horse better than anyone he knew. Yet, he always thought of her as a beautiful princess. His princess. But he'd never made a move.

I'm such an idiot. I had it all right within my grasp, and I've let her slip away. When Bishop finds out how I feel about his sister, he's going to want to strip the hide from my body.

Sven climbed the rest of the way down the ladder. He grabbed a bottle of Gatorade, opened the lid, and chugged it down. For November, the heat and humidity was unbearable.

Glancing at his watch he decided he'd done enough for the day. He'd fix a sandwich then try to Skype Connie. The troupe was leaving for Kuwait tomorrow, and she had an early flight.

Worry pinched inside him. He hoped the security team would keep the troupe safe as they traveled. Manny seemed like a capable sort. He hadn't met any of the others on staff, but Manny had assured him they'd never lost anyone. He chuckled. He certainly wouldn't mess with the giant man.

A truck rumbled down the road to his farm. His collie, Myrtle, who'd been asleep on the front porch, scrambled to life.

"Myrtle, stay," Sven commanded. The dog glanced at him then at the truck, poised to run. "Stay."

She wiggled her butt then sat with a thump, a dejected expression on her doggie face.

"You wait until the truck comes to a stop, girl. You're going to get run over one of these days."

He groaned when he saw Bishop behind the wheel. What could he possibly want at this time of day on a Saturday? Had he found out about his feelings for Connie? Darbi was on to them, he knew, but, surely, she wouldn't say anything. Besides, there really wasn't much to say. They had both decided the relationship shouldn't move forward too far at this point with her being gone so much of the time. But they had decided to talk more about how they were beginning to feel about each other.

Sven licked his lips, remembering the taste of her. He definitely wanted more than her kiss, but it would be moving way too fast. These feelings had been in his heart for a long time, but the relationship needed to grow on Connie. He could read her uncertainty. Truthfully, he wanted her to enjoy her trip, the performing. It was perfect for her, and others would soon recognize her talent. He worried a great deal this Trevor Thornton would hear her sing and whisk her straight off to Nashville for a record deal.

He reminded himself to remain patient as he strolled over to greet his best friend.

"Hey Bishop. What brings you out here?"

Myrtle barked and bounced on the porch. Sven whistled, and she flew off the porch and tumbled into the grass. She gathered her footing and charged toward Bishop. He braced for her launch, but when she reached him, she plopped on the ground, doggy smile in place, tail swishing behind her.

Bishop reached down to rub her ears. "Hey Myrtle. Good girl." He glanced up at Sven. "When did she learn to do that?"

Sven's eyebrows shot up. "Wow. I've been working with her, but I didn't really think she was getting it. Looks like I was wrong." He patted Myrtle, praising her.

"You gotta cold beer?"

Sven lifted an eyebrow. "Uh-oh. What's wrong?"

The men walked into the small house. Self-conscious thoughts often plagued Sven when he invited Bishop into his small home. Tidy and functional, his fifteen hundred square feet didn't even compare to the five thousand Bishop had. His décor a bit more modest and masculine in taste. Sven preferred simple to grandiose. Not that Connie had furnished their home over-the-top by any means, but she'd had a taste for nice things. The quality of furnishings she'd chosen for the Champion mansion, as he secretly called it, ranked much higher in quality.

He led his friend through the small foyer, past a sparsely decorated living room on the right and an all but empty dining room on the left, and into a kitchen/family room combo. Their boots tapped softly on the oak hardwood floors then onto the stone tile in the kitchen. The one thing Sven had spent a great deal of money on when he'd built the house was the kitchen and the bathrooms. If he decided to sell or move to something larger, he wanted this place to sell. So, he'd sprung for the black- and white-flecked granite countertops, windows in the white cabinets on the wall, and high-end chrome appliances. Connie had insisted he paint the walls a soft lemon, so he had. At first, he'd balked, thinking it too girly, but now when he entered the kitchen, he appreciated the brightness the paint color added to the room. Especially in the mornings when the eastern-facing kitchen had the early morning sunbeams gleaming through.

Bishop hopped up on a bar stool while Sven went to the commercial-grade refrigerator. He pulled two bottles of beer from the top shelf, reached into the drawer next to the fridge and removed the bottle opener.

"Looked like you finished the roof on the barn today," Bishop commented.

Sven popped the tops on the beer and set a bottle in front of Bishop. He pulled a long swig from his own before he answered.

"Ah, good. It's hotter than hell out there for November."

Bishop nodded then took a swig from his own bottle.

"I did get the roof finished, so she's finally water tight. Now I need to finish the stalls inside, so I can finally move the horses in. It'll get cold soon, so I need to get it done."

"Want some help? I can come out a couple evenings next week. You got power in there?"

Sven nodded, he pulled his cell phone out of his back pocket and laid it on the counter then stepped over to one of the cabinets. He opened it and pulled out a bag of pretzels and a wire basket. He put a paper towel in the basket and poured in some pretzels.

Bishop chuckled. "I coulda just eaten them outta the bag, man."

Sven made a face. "Gross. I don't even eat them outta the bag. Who knows where your hands have been?"

Bishop laughed. "True enough."

Sven placed the basket between them and settled on the second bar stool next to his friend.

"So, what brings you out here on a Saturday evening with your knickers in a twist?"

Bishop sighed. "Do you remember the rancher we sold Blue Bonnet to last spring?"

"The one in Texas?"

"Yeah, the jerk who made such a fuss about having her transported in a padded trailer?"

"Which you did."

"She's come up lame, and he wants to blame the breeding."

Sven ran a hand through his sweaty hair and cursed. "Unbelievable. He's probably over-trained her."

"I'm sure he has. He sent me videos of her workouts, and the paces he put her through shocked me. Anyway he's…"

Sven's cell phone chimed, and Connie's face popped onto the screen. Too late for him to hide it from Bishop, he slid his finger across the screen. "Hey, Connie."

"Hey, sweet man. I miss you already." Cheer filled her voice.

Bishop stared at his friend, one eyebrow raised. He mouthed the words "Sweet man."

"Yeah? Bishop's here. Say hello."

"Uh….oh, hey, brother of mine. What are you doing at Sven's this time of day? Doesn't Darbi have a nice meal waiting for you at home?"

"Hi, Connie. Nice to talk to you finally." Sarcasm dripped from his tone.

"I've been busy, Bishop. Besides, the last time I called, Darbi said you weren't home. How is she and those blessed little girls? I miss them so much."

Bishop shot Sven a look. "Not as much as you apparently miss your sweet man here."

She paused. Sven looked away trying to hide the flush creeping up his neck. He cleared his throat.

"Oh grow up," Connie snapped. "I've called him sweet man for years now. Answer my question. What are you doing at Sven's on a Saturday evening? Everything okay at the ranch?"

Since Connie was a partner, Sven so no reason not to share the issue with her. Plus it pulled the spotlight from them. "The Texan is suing for bad breeding."

"Which Texan?"

"Adam Winthrop."

"Oh yeah, I remember him. He bought Blue Bonnet. And he's suing for what?" Incredulity replaced irritation.

"Bad breeding," Sven answered. "She's come up lame."

"Oh bull crap. She's from the best stock we have. He probably over-trained her. He's such a jerk."

"I agree. He sent me some videos, and they won't help his case. Still, we have to go through the motions."

Sven shifted on the bar stool, pulling the phone closer. "Has he filed the suit yet?"

"No, but his attorney is about to."

"I'll call him tonight and see if I can talk him out of it. It will just go to arbitration anyway, but I might can get him to settle for less. Keep our name out of the papers."

Bishop visibly relaxed. After Champions Gate's battle with Darbi's father, who owned Clover Leaf Farms in Ireland, the last thing they needed was bad press. It had been a battle for the ages, and when Bishop had discovered Darbi's true identity a few months ago, it had nearly been the end of their relationship. Now they were to become family and Bishop had bailed Patrick Brennan out of a dicey situation and saved his farm, things were less strained. Sven had been proud of his negotiating skill through the transaction. He'd constructed a deal allowing Patrick to save face and Bishop to get permission to marry his daughter. He should open a dating site.

"That would be great, Sven," Connie said, her voice enthusiastic. "If anyone can do it, you can."

Bishop shot Sven another glare. "How's New York?"

"Fantastic. My feet still hurt, but they are healing. We fly out tomorrow morning early for Kuwait. I was going to call you tonight to say *adios*."

"After you called Sven," her brother commented.

"Oh give it up, Bishop," she remarked. "I'll talk to you later tonight. I'll call you later, too, Sven. Let me know how the talks with the butthead Texan go."

"I will, Connie. See ya." He disconnected the call, clearing his throat again. He took a long pull from the beer bottle.

He glanced at Bishop who stared at him. "What?"

"You know what. What happened in New York, *sweet man*?"

"I went for a conference, and saw your sister. I took her out to a nice dinner, and then we spent Saturday seeing the sights of the city."

"Yeah? What other *sights* did you see?"

Sven faced the other man squarely, temper simmering. "I'm not sure what you are trying to insinuate here, but I'm going to tell you something, and then we aren't going to speak of it again. I happen to be in love with your sister." He held up a hand when Bishop's mouth opened and his brows drew together. "Let me finish before you go off all half-cocked. I've loved Connie for years. I just never had the nerve to tell her. And this look"—he waved his hand at Bishop's face—"is why. Your family has always made me feel less than adequate, through no fault of your own, mind you, but after Connie left, I realized I had one last shot at telling her how I felt. So, I went to New York to tell her."

Bishop stood and walked to the sliding door. He gazed out over the pool. After a moment, he turned. "Why now, Sven? Why wait until she's about to embark on a trip I tried to have you get her out of? If you loved her, why in on God's green earth didn't you stop her?"

Sven read the angry expression on one of his best friends in the entire world. He hated this. Part of him wished he'd kept his feelings to himself and never pursued this rash action, but he couldn't help it. His heart had led him to tell Connie the truth, yet he vowed he wouldn't stand in her way.

He sighed, rising to get two more beers from the fridge. "I can tell you're upset, but I can't help how I feel. I know I've been foolish to keep my feelings to myself, but I wouldn't have stopped her from going anyway. She's needs this shot, Bishop. Don't head down that destructive road again. She's so talented, and she deserves a chance to let others hear her sing. I'm going to miss the heck out of her, but I need to let her go. Besides, I'm not so sure she feels the same way about me."

Bishop reluctantly accepted the second beer. Sven tossed the other two bottles into the recycle bin under the sink. They clinked as they hit the plastic. He sighed. "I know she needed to do this, but you, man? Why didn't you ever tell me how you felt?"

"She's your sister, bro. You're very protective of her. Right now, you want to rip my eyes out, and I'm not sure what's stopped you from taking a swing at me, but I appreciate it. You've got a nasty right hook."

Breaking the tension, Bishop laughed. He sat back down on the bar stool. "You know me too well, my friend." He shook his head. "I just don't get why you never told her."

"It shocked her, let me tell you. I don't think she's quite soaked it in yet. And when she does, she may not feel the same way. We've decided to take it really slow. I've waited this long, I can wait a while longer. I don't want to stand in the way of her dreams, Bishop. I really don't. But I just couldn't let her fly off to another part of the world and not at least plant the seed of how I felt about her."

Bishop's eyes narrowed. "That was the only seed you planted, right?"

Sven's anger flashed. He leaned over the bar and raised a finger to his friend's face. "You've overstepped, friend.

That's none of your business. Our love life is between Connie and me, so don't ever go there again. You got it?"

Bishop leaned back a bit, held up a palm. "Okay, okay. I'm sorry. You're right. This is just really weird for me. I never ever pictured the two of you together."

Sven lowered his hand and took a deep breath. "I'm not sure Connie did either, and she may come to the conclusion it won't work. But I took my chance. I'll just have to see how it goes."

"Good luck, man. She's a pain in the butt, and determined to get what she wants."

"One of the reasons I love her. Now, take your beer and go, so I can call the Texan. I'll let you know what I find out."

"Thanks, Sven." Bishop rose still shaking his head.

"Let it digest a bit then we'll talk about Connie some more, but I'm not ever going to tell you everything. She's your sister, for God's sake."

"I'm just going to say one thing, and then I'll drop it."

Here it comes. The great Bishop warning. Sven cocked one eyebrow. "Let's hear it."

"You hurt her, and all bets are off."

"I know, but I ask you this. What happens if she hurts me?"

Bishop stared at him for a long moment.

Yeah, big boy. I'm one of your best friends, and you didn't think of that, did ya?

"I'll have to kill her."

They both laughed, relieving the tension.

"It'll be fine, my friend. I've known Connie a long time. I know I'm the one who sprung this one her, and I'll be a big boy no matter what she decides. Don't lose too much sleep over it."

"I might. This has thrown me for a loop, Sven. You're a good man, but… Just make sure you treat her right." He strode to the front door. "Subject closed."

Sven reached for Bishop's hand, shook it. "Thanks, man. I treasure her, but let's just let things take their natural course and see what happens. I'll let you know what happens with Winthrop."

"Okay. See ya later."

His friend from childhood strode to his truck, shaking his head.

What have I done?

Connie would kill him for telling Bishop the truth, but he was happy the jig was up. He didn't like hiding things from anyone, much less his best friend. He closed the door and headed to his tiny office upstairs to first call to the crazy Texan, and then call Connie and confess what he'd done.

Chapter Ten

After an hour's drive through New York's early dawn, Connie stood on the tarmac at the John F. Kennedy airport, absorbing the sight of the C-17 cargo plane they would take to Kuwait. She'd never seen anything so big. They could drive vehicles into the back of it, which they'd done. Three, maybe four cargo vans had been loaded, and their crew buzzed around the ramp like bees, busy loading all the equipment they'd need to put on the show.

Her excitement built as she waited her turn to board. Trevor Thornton planned to meet them this morning and fly on the transport plane with the rest of the group. She couldn't wait to meet him. Secretly, she hoped he might be her ticket to something more permanent in the entertainment industry. From the time she could hold a toy microphone, she'd dreamed of being a singer. In her mind's eye, she imagined herself on stage in front of a sold out crowd in some huge arena. Her voice would echo throughout the space as she finished a song on a powerful note. People would stand and scream for more.

She chuckled to herself. This USO tour would be even better. The thought of seeing the faces of the men and women who served her country light up at the sight of what they had planned for them sent shivers down her spine.

"Are you cold?"

She jumped at the sound of the deep male voice behind her. Turning, she faced Logan Richards, the young man she'd met the other night in the rehearsal studio.

Heat flushed her cheeks. He truly was a gorgeous man, all dark and mysterious looking, with his cropped coffee-brown hair and matching eyes. His high cheek bones and slightly pointed nose gave her the impression he might have some Native American heritage in his genes. Her gaze quickly roamed his body. He wasn't as tall as Sven, and the exact opposite in coloring. He stood with his hands shoved into the pockets of his black cargo pants. A black T-shirt stretched across impressive pecks. The entire hunk of a package was wrapped in a black bomber jacket.

"Logan, right?"

He smiled, showing perfectly white teeth. It brightened his face and added a slight amber sparkle to his deep-brown eyes. "Yes, you remembered."

"Of course, I remembered. Nice to see you again. And no, I'm not cold. Just excited. This is my first time on a tour like this." She waved a hand at all the activity. "It's quite a production."

Logan nodded. "It is. This is my second tour, but I'm looking forward to it more than the first. The pace will be grueling. I hope you're ready."

"I hope so, too. I've barely recovered from all the rehearsing."

He chuckled, a low rumble in his throat. His voice reminded her a little of the actor Sam Elliott.

"They'll keep you running for sure, but it's so worth the effort. The entertainers really seem to get a lot back from performing for the troops."

"I'm looking forward to that the most," she confessed. "I was just standing here thinking about the looks on their faces when they see what we have in store for them. Should be quite impressive."

He gestured for her to move forward in the line as they boarded the plane. "Having Trevor Thornton won't hurt either."

"No." She tried to maintain her composure but couldn't resist a little happy dance. "I'm so excited to meet him."

"Fan girling a bit, are you?"

She grinned. "A bit. I hope I get to sing with him at least once."

"Darlin', once he hears your voice, he'll want you to go on tour with him. I've never heard such amazing pipes on a human before. Are you sure you aren't an angel?"

Heat returned to Connie's face. She slapped him lightly on the arm. "Stop it. I bet you tell the same to all the girl's."

"I would if they had your voice, but honestly, Connie, I've never heard anything like it."

She turned away from him and smiled, pride filling her heart. She knew her voice was a gift from God, and he'd been a troubled soul the night he'd stepped into the rehearsal hall and heard her sing "Amazing Grace." She wasn't sure what caused his sleeplessness, but her voice had allowed him a respite from whatever plagued him. She offered up a quick prayer of thanks she'd been able to reach him…soothe him.

"Thank you, Logan. That's very flattering. I just open my mouth, and God guides out the sound."

They stepped up the stairs onto the giant cargo plane. Connie's mouth formed an O.

"First time on a C-13?" Logan steadied her with a hand on her elbow.

She nodded, stunned at the number of people milling around inside the plane. She'd been told they had at least three pilots, not to mention all the other crew it took to load, unload, and set up for the shows in all the places they planned to visit. She and Logan made their way to the passenger seats which were wide and thickly cushioned with plenty of space between them. Nothing liked the cramped space of a commercial airliner. This would make the long flights much more comfortable.

Choosing a seat about two rows up from the where the crew continued to strap down the cargo, she sat.

"Mind if I sit next to you?" Logan's eyebrows arched with his question.

"Of course not, I'd love to have your company. My friend Wrynn flew ahead with Stan to start preparing for our arrival in Kuwait, and I haven't had time to make any other friends yet, so I'd be delighted to have your company."

He smiled. "Thanks." He glanced around alert.

"Always on duty?" she asked. "Surely, there's no threat here on the plane."

"You never know." He waved to Manny farther up front. "We keep an eye out all the time. When I was in Iraq…" He paused, swallowed hard. She noticed the color of his skin fade to a light shade of gray.

"You served?"

He nodded, turning his attention to stowing his gear.

"Thank you," Connie murmured.

He sat down, twisting to face her. His expression had grown hard. "Don't thank me. I wasn't very good at it."

She arched both eyebrows, surprised at the statement. She sensed there was an underlying meaning, but she wouldn't push him yet. She'd get to know him better. She had twelve hours to ferret out what troubled him. Maybe she could help. Plus, she loved his voice. Hearing him talk would be no chore.

A commotion drew her attention to the doorway she'd entered moments before. A hoard of people boarded the plan, laughing and playfully pushing and shoving each other. A few staggered across the floor, bumping into some of the cargo.

"Hey, guys, ease up. Act like you've got some manners." The man stood just outside the doorway, beyond Connie's line of sight. She stared at what must be the band for Trevor Thornton. The dead giveaway was the country singer's name plastered across the front of a chesty blonde woman. She grinned stupidly and waved at everyone on the plane.

"Hi, y'all," she yelled, her speech slightly slurred.

Logan rose. "Oh, boy, here we go. I was hoping this was going to be an easy tour."

"Are they drunk?"

"Some of them appear to be a little inebriated, yes. I'll be back after I get them seated. Save my place." He smiled down at her.

Connie's heart fluttered. *Wow, what a look. You turn it on too many women, buddy, and you'll have a problem. You're downright hot.*

Logan stepped across her, and she caught a whiff of his rich, woodsy cologne. Again, her heart gave a little thump. *Stop it, girl. You've got a great man waiting for you in Brooksville, and what might be a forever relationship just getting started, and here you go mooning over the security guard.* She snorted and rolled her eyes at her thoughts.

"Hey, folks." Logan approached the band members. "Move along this way and we can get you seated."

He grasped the tall, leggy, busty blonde by the arm to steady her. "This way, miss."

"Oh, aren't you dreamy?" she drawled. "Trevor, you've got some competition here. What's your name, darlin'?"

"I'm Logan Richards, ma'am. Please step this way." He tugged on her arm. She leaned into him.

"I'll follow you anywhere, sweetie."

Logan tipped his head back. "I believe coffee might be a good choice when they ask about beverages."

The woman barked out a raucous laugh. "I'm a nervous flyer. I needed a toddy just to get on the plane."

"Smells like you had more than one." As he led the blonde past Connie's row, he gave her an eye roll. She covered her mouth with her hand to hide her grin.

She twisted in her seat hearing a male voice from the back of the plane again. "Angel, you behave. We probably shouldn't have given her that extra drink. Oops."

A tall, sandy-haired man stood just behind the last row of seats. In comparison to Sven, he wasn't quite as tall but close. A tight pair of jeans covered his impressive butt, and his chest strained against a navy graphic T-shirt imprinted with a white guitar. Connie bet his name was spread across the back. From where she sat, his eyes looked hazel, about the same color as her own. His hair hung almost to his shoulders, and the ends flipped up under his black cowboy hat. She could tell he spent plenty of time in the gym. *One strike against him*. Men with bodies like that normally had an ego just as big.

Now, don't go judging the man before you even meet him. He might be your ticket to the big time. You can put up with a little bit of ego for the chance, she chastised herself.

Trevor Thornton followed Logan up the aisle. He stopped when he saw Connie. She smiled, stood.

"And who might you be?"

She gave her hair a nervous toss. "Um…I'm Connie Champion. One of the singers."

He clasped her palm in both his hands. His fingers were calloused from all the guitar playing, but his palms were warm and smooth. "I'm Trevor Thornton. Pleased to meet ya."

"Oh, I know who you are," she stammered. Heat flamed in her cheeks. "I've been a fan for a long time."

"Nice to hear. So, you're one of the singers?"

She nodded, swallowing.

He gave her a once over glance, his lips stretching into a smile. He winked. "Twelve hours is a long flight. Maybe we can…um…sing a song or something."

Connie drew her brows together, not quite understanding the meaning of his strange statement. "Uh…sure."

He nodded, winked again, then moved up the aisle to join the rest of the band at the front of the plane.

"Okay," she muttered. "That was weird." From all she'd read about Trevor Thornton, he appeared to be a perfect gentleman. Had he just hit on her? Really?

Oh don't be an idiot, Connie. He probably had a few nerve settling drinks, too. He's just a little loose-lipped. He just meant we can jam on the flight.

How fun. Just sitting around and singing with Trevor and some of the other performers. She sat down and settled into her seat. She saw one of the pilots step out of the cockpit and pull a PA microphone from the wall.

"Good morning, all. If you'd go ahead and take your seats and buckle up, we will get this show on the road…or in the air." He chuckled at his own joke. "If there is anything you need to make your flight more enjoyable, just let us know."

He glanced at Trevor's band. "And just so you know, no alcohol is allowed on military flights."

A large groan escaped the group.

Trevor stood. "Hey, y'all, listen up. This is a great opportunity to serve our troops who protect our country. Settle down and don't behave like a bunch of animals." He glanced at Connie, winked again.

She sat up straighter in her seat. *Oh great. I'm going to have to be on my toes with this guy.*

Trevor looked at the pilot. "You won't have to worry about my band. They're a great group of folks. They will behave." He twisted toward the band members. "Right?"

They all nodded, muttering, "Right," "Sure, Trevor," and "No problemo."

"Glad to hear it." The pilot offered them a smile. "Let's all get buckled up, and we'll be in the air shortly. Once we reach a safe cruising altitude, I'll come back out and check on you. If you're the praying sort, shoot one up for a safe flight."

Connie fingered the tiny gold cross necklace she wore. She pulled it to her lips and gave it a quick kiss, then said a quick prayer for their safe arrival in Kuwait.

Excitement rolled through her like a wave. This was it. She was really going to do this. She knew she must have been beaming when Logan rejoined her.

"Excited?"

She nodded. "I am. This is going to be a wonderful trip. I just feel it."

"I'll make sure of it."

The plane rolled down the tarmac. She briefly wondered how such a large plane could possibly take off, but soon, they were soaring above New York on their way to the biggest adventure of her life.

Chapter Eleven

The plane soared to cruising altitude. Connie relaxed her grip on the arm rests and settled more comfortably in her seat.

"Convinced we aren't going to fall from the sky?" Logan asked, a smirk on his handsome face.

She puffed out a breath. "I'm still in awe of the fact something this heavy, loaded down with this much stuff, can actually fly."

"Modern marvels, right?"

She agreed, studying his face. His eyes drew her in, like staring into a mug of dark hot chocolate. His smile sat easily on his lips when he chose to use it—which he did now. She couldn't place the scent of the cologne he wore, but she liked the subtle earthy scent. How had this guy not been swooped up by some girl? Or maybe he had. She didn't think so though. His gaze held secrets. Her curiosity overcame her manners.

"Do you have a girlfriend, Logan?"

The brightness in his eyes dulled a little. "Not at the moment, no." He glanced away, and when he faced her again, the twinkle was back. "Why, are you applying?"

She laughed. "I barely know you."

"The tour is young. Although, I can't compete with the fabulous Trevor Thornton."

Connie shot a glance at the back of Trevor's head. So far, his crew had settled down and were conversing quietly at the front of the plane. She met Logan's gaze. "I'm not so sure about him. Our first interaction wasn't what I thought it would be."

Logan's brows drew together. "What do you mean?"

"I don't know. Perhaps I'm drawing too impetuous of a conclusion this early."

"Wow, what a mouthful. Was he a jerk?"

She laughed again. "You have such a simple way with words."

His gaze remained intent. She squirmed a little in her seat. Clearly, he awaited an answer.

"No, not a jerk exactly. I'm probably over analyzing because I'm such a big fan, but he seems a bit…" She wanted to choose the right word. This could be a long tour if word got back to Trevor she'd said something negative about him.

"Smarmy?" Logan supplied.

His insight surprised her into a snort. She placed a hand over her nose and mouth. When she'd recovered, she said, "That's a good word. I'm going to remember it. What does it mean, exactly?"

"You know what it means. You're just too polite to say it. I saw the way he gave you the once over. Maybe giving him a wide birth might be a good idea."

Heat crept into her cheeks. She didn't want to believe Trevor had made a pass at her, no matter how subtle. Her goals depended on him liking her. If she impressed him, he might be able to open some doors for her singing career. Maybe she'd imagined the look he gave her, and misinterpreted his words, but if Logan had seen it, too, then she'd not been too far off the mark. The last thing she wanted to do was avoid him, for heaven's sake. But she absolutely didn't want to give Trevor the impression she was interested in him in any other way but professionally.

"I'm sure he was just being friendly," she said. "I've never met a celebrity before. Maybe they all greet people that way."

"Humph," Logan grunted. "I've met plenty, and no they don't."

What was that tone? Anger? Disgust? She couldn't quite place it, but he might be a bit biased.

"So, are most celebrities you've met so bad?"

He glanced at the back of Trevor's head. "Some. You have your good ones and your bad ones. The jury is still out on him." He jerked a thumb in Trevor's direction.

"Wow, you form first impressions fast."

"Have to when you're in the security business. You've got to get a sense of how difficult someone will be to deal with."

Connie looked out the window at the clouds sailing by. She supposed Logan had a point, but she didn't want to start the tour suspicious of everyone. Granted, she may be a little out of her league, but she'd dealt with enough admirers back in Brooksville to know which ones to avoid, and she didn't feel Trevor had hit the mark just yet. She'd be cautious though.

She turned toward Logan who'd propped his head against the head rest and closed his eyes. He must have felt her gaze on him for he rolled his head to face her.

"Tell me how you got into the security business," Connie said. "You said you served in the military. Was it a connection from there?"

Logan nodded. "A friend of Manny's was in my platoon in the Marines. When I was discharged early for medical reasons, Glenn hooked me up with Manny."

"Were you wounded?" Sympathy filled her expression, until she saw his eyes grow dark and the lines around his mouth harden.

"In a manner of speaking. Let's talk about you. What's it like to live in Florida? Did you go to the beach all the time?"

His abrupt change of subject startled her. Clearly, he didn't want to discuss his time in the military. From the first time she met him, she'd sensed a troubled soul. People with a clear mind and heart didn't roam the halls in the middle of the night or have trouble sleeping. She'd heard stories of what went on in countries like Iraq and Pakistan. She hoped nothing horrible had happened to him, but she suspected it had. And he blamed himself for whatever it was. Her fixer's heart set a course to help him. He seemed like a super nice guy, and one in need of a friend.

"I live in an area not too close to the water, so no, I didn't go to the beach all the time. My brother and I own an Arabian horse farm. In fact, Champions Gate is well-known for breeding champion racers. We sell them all over the world."

Logan raised his eyebrows. "Impressive. I like horses. Arabians have a reputation for being sweet tempered. Is that true?"

Surprised he knew this much about horses, she nodded. "They do. They are very sweet natured, but they can be determined and stubborn, too. They're bred for stamina, so they sort of come with a permanent can-do attitude."

"What got you into the horse breeding business?"

"It was my brother's dream really. We had a small farm growing up, and Bishop got it in his mind he'd put us on the map. He and his wife started Champions Gate along with his best friend, Quinton Gates. They were very young, but had some great stock. Then when Bishop's wife died during the birth of his triplets, he sank his heart and soul into the ranch. He's traveled all over the world, selling the horses and their sperm for breeding."

Logan shifted in his seat. "Tough break. Triplets, you said?"

Connie nodded. "I stepped in and took over raising the girls." She sighed. "I don't know if it was the right thing to do or not, but it seemed right at the time. He was so lost."

"I know what that feels like," Logan muttered, under his breath.

Her heart ached for him. He had a story, and it weighed on him. She gazed at him for a moment. *Nope. Still too early to push. I'll have to ease it out of him.*

"It was so sad. Bishop couldn't connect with the girls because of his pain over losing Laura. And as they grew older, they looked so much like her, he couldn't move past his grief."

"Wow. What are they doing now that you're on tour with us?"

"That's a great story." Connie told him all about how she'd brought Darbi, her new best friend, from Ireland to be a nanny for the triplets. "Who knew Facebook could foster such lasting friendships? And they're getting married. When I go home at New Year's, they're having the wedding."

"Some story. I guess it just takes the right woman sometimes." He glanced ahead, his expression wistful.

Connie let his statement hang in the air for a moment. So far, she really liked Logan. He treated her with respect, and she felt surprisingly safe with him. He radiated confidence, yet seemed entombed in a deep sadness. She'd seen the same thing in Bishop when Laura died. Perhaps Logan had lost someone close to him.

Tentatively, she reached out to touch his hand. "Did you lose someone close to you?"

He jerked at the contact, then clumsily patted her hand. "In a manner of speaking, but not the way you think."

"I'll listen if you ever want to talk about it."

He held her gaze for several seconds, then offered her one of those dazzling smiles. "I believe you would. Thanks."

Connie returned his smile, hoping she'd broken through maybe one layer of his tough exterior. She looked forward to knowing him better. He intrigued her. Obviously, he'd been through some type of trauma. She couldn't relate to going to war and living through what she'd heard some of the soldiers had witnessed in the Middle East. She wanted to be Logan's friend. It appeared he needed one.

Suddenly, thoughts of Sven popped into her mind. Since boarding the plane, she hadn't given the man much thought with all the other issues filling her brain. Mentally, she compared him with the man sitting next to her. Both were equally good looking, polite, and careful with the way they treated women. Sven, however, lacked the sadness she saw in Logan's eyes.

She didn't like the way she'd not thought of Sven when these exciting things had started happening for her. This relationship developing between them was still so new. Maybe it was why he hadn't immediately jumped to mind after she'd met Trevor.

Her growing affection for Logan worried her a little, too. She could see them developing a strong friendship on this tour. That wouldn't be fair to Sven, who'd loved her practically since elementary school—or so he'd told her.

She removed the band holding her hair and drug her hands through it, frustrated. Perhaps telling Sven she'd give them a shot had been a mistake. There was so much more to experience on this tour and in her life if all went well with Trevor.

She glanced at Logan as she pulled her hair back up into a loose pony tail. Knowing how Sven felt about her, how could she have this affection for the wounded soldier next to her? Didn't take her long to figure it out. Because he was charming as a furry kitten, strong as a bull, and more handsome than any man she'd ever met. Plus, deep in her heart, she knew he needed someone.

She stared out the window. *Crap. I need to cut this out. I cannot allow Logan Richards to screw up what I have growing with Sven. But will Sven be able to handle the long distance and struggles with a career choice like mine?* She wasn't sure. Sven had his roots firmly planted in Brooksville. She wanted to travel the world. *Slow down, Connie. Take it one day at a time. You don't have anything developing with Logan. He's not shown a romantic interest in you.* But what if he did?

One of the crew interrupted her musings, announcing the service of a meal. They passed out trays of food. The passengers had their choice of chicken marsala or Mongolian beef. She chose the chicken, and Logan chose the beef.

"This is very good," she said between bites.

Logan agreed. "The USO doesn't skimp on food. You'll eat well on tour. We may drag you out of bed at the butt crack of dawn and sling you all over the world in a matter of weeks, but you'll eat well."

Connie laughed. "Good. I love to eat."

They clicked their plastic forks together and continued their meal.

Once the food service had been cleared, Trevor rose from his seat and faced the rest of the passengers.

"Who's in the mood for a sing-a-long?"

Angel jumped up. "Me, me."

Connie rolled her eyes. *Like that's a surprise.*

Some of the other performers raised their hands. Trevor passed them and walked up to Connie. "How about you, pretty lady? Want to join us?"

Connie couldn't control the heat that crept into her cheeks. "Um…sure."

Trevor graced her with a huge grin. "Excellent. I'll get my guitar."

"He's in for a real surprise," Logan commented in a hushed tone. "You're going to blow him away. Take it easy on him, will ya? His ego might not be able to handle it."

Connie slapped him playfully. "Will you stop?"

Logan shook his head. "I'm just sayin'."

Trevor retrieved his guitar from a case at the back of the plane. He slipped it over his shoulder, strummed it a few times, and took his place in front of the plane.

"Let's see. How about we start with something we're all familiar with. Any suggestions?"

"How about 'God Bless America'?" someone shouted.

"Good one." Trevor strummed a few chords then started singing in his clear country twang. The rest of the group joined in. Some moved out of their seats closer to the front of the plane where Trevor stood. One of the band members pulled out some drum sticks and tapped a rhythm on the back of the seat.

Connie and Logan joined the group. Her voice rang through the belly of the plane. Trevor glanced at her, surprised, his eyebrows raising as he sang.

A few more songs were suggested, and the group belted them out, laughing and enjoying themselves. Connie ignored Trevor's glances, but inside she bloomed with pride each time she'd hit a note which drew his attention. She didn't miss Logan's expressions either. He wasn't singing, but he kept a close eye on the country singer and his reaction to Connie's voice. He seemed…protective. Inwardly, Connie beamed. She liked Logan Richards, a lot.

When the group paused to catch their breath, the crew passed out water bottles. They all drank, then Trevor said, "Hey, Connie."

She nearly choked on her water. "Hmm?" She didn't realize he would remember her name. He'd met so many people on the plane.

"Do you know my song 'You're A Wonder'?"

"Boy, do I," Connie replied. "I love that song."

"Sing it with me? You can do Angel's part."

Connie's insides turned as liquid as the water she'd just finished drinking. *The Trevor Thornton wants me to sing a duet? I think I'm going to pass out.*

She felt a firm grip on her elbow.

"Easy there, tiger," Logan whispered in her ear. "You don't want to faint in front of your idol."

She almost snorted but cleared her throat instead. "Um, sure."

"Come up here with me."

Connie glanced at Angel. The woman who'd been so friendly upon her arrival didn't appear so now. Perhaps, lingering effects of alcohol caused her reaction, but Angel scowled openly at Connie.

She hesitated a moment, but Logan pushed her forward. "Go on," he urged. "This might be your shot."

She glanced back at him, drawing courage from his smile. Nodding, she wormed her way through the performers up to the front of the plane.

"Key of G okay?" Trevor strummed the guitar.

"Sure," Connie replied. It would be so embarrassing to screw this up or, worse, to pee her pants in front of this crowd. She took a deep breath to calm her jangled nerves. Most of the other performers smiled encouragingly. Angel didn't.

Trevor began the song. Before he'd finished the first verse, she relaxed. It truly was a beautiful song, and she couldn't count the times she'd sung it to herself while working in the barn at home. He finished his part of the song, telling the story of a broken heart trying to heal.

She swallowed, sucked in a breath of air, and sang the woman's verses. She watched the faces of the band. The rest of the troupe had heard her sing, so they weren't surprised any longer, but the band members all nodded and cheered enthusiastically. Except Angel.

When she joined Trevor at the chorus, Connie easily harmonized the parts. Trevor raised his eyebrows, smiling as he sang. She hoped she impressed him. She shot a glance at Logan for reassurance. His eyes were closed as he swayed to the music. For the first time since they'd boarded the plane, he seemed relaxed. Pleasure filled her. She loved seeing people enjoy her singing. She always prayed it brought them as much joy to hear her as it did for her to sing.

The song ended way too soon for Connie. She'd liked the way their voices melded together, his Southern twang with her bright, clear tones. Excitement shot through her. She hoped Trevor thought it sounded as wonderful as she had.

"Holy crap, Connie," he said, putting the guitar aside. He pulled her into his arms for a hug then released her.

Okay, nothing funny there. Just a friendly hug. She smiled up at him.

"That was amazing. We're going to have to do that one on this tour. Would you do it with me?"

Connie heard Angel clear her throat. Trevor glanced her way, clearly caught the angry expression on her face, then smiled at Connie. "At least once?"

"Um, I don't know. Your fans are used to you and Angel doing that song."

"I know, but you brought a depth of soul to it I've never heard before. It'll be fun. Whaddya say?"

Connie didn't look at Angel. This was a shot for her career, and she knew it, yet she sympathized with the other woman, whose feelings were clearly stung. *Maybe that's how this business goes. A person is only great until somebody better came along. Am I the someone better this time? I hate it for you, Angel, but I've got to take my shot. I know I'll regret it if I don't at least try.*

"Okay. If you insist."

The group on the plane cheered. Her heart warmed at their reception of her. She'd slowed the group down in rehearsal, so it cheered her to know they were so supportive. All but Angel, of course.

The captain's voice came over the intercom.

"Hey, folks, that was awesome, but I'm going to have to ask you to return to your seats. We're heading into some bumpy air. I'll let you know when you can move around safely again. Thanks."

Connie and Logan sat down and buckled up. Her stomach twisted with nerves. Bumpy air didn't sound like something she wanted to experience.

Logan laid a warm hand over hers and squeezed. "It'll be okay. Just a little turbulence. Very common when flying over the ocean."

"If you say so," she replied.

"You sang amazing. You sounded better than the original version."

Glad to have a distraction, she replied, "Really? Angel has more of a country vibe than I do. She does it beautifully."

"Yeah, but you did it better. She knew it, too. Did you see the look on her face?"

Embarrassment stabbed Connie. "I did. I feel awful. Trevor really shouldn't have done that to her."

Logan shrugged. "Maybe, but now he knows what your amazing voice sounds like. I'd say you're headed for great things.

She stifled a giggle. *I hope you're right, Logan Richards. I hope you're right.*

Chapter Twelve

Twelve hours later, they arrived in Kuwait. They were shown to their quarters on the base for a few hours of sleep before they began setting up for the show. Connie was too excited to sleep. Guilt tugging at her, she pulled out her phone and called Sven. She activated the video function because she desperately wanted to see his face when she told him about the flight and singing the duet with Trevor.

The phone rang a few times then his features popped onto the screen.

"Hey there, world traveler. Are you in Kuwait safe? How was the flight?"

She smiled. Seeing him warmed her heart but gave her a quick pang of homesickness all at the same time.

"The flight was fantastic. It got a little bumpy at times, but let me tell you what happened."

She relayed the events of her initial meeting with Trevor.

Sven frowned, his brows drawing together. "You be careful with him, Connie. He might be a little too slick for his own good."

Is he jealous? "Don't worry, Sven. I can handle him. You act like I've never had to ward off unwanted attention before. I'm a horsewoman in a horseman's world, remember."

Still frowning, he said, "Yeah, but this guy is famous. He's your idol. Don't let it go to your head. Be careful."

She bristled a bit but tried not to let it show. She wouldn't allow him to bring her off the high of singing with Trevor Thornton. She proceeded to tell Sven about the sing-a-long. "And you'll never believe what happened next. He asked me to sing his duet with him, you know the one… 'You're a Wonder'? And Angel, the woman who sings it with him on the record was sitting right there."

Sven grinned. "I bet that went over well with her."

"Yeah, she didn't like it much. I felt kinda bad for her, but I sang it anyway. And you know what? I sounded better. Trevor even said so. He wants me to sing it with him on this tour. Sven, this might be my shot."

Sven struggled through a few different emotions. Finally, he smiled, although it didn't totally reach his eyes. "That's great, sweetheart. I know that's why you went on this tour. Lord knows you've got the pipes for it."

"Um…you didn't sound all enthusiastic." She hadn't expected him to be as happy about it as she was, but she didn't like the reservation she sensed in him. Had he changed his mind about supporting her dreams?

"I'm happy for you, really. I just don't like what you said about the way Trevor eyeballed you."

She grinned. "You're jealous."

"Am not," he declared.

"You're jealous, you want to sock him," she sang.

Sven sighed. "Okay…maybe I'm a little jealous. You're thousands of miles away, in a foreign country with the most famous country singer on the planet, who's making passes at you for cripes sake."

Inwardly, his jealousy pleased her. As long as it didn't consume their budding relationship. She wanted to tell him about Logan and her suspicions about something bad happening to him, but she held back. He might have had enough with just the Trevor issue. No reason to overwhelm him on the first call home.

"I'm a big girl, Sven. I know what to do if Trevor gets too fresh. Besides, I'm the one planning on using him, remember?"

Sven shrugged. "I hope so. Do you think all this is worth it, Connie? Have you considered what you might have to go through to get where you want to be?"

She sighed. "I know I'm new to all this, and you're worried about me. I appreciate it, I do. But Sven, I'll be okay. The joy that fills my soul when I sing and see the expressions on the people who enjoy my voice is indescribable."

His features relaxed a little. "I know, baby. I know how much this means to you. And I don't want to make it harder." He glanced at his watch. "What time is it over there? Isn't it like almost 4:00 a.m.?"

She nodded. "It is, but I'm too wired to sleep. We have to gather this afternoon to set up for the show tonight. I'm a little nervous. I can just see myself tripping over these two left feet of mine and throwing everyone off."

"From what I saw when I was in New York, you've got this down. Stop worrying. Hey, you should call Darbi. She's got some news for you."

"Oh no, are the girls okay?"

"They're fine. In fact, there's going to be one more."

The blood drained from her face. "She's not…"

Sven must have realized how his words sounded. He laughed. "No, Darbi isn't pregnant. Sorry I made it sound that way."

Connie's hand flew to her heart. "Oh, gosh. You scared the stuffing out of me. I was going to have to have a serious talking to with Bishop. They're getting married in less than two months. Sheesh."

A flush crept up Sven's neck into his cheeks. "Nah, not what I meant. As far as I know, and I don't know this for sure, they aren't sharing a room. He wouldn't do that with the girls in the house."

"Well what did you mean?"

"She probably wants to tell her yourself."

"Oh, don't you dare. You've let the cat out of the bag now. You've got to tell me."

So, he did. Sven explained all about Mia and the temporary foster care Darbi and Bishop would be providing. Connie's heart warmed. She'd made the right decision when she'd convinced Darbi to come across the pond.

She swiped a tear from her eye. "How sweet. A year ago, Bishop would have never considered it. She's really softened him up."

"I'll say. I know he loved Laura, but I believe he loves Darbi just as much."

"I know. I can't wait to come home for the wedding."

"I can't wait for you to come home either. Where all are you going?"

"I'll email you the itinerary. I can't remember all the spots. I just walk in the direction they point me in. I know we will be in England by Christmas." A thought occurred to her. "Sven, do you think you could come to England for Christmas? A lot to ask, I know, but it would be so cool. We could take a few days and then fly back home together for the wedding."

His expression grew thoughtful. She loved the way his eyebrows squished together when he concentrated.

"Let me check my calendar. Courts are usually closed for two weeks, and I'll make sure I have nothing pressing. I think I could make it work."

She jumped up and down on the bed. "Yay. Now I've really got something to look forward to."

He smiled, his crystal-blue eyes twinkling. She knew her comment pleased him. "Me, too. You get some sleep if you can. I don't want to get a report you fell off the stage in front of Trevor Thornton."

"Oh God, wouldn't it be horrible? I'd die of embarrassment."

They both laughed.

"Good night, Connie. I miss you, sweetheart."

She didn't miss the fact he didn't say he loved her. That was okay. It was a bit soon. "I miss you, too, Sven. Talk to you soon."

She hung up and flopped back on the bed, a swirl of emotions running through her. Sven had been her rock through some really tough times. He was a man she knew she could count on. The fact he looked like Thor didn't hurt either. But something nagged at her about pushing the relationship forward. Her feelings weren't as strong as his, but this was so new to her. Thinking about him in a romantic way still seemed a bit strange. And the fact Logan had begun to catch her attention hadn't escaped her.

She huffed out a breath. She'd gone for years without a man so much as winking at her, and now she had three interested all at the same time. Trevor, she'd mark off the available list. It wouldn't be wise to have lustful thoughts about the man she wanted to hitch her professional wagon to. It could only lead to disaster. But Logan wasn't in any danger of an attachment. She couldn't say for sure she'd like to explore more than friendship with him without knowing him a lot better, but the man had potential.

Then there's Sven. My mighty Norse god for the asking. I can't believe I didn't jump on that horse and ride it all the way to the altar. He's a definite catch, but I'm not so sure he can be supportive of my career.

She snorted. *What career? You're singing on one USO tour, and, yes, you sing well, but you're no Whitney Houston. Cool your jets, Connie girl.* She smiled remembering Darbi's favorite saying to her. At that moment, she knew who she needed to talk to about her man problems. She looked at the travel alarm clock on the bedside table. 4:15 a.m. If she didn't get some sleep, Sven's prediction of her falling off the stage would come true. She yawned. Perhaps sleep would come after all. And some very nice dreams.

Chapter Thirteen

Logan arrived at the hangar where the show would take place just before five in the afternoon. The crew had completed most of the stage construction. He still marveled at the speed at which these people could work. He waved at Dave Kapinski, the manager in charge of the setup crew. If any man knew how to stage a show, Dave did. He'd worked in show business in one fashion or another for thirty some odd years. He generously volunteered for the USO tours.

Manny shouted to Logan from across the warehouse. The two men reached each other and exchanged a quick hug and pat on the back.

"How did you think the flight went?" Manny asked.

"A bit bumpy, but the entertainment was fantastic."

"Yeah, wasn't it?"

"I tell you, Manny, she can sing like nobody I've ever heard."

"She sure can. Maybe she'll get her shot if Trevor likes her."

"Maybe." He touched Manny's sleeve, drew him in closer. "Listen, I observed Trevor making a couple of passes at Connie. She may be a little too star struck to know what's going on, but I've seen such a leer before on a man. Help me keep an eye on her, will ya?"

The large man nodded. "Yeah. Thanks for telling me. I promised her boyfriend I'd look after her."

Logan sucked in a breath. He struggled not to let his surprise show. *Boyfriend? She never mentioned any boyfriend.*

"Um," he managed. "Okay. Good. You be sure and do that."

Manny eyed him until he blushed. He glanced away to the crew still building the stage.

"You got a thing for Connie?"

He jerked back around. "What? Me? No. What would make you say so?"

"Because when I said the word boyfriend, you looked like somebody'd socked you in the gut."

Logan tried to laugh, but it sounded forced. Manny never did beat around the bush. He went straight for the heart of things.

"You know the tour rules. No fraternizing. Besides, she's a sweet girl and could easily be a heartbreaker without meaning to."

"Like I need love advice from the likes of you?" Logan tried to make light of the situation. He did feel something for Connie, even if in the very early stages of attraction. No one could soothe his troubled mind like she could with a song. He knew the rules about not dating members of the troupe, and the solid reasons behind them. His head planned to follow them, he just hoped he could get his heart and soul to follow suit.

"Looks like ya might," Manny commented, only half teasing.

"Nah. I'm good there. I know the rules, Manny. She's just a pretty special person is all. I'd like to think I've made a new friend, and Lord knows I don't have many of those."

"Your own doin', Logan. You keep yourself so closed off all the time. You're a pretty likeable guy. You should step out there more. Ya know who I think is pretty?"

Logan struggled not to laugh. Here he'd just gotten a lecture on not fraternizing, and Manny pops up with a statement like that. "No, Manny. Who do you think is pretty?"

"Wrynn."

Logan nodded. Wrynn's looks hadn't escaped his attention either. "Same rules apply. No fraternizing."

Manny chuckled. "Touché my friend. At least Wrynn would be a more permanent fixture. I think Connie's gonna move on after this tour. I agree with you about the way she sings. An angel on Earth if there ever was one. I wouldn't be surprised if Trevor doesn't hook her up. She's just that good."

Logan sighed. "Yeah. I'm afraid that's what she's after, but I think she's playing with fire by messing with Trevor Thornton. I ran a background on him before he joined the tour, like I'm supposed to, and I didn't much like what I found out."

"Oh? Care to share?"

"I'm not keeping anything from you, Manny. He doesn't have anything bad enough to keep him off the tour, but there were a few drunk and disorderly misdemeanors, and some sexual harassment issues floating around in his past. I hope he doesn't try anything with Connie…um….or any of the other women."

Manny grinned. "Oh boy, you're toast. I can see it all over your face. You've fallen for the horsewoman from Florida."

Logan pushed his shoulder, causing the larger man to stagger a step. "Cut it out. I've fallen for her singing, that's all."

"Ah, the siren's song. Better guard your heart there, buddy. She might bewitch you."

Logan laughed. *She already has.* But he replied, "I'm no catch. A woman falls in love with me and she's getting a basketload of trouble."

Manny started walking the perimeter of the warehouse. Logan followed.

"Don't say that, Logan. I don't want to hear any negativity. You still having those nightmares?"

This man had become one of the few people Logan trusted with his deepest secrets. "Yeah, some. It's gotten better over the last few months."

"Maybe you should have the doc adjust your meds. Ya know, give ya somethin' to help ya sleep or something."

Logan shook his head. "I don't want any more medicine, Manny. I feel like I'm carrying around a pharmacy as it is. I know I can beat this. I'm still doing the counseling through Skype, and it helps a lot."

"I'm glad. No one should go through what you went through and not have support. It was a tough time, and I'm worried you being back here might trigger an episode. You got all that under control?"

Logan nodded. At least he hoped so. Sometimes, his outbursts snuck up on him. "Where all that happened was in Afghanistan. We won't be close to there. I'll be okay, Manny. Don't worry. I appreciate you thinking about me though. If I feel an urge, I'll get somewhere away from all the others and let you know."

Manny placed a big hand on his shoulder and squeezed. "You do that, son. I want to look after those who stand on the wall."

"Stood on the wall, Manny. Stood."

"Makes no difference to me. You served your country proud. Wasn't your fault all the crap that got thrown at ya."

Logan fought the clogging of his throat. He wished he could agree with his friend. Even after several years had passed and he'd had plenty of therapy, it was still difficult for him to let go of the responsibility which plagued him and was often the subject of his nightmares. But Connie's singing really helped. This evening at the rehearsal, he planned to use his phone and record a song or two. He could play it just before he went to sleep. Instinct told him he'd sleep like a baby.

"I'm going to check on the celebs. You want to continue the perimeter walk? I let Walker sleep in and take the concert."

Logan nodded. Manny left without saying anything else about Connie or Wrynn. His boss was only half kidding about the fraternizing. It happened behind closed doors all the time. What Manny was more concerned about was Logan's heart. Coming out of one bad break up was enough for anyone to handle. He didn't need to go through a second when Connie took off for fame and fortune, which, from the look on Trevor's face on the plane yesterday, would no doubt happen. For the first time in a long time though, he had a friend and that was what mattered most. A friend he could keep. *As long as you can keep yourself under control.*

At seven o'clock, the performers assembled on stage to do a fast run through. The soldiers had already lined up at the door, and it promised to be a packed house. Trevor strolled in to cheers and shouts. He waved at the troops before allowing the door to close behind him. Logan watched him saunter on stage. The lanky man seemed nice enough, but instinct warned him to keep a sharp eye. He wasn't sure Trevor had the god complex he'd seen with some celebs who'd been on the tours, but his ego was large enough. He hoped Connie knew what she was doing. Playing with fire could get her singed. He chuckled to himself. He should suggest it to her as a name for a song.

Suddenly, a small pair of hands covered his eyes. His body went rigid, automatically preparing to fight. He grabbed the wrists and spun around, Connie now facing him. She let out a terrified squeak. He dropped her hands immediately.

A red flush crept into her cheeks, and she meekly said, "Guess who?"

The tension immediately drained out of his body. "I'm sorry."

She laughed, but it wasn't her full-on high-pitched tone he was used to. "I guess I should know better than to sneak up on an ex-military security guard."

He huffed out a breath, forced a smile to rid the last of the adrenaline. "Yeah, probably not the best plan." He wanted to change the subject quickly. "Did you get any sleep?"

She nodded, her blonde hair slipping over her shoulders. *God, she's gorgeous. I swear she's an angel sent straight from Heaven.*

She wore a long thigh-length gray T-shirt with the USO emblem plastered across the front over a pair of black stretchy pants. He recognized the uniform of the dancers. It hugged her body in all the most delicious places. He glanced away, trying not to stare.

"Looks like they're about ready for you. Are you wearing that the entire show?"

Connie shook her head. "No, I've got this cute autumn-colored dress to change into for my solo part."

"Are you singing with Trevor tonight?"

"Only for the group parts. He said we needed to rehearse a bit before we put it in the show."

"I'll be he did," Logan muttered.

"What?"

"Nothing. I'm looking forward to the show."

She grinned. "Me, too. I'm so excited and really nervous, too. I hope I don't fall off the stage."

He laughed, picturing it. "You won't. Just stay away from the edges. And if you do, I know a desert full of soldiers who will be more than happy to catch you."

She laughed, and her shoulders relaxed.

"You're going to be amazing. Just take a deep breath and have fun."

She reached out and squeezed his hand. The bolt of electricity that charged through him at the contact surprised him, but he managed to keep her from noticing. His attraction to this delightful woman multiplied.

"You're so sweet. Thank you."

He grabbed his cell phone. "Let me grab a picture pre-tour. You look amazing by the way. I really like the way your hair looks down."

She offered a shy smile, and he snapped a quick picture.

"I'll take one post tour and we'll compare the energy level." He chuckled. "Oh by the way, would you mind if I record a song or two of yours when you sing tonight?"

Her eyes widened. "Well, no, but why?"

He led her toward the stage for he'd heard them calling for her. "It helps me sleep."

Connie smiled so beautifully he had the strongest urge to pull her into his arms and kiss her right there in front of God and everybody. He resisted.

"You're a good man, Logan Richards. Of course, you can record my songs, but you have to promise to delete them if they stink."

He laughed good and loud, grateful for the break in mood. "Oh, they won't stink. I know it. These soldiers are in for a real treat."

He turned her over to the stage manager, and they quickly rehearsed a few songs. She sounded amazing as always, and he watched Trevor's facial expressions during her performance. His heart sank. From the look on the country singer's face, and the way he whispered to his band manager, Connie had a solid future in country music if it was what she wanted.

He glanced at the photo he'd taken of her and sighed.

Chapter Fourteen

Later that night, Connie and Wrynn sat in their quarters going over every moment of the show. It was late, and she was exhausted, but so high on post-show adrenaline, she couldn't sleep. They sipped on soothing lemon chamomile tea and giggled like girls.

"You were fantastic." Wrynn hugged her mug with both hands. "Of course, you know. I don't need to tell you."

"Oh, yes you do. My dancing was atrocious." Connie rolled her eyes. "I was off-step more than a newborn colt."

"I didn't notice." Wrynn hid her mouth with the mug.

Connie slapped at her playfully. "You did, too. Was it bad?"

Her friend laughed. "No, not at all. Barely noticeable, and you weren't the only one to mess up."

"Really? I feel a little better."

"It was a great show. The soldiers couldn't stop raving about it. When we do this in the states, all their families will come. When Stan gets a good idea, boy, he really gets a good idea."

Connie nodded, settling more comfortably on the cot. She wanted to call Darbi and tell her all about the show, but it was still nighttime in Brooksville. They had a day off today for rest, so she'd call her after she woke up—if she could ever go to sleep. The concert had been amazing, and, to her utter joy, she pleased the crowd with her songs. Once or twice she'd been a little pitchy. It had been hard to hear the band over the screaming soldiers, but once she started singing, the silence which filled the warehouse had been deafening. Only her voice and the music floated through the rafters of the high metal ceilings. She'd even noticed a few soldiers swiping at their eyes.

After the concert, they'd formed a receiving line with Trevor at the front and her at the back. She'd been stunned at the number of men who wanted her autograph as well. The pride in her own gift shamed her a bit, but she ignored it. Flying high on the flattery and praise would be okay for one night. She hadn't missed the approval on Trevor's face when he'd heard her sing. She offered up a quick prayer of thanks to ease her conscience.

"I've never seen so many people in one place," she commented to Wrynn.

"It was quite a turnout. I think we plan to do one, maybe two more shows for the guys who were on duty and couldn't attend. When word of this show gets around, it'll be suicide if we try to leave too soon."

"Great. Will it put us behind getting to Japan by Thanksgiving?"

"I don't think so. I'd built in a few rest days we can use for travel. Not much to sight see here." She chuckled.

Connie shook her head. "No, I don't think I want to leave the base."

"Nor can you."

"Sounds like a plan. I'm surprised I'm not more sore and tired. I guess all the rehearsing paid off."

"Give it a few shows," Wrynn commented, settling down on a cot opposite Connie. "You'll feel it soon. These tours are exhausting."

Connie leaned against the wall, her legs stretched out across the cot. She wiggled her still sore toes.

"Have you spoken to your boyfriend since you arrived in Kuwait?"

"I'm not sure I'd call him my boyfriend yet. We just started thinking about getting romantic. It's still a bit strange to think of Sven that way." Connie leaned forward. "Can I ask you something, Wrynn, and you not think me a terrible person?"

Wrynn smiled. "The last thing anyone could accuse you of is being a terrible person. What's up?"

"How much do you know about Logan Richards? We were able to spend some time together on the plane on the way out here, and I think he's a super nice guy, but he really seems to have a lot of underlying sadness in his life."

Wrynn cocked her head and went straight to the point. "Are you interested in him?"

Connie blew a raspberry with her lips. "Boy, you don't mess around. You get right to the heart of it."

Her new friend laughed. "Saves time. So?"

Connie scanned Wrynn's face. The laugh had sounded a bit forced to her ears and the cheerfulness hadn't quite reached her eyes. She decided not to get too deep into the subject. "Not really. I mean I'd like to be his friend. He doesn't seem to have too many of those."

"How do you know? He may have a whole host of friends back in the States."

Connie shook her head. "No…I don't think so. I think he struggles with something. He's told me he has trouble sleeping and my singing soothes him. Not a comment I normally hear about my singing. He has this lost look about him. Have you ever noticed it? He said he'd served on a few tours before."

"I've worked with him for about two years. You're right. He is a really nice guy, and I can definitely see why he'd be interested in you. You're beautiful, you sing like an angel…"

"Whoa, wait a minute. I didn't say he was interested in me. I'd like to get to know him better as a friend. I've got Sven to consider after all."

"You could have fooled me. I watched him watch you sing tonight. He was recording you on his phone. Did you know?"

Connie noticed the sharpness of Wrynn's tone increase. *Is Wrynn interested in Logan herself?* Instinct told her to tread lightly.

"I know. He asked my permission, and I told him it was okay. He said my voice helps him sleep."

"I think he may have experienced some bad stuff in Afghanistan. Maybe it haunts him some."

Connie nodded, ready to change the subject. "My brother is getting…."

Suddenly, a man's yell from the room across the hall interrupted her. They both sat up straighter on the bed.

"What the heck?" Connie scooted to the side of the mattress, craning her neck toward the door.

There were a few moments of silence, then they heard it again. An agonized, desperate wail.

The women shot to their feet and ran out into the hall.

"That's Logan and Manny's room. Manny's on duty tonight, so it must be Logan. Either he's having a really good time with someone, or he's having a nightmare."

The yelling increased. Connie leaned against the door to listen. She couldn't make out the words, but she sensed a high level of distress. "I think we should go in there."

Wrynn agreed and tried the door knob. It was unlocked. She opened the door slightly, Connie leaning over her shoulder.

"Logan? Is everything alright?"

Through the dim glow of an outside light, Connie could see the figure of a man thrashing about in the bed.

"God no! No! No! Don't go there!" Logan screamed.

"We need to wake him up." Connie shoved Wrynn out of the way.

"No wait." Wrynn grabbed her by the elbow. "If he has PTSD and is in the middle of a flashback or related nightmare, he might hurt you. He's very strong and could grab you around the neck or break your arm or something. He'll act on instinct."

Wrynn rubbed her neck absently. "My brother has PTSD."

"Get down! Get down! Incoming!" Logan curled up in a ball on the bed, his arms covering his head.

"What do we do? Should I throw some water on him or something?"

Wrynn stepped closer to the bed. She spotted his revolver on the nightstand. "I'm going to get his gun. Then we can try to wake him up. I just don't want him to grab it and start shooting.

Connie sucked in a breath. *Gun? Oh boy.*

Wrynn tiptoed to the bedside table and gingerly lifted the revolver and stepped back. She passed it to Connie who, no stranger to guns but still not comfortable with them, placed it on top of the dresser.

"Logan," Wrynn said, loud and firm.

He continued to moan and writhe in the bed. Suddenly, he stiffened. His legs and arms shot out from his body, every muscle rigid.

"Oh no. No. No. Please no," he moaned.

"Good Lord, what happened to this poor man?" Connie whispered. "I can't stand this anymore, I'm going to—"

"No," Wrynn responded sharply. "I'll do it. I know what to do. You just be ready to go grab somebody if he attacks me."

Oh crap. This is crazy.

Connie nodded, standing near the door.

Logan started to sob. His muscles loosened, and he covered his face with his hands and rolled back and forth on the bed. Wrynn took this as the opportunity to try and wake him.

She stepped up to the bed, leaned in, and took a firm hold on his shoulders. "Logan," she shouted, shaking him hard.

He continued to sob.

Wrynn dug her fingers into his shoulders and shook him more firmly. "Logan, wake up. You're having a nightmare."

He started to fight against Wrynn's hold on him. "No, let me go. Get away."

"Logan! Wake up!"

His eyes popped open. An expression of total disorientation filled his face. Tears streamed down his cheeks.

"Logan, it's me, Wrynn. Do you recognize me?"

His head turned slowly to face the woman holding him down on the bed. Wrynn sat beside him.

"You're okay, buddy." She stroked the damp hair from his forehead. He rolled away from her continuing to sob.

"Connie, will you sing something for him?"

Connie blinked. "What?"

"Sing something you think he'll like. It will help bring him to the surface faster."

She sang the first thing that came to mind. "Amazing Grace." The song he'd heard her sing the night he walked into the rehearsal hall.

Approaching the other side of the bed, she sang softly. Wrynn rubbed his back while he cried.

Connie sat on the bed and reached for his hand. She held it loosely and continued to sing. He relaxed a little, his sobbing eased.

Wrynn murmured into his ear, trying to bring him around. "It's okay, Logan. You had a nightmare. Connie and I heard you yelling from across the hall." She continued to stroke his back.

His eyes flickered open. She kept singing, unsure of what to do next.

Wrynn reached around and urged him to face her. He rolled over. She pulled him into her arms, holding him like a mother would a child. She stroked the back of his head.

"Wherever you were, you're not there now. You're back, here with us."

Logan nodded, sighing deeply. Connie finished the last verse of the song. Logan lifted his head and glanced from Wrynn to Connie.

He offered a weak smile. "Thanks." He cleared his throat and struggled out of Wrynn's hold to sit up. "You all can go now. I'm fine."

"Logan, are you—"

Wrynn shook her head sharply, so Connie stopped talking, a little offended at her friend's reaction.

Wrynn rose from the bed. "Okay. We're going. We're right across the hall if you need anything. Try to get some rest."

Connie realized she still held Logan's hand. She gave it a quick squeeze, but he pulled it away.

"Thanks again." He shifted to a more upright position. "I'll see you tomorrow."

Realizing they'd been dismissed, she followed Wrynn out of the room. When they'd shut the door to their room, Connie said, "Why did you shush me?"

Wrynn plopped on her cot then ran a hand through her chestnut hair. "I'm sorry. I'm just used to dealing with this, I guess. Most men with PTSD are highly embarrassed by it. They see it as something they should be able to control, but they can't. I'm not sure what happened to Logan, but it must have been bad. That was some grip the nightmare had on him. Thanks for the singing. I think it eased him to the surface a little better."

"Music soothes the savage beast," Connie mused.

"Something like that."

"I wonder what happened to him?" She sat on her own cot.

"No telling. Maybe Manny knows. We may never know."

"I know Logan doesn't like to talk about his military service. He doesn't seem to think he was a very good soldier."

"He said so?"

"Not in so many words, but he gave me that impression. Maybe someone died he was responsible for," Connie said.

"Maybe." Wrynn pulled off her sneakers. "I'm going to get a shower and then try to go to sleep.

"Yeah, I guess you're right. I'm still adjusting to the time difference."

Wrynn chuckled. "Wait until we get back home to the States. Your body will be so messed up."

Connie's friend gathered her belongings and stepped into the small bathroom. When she shut the door, Connie leaned back against the wall. She studied her still trembling hands. This was turning into an interesting trip indeed. Her heart bled for the man across the hall, who was haunted by who knew how many ghosts. She wanted to be his friend even more now.

Chapter Fifteen

Thanksgiving morning dawned bright and sunny. The Florida sun was warm but not hot, and the humidity remained low. The sweet scent of some flower Dusty couldn't identify floated through the light breeze. She rode Sweet Mountain Laurel, her quarter horse she boarded at Champion's Gate. Quinton rode ahead of her on Bullet, the frisky colt he'd been working with for the last several weeks. He reined in the horse, his biceps flexing with the effort to hold him in. Clearly, the young stallion wanted his head.

Quinton had to be the handsomest man she'd ever seen, and the dumbest. With his strong Native American heritage, he reminded her of the actor Lou Diamond Phillips, only much larger. Quinton stood about six foot four if he was an inch, something Dusty loved in a man. She'd have to stand on a stool to kiss him, if she ever got the chance again. Today, he wore his usual horse training uniform—blue jeans and a Champions Gate polo even though it was a holiday. She rolled her eyes. Men and their thoughts of acceptable family dinner attire. She'd make sure he changed his shirt before going to Bishop and Darbi's for dinner later this afternoon.

Dusty loved Thanksgiving at Champions Gate. Growing up in the foster care system hadn't given her a real sense of family. She'd enjoyed, even loved, a few of the families she stayed with as a girl, but it was nothing like being with her best friends Quinton, Bishop, and now Darbi. She missed Connie more than she could say. This Thanksgiving would be so different. One, because Darbi was celebrating her first one, being from Ireland. Two, Connie was missing. And three, the family had Mia with them. She offered up another prayer of thanks for Darbi Brennan. Thanks to her new friend, Mia had a home, even if it might be temporary, but she'd didn't think it would be.

Dusty had stopped by a few afternoons ago, and had found Mia grooming one of the horses in the barn. She proudly showed Dusty what she'd been taught and prattled on about the new riding school Darbi planned to start next month.

"Hey, Dusty." Quinton's shout brought her out of her reverie. She noticed he'd ridden several yards ahead of her. "You gonna sit on that horse all morning, or are we going to ride? Bullet here has an itch he needs to scratch."

She grinned at the smiling rancher. *God he's so beautiful. I wish I didn't love him madly, but I do.*

"Coming," she called, digging her heels into her horse's sides. "Giddy-up."

Mountain Laurel sprang into action, racing toward Quinton and the pitch-black Arabian. As she flew by, the man she loved whooped for joy. He let the colt have his head, and they raced past her.

What a pretty pair. A dark haired man on a dark horse. One of these days, Dusty you idiot, you just need to tell him how you feel. He's obviously not going to get it. He's just too shy. A brick in the head's what he's going to need.

She smiled, enjoying the horse's bunching muscles beneath her, the wind in her face, blowing her auburn hair behind her. She mashed her Stetson tighter on her head. She'd just paid a fortune for it and didn't want to lose it.

They raced across the meadow until they reached the pond. A bench sat under a willow tree near the edge of the water. Bishop had built the small oasis for his wife Laura. When she died, he'd let the place become completely overgrown for years. Now, the bench gleamed white in the early dawn, and she knew Bishop enjoyed it again with his new love, Darbi.

"Can we stop here for a bit?"

Quinton reined in Bullet and nodded. "Sure. I think he's a bit winded anyway. Although you'd never convince him. We've got a winner here. I just need to break the stubborn streak in him."

Dusty dismounted and let go of the reins. The horse shook her head and walked into the meadow to graze.

"You think he'll hang around with Laurel here, or will you need to ground tie him?"

"Tie him, definitely." Quinton led the horse behind the bench to the willow tree. He looped the reins over a low branch and gave Bullet enough slack to graze. He joined Dusty.

He sat on the bench, stretching out his legs, draping both long arms over the back. Dusty sat next to him, snuggling into the crook of his shoulder. She dropped her head on his chest.

"I love it here, don't you? It's such a beautiful morning. We have a lot to be thankful for."

"We do."

Oh, please don't let this be one of those days where he has hardly nothing to say.

"Mia seems to be adjusting well, don't you think?"

"Seems to," he said.

Dusty rolled her eyes. "We used to play this game on Thanksgiving Day at one of the foster homes I lived in. We'd each have to go around the table and tell at least one thing we were thankful for. Back then, it was hard to think of something, but today, I have about a million things I could say."

"Yeah? Like what?"

Boy, he really is thick sometimes, but I believe that's part of what I love about him.

"There's the family-like love I share with Bishop, Connie, the triplets, and now Darbi. There's Mia and her newfound support and apparent happiness."

She'd deliberately left him out of the family-like love statement, yet he hadn't seemed to notice. He continued to stare across the lake. How could one man be so oblivious?

Damn it. I'm going for it. It might a bit uncomfortable for him, but I doubt things will be much different than they are now. I hope so, but I doubt it.

"Are you even listening to me?"

He nodded, raised eyebrows indicating his curiosity.

She continued, bolstering her courage. His rejection could make things between them very awkward. Having grown up the way she did, she halfway expected it. Foster kids got used to things being temporary or never coming into full bloom before they had to move on in life. She took a deep breath, blew it out. She just couldn't hold her feelings in any longer.

"I'm thankful for my job. I have my health, and…"

She paused, gazing up at him. She could stare into those soft-brown eyes forever. He'd been her rock during some of those tough times in foster care and afterward. Quinton had given her courage when her life seemed just about hopeless. He'd encouraged her to go to college and get her social work degree so she could help other kids in her situation. Help them have it a little better than she did.

"And…?" he prompted.

She took a deep breath, let it out. "And, my *love* for you."

There she'd said it. Emphasized the word even. Would he catch her meaning or continue to be the oblivious dunderhead she knew him to be?

A moment passed then another. Her heart skipped a beat then her breath hitched.

He wrapped an arm around her neck, rubbing the knuckles of his other hand into her head.

"You're such a squirt," he said.

She jerked away from him, stung by the use of her childhood nickname. What the heck did that comment mean? Had he not understood her? Or was he still thinking of her as a little sister?

She moaned. *Oh God, what have I done? Actually, you idiot, probably nothing as he doesn't seem to have a clue what you meant. Should I press it? Make sure he understands? I Love Him!*

"What's wrong? You look like you just ate a bad persimmon. Is your stomach upset?" He rose. "Maybe we should get back to the house."

Dusty stood, turning away from him. "I'm fine." She cleared her throat.

He touched her shoulder, but she stepped away. Just then her phone chirped. *Saved by the bell.*

She yanked it out of her back pocket. The screen showed she had a text

Darbi: *I don't know what to do with this bloody bird. HELP!*

Dusty: *Hold on. I'm coming.*

She whistled for Sweet Mountain Laurel. The horse trotted to her obediently. "I need to go back. Darbi needs help with the turkey."

"Uh, okay. Are you sure you're all right?"

"Fine." She mounted, jerking the horse around by the reins. She took off toward the ranch before he could see her tears.

"Dusty, wait up."

She didn't stop. She kicked Laurel in the sides, perhaps more viciously than she'd intended. The horse sprang forward.

"Sorry, girl," she told the mare. "I just can't believe Quinton can be so thick. I think I'll just give up and start looking for someone else. It's obvious he doesn't love me the same way I love him. I'm just whistling in the wind."

Quinton still called her name behind her. Bullet was fast but no match for Sweet Mountain Laurel when she detected urgency from her rider. Dusty gripped the reins tighter, leaned down to keep the wind resistance low, and shouted, "Hah!"

Quinton remained in her wake of flying sand and dirt. When she arrived at the stable, she jumped off and asked one of the stable hands to rub her horse down and feed her. She did not want to be in the barn when Quinton rode in. It would be hard enough to face him across the Thanksgiving Day table. Maybe she'd help Darbi with the turkey and then fake an illness. Go home and nurse her sore heart with a bottle of Pinot.

Hooves pounded behind her, so she scuttled out of the barn to the path to the house. Quinton wouldn't come looking for her until he'd seen to the horses. She'd need to have an excuse for her reaction. He clearly didn't get it. *I'm such a fool. Why did I have to fall in love with a man who doesn't even know the meaning of the word. I'd have to sprout long ears, a mane and a tail before he'll ever notice me.*

She walked in a circle at the bottom of the deck, getting herself under control. She couldn't let Darbi see her this way. She'd see through her in a heartbeat.

She sucked in a few deep breaths, swiped at eyes. Then, squaring her shoulders, she pasted what she hoped was a happy smile on her face and headed up the stairs.

Kelly Abell

Chapter Sixteen

Dusty occupied the rest of her morning helping Darbi prepare the Thanksgiving Day meal. Together, they wrestled the nicely stuffed and trussed twenty-pound bird into the oven. Darbi had chosen a few Irish dishes that had been her mother's favorite for holidays and started to prepare those. Dusty worked on the pumpkin and apple pies.

Grateful for busy hands, she had little time to dwell on her earlier conversation with Quinton. He'd already arrived at the house about an hour ago, and he and Bishop sat watching sports on the television with the triplets. They argued over the plays and yelled at the teams on the screen.

"You'd think they were the bloody coaches the way they carry on. Do ya think they know those boys on the field can't hear them?"

Dusty sliced some apples. "I know, right? I guess it's turned into a family tradition. I remember when the triplets would force themselves to watch football just so they had some time with their Dad. They used to hate it, but now it seems they're getting into it."

"They must be. Bishop has this plastic serving tray with all the helmets of all the teams on it. He uses it to quiz the girls on the cities where all the teams are from. They fight over who's goin' to get the most names right."

Dusty rolled her eyes. "Oh, good grief."

"I'm not fond of the sport myself. Too rough-and-tumble for me. My brothers like playing rugby. Now, that's an even rougher game."

"It definitely is. A real man's game," Dusty commented.

Darbi pointed at her with the knife in her hand. "Daft. All of them. Men have barely enough brains in their heads to get through the day. They don't need to be crushing their skulls, makin' it worse."

Dusty laughed but noticed a bitter edge to it. She struggled to control her hurt and anger, but she couldn't quite manage it. "Ain't it the truth." Quinton sure didn't have many brain cells left apparently.

Darbi watched her as she finished slicing the apples a little more viciously than she'd intended.

"Um…Dusty."

She chopped on, trying to get the word "Squirt" out of her brain. He'd blown right past her declaration of love. Acted as if he hadn't even heard her. And hadn't it just made her day?

"Dusty."

A sharper tone pushed through the fog of the morning, and she glanced up.

"The apples should be sliced not minced."

She glanced down and sucked in a gasp. A pile of apple mush, closer to applesauce, instead of clean neat slices covered the cutting board. Heat crept up her neck, around her ears, and into her cheeks. "Oh no. I'm sorry. I guess my mind wandered. Do you have any more apples?"

Darbi went to the pantry and brought back two bright-red apples. "Wandered, is it? Appears it went to China. What's eatin' at you, girl?"

Her eyes turned liquid. She blinked several times. She would not do this here.

Darbi glanced at the group in the family room munching on the chips and dip she'd provided to tide them over till dinner. She put down her own knife, wrapped an arm around Dusty, and steered her toward the door to the deck.

The women stepped outside into the cool November afternoon. The oak trees, so plentiful on the farm, dropped their acorns but not their leaves. A few struck the deck, as the local family of squirrels chased each other through the branches.

"I'll never get used to a Florida autumn," Darbi commented. "I miss the change of colors."

Dusty swiped at her eyes, furious with herself for allowing her emotions to have the upper hand. She'd made it her purpose in life to keep a tight rein on her feelings. It made her the perfect social worker. But today, she struggled.

"What's the matter, girl?" Darbi led her to an Adirondack chair.

"I'm sorry, Darbi. I'm ruining your first Thanksgiving. I should go."

"You'll do no such thing. You were in such a good mood this morning before your ride with—"

Dusty fought the embarrassment. Could she tell her friend what she'd done and how it had been received? Knowing Darbi, she'd drag the man out here and give him a good tongue lashing, and he'd look at her like she'd lost her mind, because he just didn't get it.

"Did you and Quinton have a fight?"

Leave it to her Irish friend to get straight to the point. At least she could answer the question honestly. She shook her head.

"I'm no eejit, so I know somethin's happened. What was it?"

Dusty wanted to run away. Hide under her covers for the rest of the day, but Darbi would dog her until she told her something. Then, eventually, she'd worm the truth out of her, so she decided to save the time.

"I told Quinton I loved him this morning."

Darbi stared at her for a moment, eyes wide. "Oh?"

Dusty nodded.

Her friend knelt in front of her. "Obviously. it didn't go over as you'd hoped. Am I right?"

She nodded again, emotion choking off her words.

Darbi smacked her palms on her flour-stained jeans. "That eejit. What happened?"

Dusty swiped at her leaking tears, took a deep breath. "He wrapped my head in a wrestling hold, rubbed his knuckles in my hair and said, 'You're such a squirt.'"

The look of complete bafflement on her friend's face would have made her laugh if she weren't so miserable.

"Huh?"

"Squirt was the childhood nickname the guys had for me because I'm so much smaller than everyone. Never had it hurt my feelings until today. He acted like I was his little sister. What do I have to do, Darbi? Draw him a map?"

Darbi reached for her hand and squeezed. "It probably wouldn't help. I swear the man's thicker than a sheep. At least they know how to follow the dog's lead. This man couldn't follow a trail if you painted red arrows on it."

Dusty wanted to smile at her friend's quip, but her misery overrode her emotions. "I just don't know how to get him to take me seriously. Maybe he just doesn't love me in that way and never will. I'll just have to get used to it, I guess."

"Now, darlin', don't give up. Most men don't know a good thing till it's bit them in the butt. He'll come 'round.

Why don't ya back off for a bit. Don't come over, don't call him. Let him see what it might feel like to do without ya for a spell. When he does call, say you're busy with somethin'. I know it'll be tough, but playin' a bit of hard-to-get might do the trick."

Dusty stared at her friend. Perhaps Darbi was on to something. She'd always been at Quinton's beck and call. Not that he called that often, but when he did, she came running. Her frequent calls to him would stop immediately. No more catching up on his day or blathering on about hers.

"It just might work."

Darbi tapped the side of her temple with her index finger. "I've raised plenty of men. Not that I was smart enough with Bishop, mind you."

"You took off to leave for Ireland, and he couldn't come after you fast enough."

"True, true, but it wasn't really calculated on my part. I was hurt, see. I wanted to run away."

"But he couldn't let you."

"Sometimes, it's the chase that gets them moving, I guess."

Dusty thought about it. She sniffed. *Couldn't hurt to try.*

"Seems like your chin just lifted a bit," Darbi commented.

"Thanks to you. Come on." Dusty grabbed her friend's hand. "Let's go finish cooking a wonderful Thanksgiving dinner."

As they stepped into the warm kitchen, Dusty heard Darbi mutter, "Bloody bird. Why can't they have beef and potatoes?"

She laughed. She'd try Darbi's suggestion and perhaps things would turn around. In the meantime, she planned to enjoy a lot of family camaraderie and a good meal.

Kelly Abell

Chapter Seventeen

Japan had to be the most beautiful country Connie had ever seen. A stark change from the desert sand and blowing winds of the Middle East. The ocean breezes, salt air and beauty of the people and her surroundings amazed her, but today, it couldn't lift her spirits.

She sat on a bench in a small park facing the sea at the edge of the military base. She'd snuck away from the crowd in the mess hall enjoying their Thanksgiving Day celebration. She missed home. She missed the triplets, Quinton and Bishop yelling at the TV, the aroma of turkey cooking in the oven. She wondered if Sven would join them today. He had his own family, so he'd probably eat with them, then maybe come over to enjoy the games with the guys. She glanced at her watch. She needed to call him soon.

I hope talking to Sven makes me feel better. Who knew missing home could be so painful?

She remembered signing up for this tour. At the time, she could hardly contain her excitement. She'd worked so hard to find Darbi and bring her to the U.S., and after she got there, life had been chaotic as she prepared to leave. She hadn't thought about being homesick. *Boy, I'm thinking about it now.*

She glanced over her shoulder at the sound of approaching footsteps. Trevor ambled toward her. She smiled and waved. That man never seemed to be in a hurry. Her heart bumped in her chest. *He's a handsome devil, alright. Guard yourself, Connie. Don't let your desire for fame run away with your good sense. Use your brain.*

"Hey there," he said.

"Hey."

"I missed ya inside. What're you doing out here all by yourself?"

She turned to face the sea as he sat on the bench next to her. His arm draped casually over the back of the bench. Aware of his closeness, she scooted away from him just a bit. Over the last few weeks, Trevor had flirted with her often. She enjoyed the attention, but there always seemed to be an underlying edge to his advances. It put her off a bit, made her wary. She wanted to talk about it with Logan, but he'd avoided her since the night she and Wrynn woke him from his nightmare. She hoped it hadn't ruined her chance at friendship with him.

"You seem a million miles away," Trevor interrupted her musings with his Tennessee twang. "Penny for your thoughts."

She sighed. "I guess I'm a bit homesick. I miss being home for Thanksgiving."

He wrapped his arm around her shoulders, squeezed her close. She stiffened, but he didn't seem to notice.

"Aw, I know. Me, too."

Her jaw dropped and she raised her eyebrows. "I would have thought you'd missed a ton of Thanksgivings being on tour and all."

"I have, but it doesn't mean I don't want to be home."

"True."

"You'll see how it is once you start tourin'. You get homesick some, but you get used to it. All those screaming fans make up for it."

She huffed out a laugh. "I don't have any screaming fans."

"Aw darlin', I don't know about that. These soldiers sure seem to love you to pieces. No wonder. You're prettier than a rose, and your voice? Woo-wee. I've never heard anything like it. It's a gift, Connie. Truly."

Warmth crept into her face. High praise from someone who knew the business. Flattered, she smiled.

"I mean it. You raise the rafters every time we perform. Adding my duet with you was a smart move. The soldiers love it."

"Angel's not too fond of it," Connie commented.

"Aw, she'll get over it. She's a pro. She knows how this business works. You're better than her. Just the way it goes. In fact…" He squeezed her against him again.

She squirmed to loosen his grip. He resisted a moment then moved away, but only by an inch.

"I've been meanin' to talk to you about somethin'."

Her heart fluttered. Could this be her chance? Her opening into the big time? She raised her eyebrows, waiting for him to finish.

"You're so cute." He touched a finger to her nose, then slowly slid it down the side of her face, then her neck until his hand rested on her shoulder.

She shuddered involuntarily, unsure if she liked the caress. She didn't have much experience with men aside from the local farm boys in Brooksville. A man like Trevor Thornton unnerved her. She cleared her throat. "You wanted to ask me something?"

"Oh yeah." He brushed his thumb against her neck, his blue eyes deepening to violet. "How would you like to join my summer tour? We get through this USO thing then you rest up at my home in Nashville while we rehearse. I've got some great new songs we can sing together, plus a few I think you might sound great soloing."

Shock bolted through her. She'd hoped to be able to sing with him more, maybe get an introduction to an agent, but not this. Trevor was handing her dream to her in a basket with a bow on it.

"I just love it when those hazel eyes go all wide with wonder." He leaned in close. "You're a beautiful woman, Connie."

He briefly touched his lips to hers. She sat back quickly, stunned. Her hand went to her mouth and touched her lips. The kiss, brief as it was, hadn't been pleasant. Trevor's lips were dry, and he hadn't shaved in days.

"Um…" She rose, took a few steps away. "Trevor, I'm beyond honored. Really. But I've signed a contract with the USO for a year. I won't be released until next October. You probably can't wait that long."

He frowned. Was it because she'd walked away from him or because of the contract? Her stomach pitched, the turkey she'd had for dinner rolling around, making her nauseated. *This man is offering me the chance of a lifetime. Just what I wanted. But why do I feel like the strings attached are more like steel chains?*

Trevor waved a hand, his smile returning. "Don't worry about your contract. My lawyers can get you out easily. Do you have an agent?"

A picture of Sven entered her mind, and a pang of guilt struck her. She glanced at her watch. She'd promised to call him. Okinawa was thirteen hours ahead, so she still had time.

"No, I don't have an agent, but my boyfriend is an attorney. I'm sure he'd have some thoughts."

Trevor frowned again. "Boyfriend, huh? I didn't know you had a boyfriend. How cute."

She didn't like his sarcasm, but desiring this opportunity, she didn't comment. Being a country singer was her lifetime dream, but not if she had to get it by any other means than her voice.

"I'd like to tour and record with you, Trevor. It'd be fantastic, but I really feel I should fulfill my commitment to the USO. I don't want to start off a singing career breaking my word."

He rose and approached her. "Connie, my sweet little bird. You are so naïve about how things are done in the music business. With a voice like yours, you could write your own ticket, but there are a lot of people who will take advantage of you, rob you blind. I'm offering you a fair deal. We can have our lawyers talk through all the particulars, but I want you to sing with me. We can make a fortune together. Our chemistry is…" He touched his head with a hand on either side, then fanned them out making an explosion sound. "You get what I'm sayin'?"

Oh, I get what you're sayin'. I'm not the little bird you think I am.

"Let's get through this tour," she said. "I want to see my family over New Years, then can we talk about it again?"

He smiled, stepped up to her, and placed his hands on her shoulders. Was he about to kiss her again? And if so, would she let him? How far should she let this flirtation go before she put him in his place?

"Connie!" She glanced around Trevor, and a breath escaped her. Logan strode down the path from the mess hall.

Trevor growled. His hands fell away from her shoulders.

"We'll talk more about this later," he muttered, strolling away.

"Thank you, Trevor. I'm really flattered," she called after him.

He waved a hand.

Had Logan just blown it for her? Somehow, she didn't think so, but she was glad to be away from Trevor's advances. *Am I nuts? He's Trevor Thornton and he wants me. Me. I could have all I ever wanted. But why does it feel so skanky?*

Logan reached her. "Are you okay?"

"I'm fine, Logan. Why?"

"I saw you out here with Trevor, alone. I don't trust him, Connie. There's something off. What did he want?"

Still irritated at him for ignoring her for the past week, she said, "I'm not sure that's any of your business."

He sighed. "Okay, I get it. You're mad at me."

"I'm not mad at you. What reason would I have?"

He raised an eyebrow.

"The fact you've ignored me for the past several days? Could that be what you're referring to?"

His face flushed in the low light of the day. A breeze blew in from the water, ruffling the top of his short hair. He'd hurt her feelings, and she wasn't going to let him off easy.

"Listen." He ran a hand through his hair. "I need to talk to you about what happened in Kuwait, but I just don't like discussing it. It's embarrassing, you know?"

She walked over to the bench and sat down again. He joined her.

"Logan, Wrynn told be about your PTSD. That is what it is, right?"

He nodded.

"I don't begin to understand it, but I know what I saw that night. We only want to be your friends. To help you through this if we can. There's no reason for you to be embarrassed."

He stared out at the ocean, the blaze of the setting sun lending its golden hue to the water. She wasn't sure if he was still blushing, or if it was the sun's glow reflected from the sea.

"I'm still dealing with the shame part of this. I know what you say is true, but I can't seem to make myself believe it. Besides, you don't know the whole story."

She placed a hand gently on his arm. "I'm here if you ever want to talk. I enjoyed your company on the flight, and I thought we'd be able to be good friends." *Maybe something more?*

"I know. I really like you, too. I was worried Trevor was putting the moves on you. I'm sorry if I interrupted anything important."

Excitement built in her when Trevor's offer entered her mind, but she wasn't sure she wanted to share it with anyone before she spoke with Sven. He deserved to know first.

"No worries. I'm just glad you're talking to me again. Do you want to tell me about what happened in Iraq?"

He shook his head. "You don't need to hear about all my crap. Let's go get some dessert."

She rubbed her tummy. "I think I've had enough. You go ahead though. I think I'm going to the barracks to call Sven."

Logan frowned. "Oh. Yeah. The boyfriend. I forgot about him."

She laughed. "He's not exactly my boyfriend. We are just testing out the waters to see if there's anything there."

"And?"

"Could be. Long distance makes the heart grow fonder, so they say."

He shrugged. "They also say, 'if you can't be with the one you love, love the one you're with.'"

She slapped his arm. "You're funny, Logan Richards." She rose, and he stood with her. She wrapped him in a warm hug. "I'm glad you talked to me again. I've missed you."

He squeezed her tightly. "I've missed you, too. I listen to you sing every night before I fall asleep. Is that creepy?"

She pulled away, a smile on her face. "Not at all. I'm happy my voice gives you some comfort. Hang in there, buddy. You've got this, but if you need me, all you have to do is call."

She reached in her pocket, pulled out her phone, and waggled it at him.

"I'll think on it," he said.

"Don't you need my number?"

He pointed to the badge on his chest. "Security, remember?"

She laughed. "Okay, now you're creepy."

Chapter Eighteen

Connie positioned her laptop on the bed in front of her, adjusting the little camera so it pointed to her face. After checking her watch, she stared at the tiny projection on the screen. It was just after 9:00 a.m. in Japan, so it should be around 8:00 p.m. in Florida. She should have fixed herself up some, brushed her windblown blonde locks, freshened her makeup, but she wanted to talk to Sven. Needed to. After a restless night, she wanted his advice.

She pressed the button on the video chat. It rang only twice, and, with a *pop*, she saw his handsome face on the screen. He sat at the dining room table in her house in Brooksville. Behind him the triplets jumped up and down, screaming her name. A pretty young girl with blonde hair and a smooth round face, stood to one side. It must be Mia, the girl Sven had told her about. Bishop walked up along with Darbi, and Quinton, with Dusty stood to the other side of the triplets.

"Surprise!" they all shouted at once.

Sven grinned. "I thought you might be a little homesick, so I came over here. I knew you'd call tonight, and I thought you might enjoy seeing us all together."

Connie's heart swelled, and her eyes filled with tears. Was there no end to the goodness in this man? This man who had professed his love for her? Who apparently thought of her before all others? What a sweet thing to do.

149

She swiped at her eyes. "Aw, Sven. This is awesome. Hi guys!" She waved at the camera. "I miss you all so much."

"We miss you, too, Aunt Connie," Violet shouted.

"What's it like in…" Scarlet craned her head to look up at her father. "Where is she again?"

He ruffled her hair. "Japan." She pushed his hand away, an irritated expression on her face. "Yeah, Japan." She faced the camera again. "What's it like in Japan?"

"It's beautiful, nugget. I'm in Okinawa, and it's on an island. It reminds me a lot of Florida, only not quite as humid. The ocean is beautiful here."

"Cool," Scarlet replied.

"How's the tour going?" Ivory said, before Scarlet could say anything else.

"It's amazing," Connie replied. "When you three get older, I'm going to make sure you get to see some of these places I've seen. You'll find them fascinating. We're on to England soon, after Germany and Italy." She glanced at Sven, who winked. Her heart soared. He was going to meet her there. He'd been able to work it out.

"Will you get to see the Queen?" Violet asked, eyes wide.

"I don't think so." Connie laughed. "We're there to perform a holiday show for our soldiers. I doubt the Queen cares much about it."

"You might see her though. And Harry and Megan, and the new baby, and William and Kate." Violet sighed.

Her sisters rolled their eyes. Connie laughed. She missed these girls more than anything.

"I cooked my first bird," Darbi piped up.

Connie laughed again at the expressions on everyone's faces. Bishop drew the corners of his mouth down in an exaggerated frown. The triplets all made gagging sounds, and Quinton raised his eyebrows.

Darbi glanced around at everyone, her expression pained. "Aw, come on. It wasn't that bad." Her Irish accent still adorable.

"You all stop," Dusty spoke up. "It was wonderful, Connie. She did a marvelous job. We're all gobsmacked at her talent with a bird." The last sentence was spoken in a mock Irish accent with a Southern twang.

Connie laughed so hard the laptop shook on the bed. "You guys. This is just what I needed. I miss you all so much. Thank you, Sven. For being there. I can't tell you what this means to me."

He smiled. "I miss you, too."

"Okay crew, let's go. Give them some privacy," Darbi said. "Move along now."

"Bye, Connie," they all called. "We love you."

"Bye. I love you, too. I'll call again soon."

Darbi glanced over the top of Sven's head and mouthed, "You better."

Connie sighed. A good dose of family had been just what she needed. God bless this man.

Sven picked up the laptop and moved outside to the pool. He carried it facing away from him so she could see the kitchen, filled with dirty dishes, half-eaten pies, empty wine glasses, and a picked-clean turkey carcass resting on their white serving platter. Grateful she didn't have to clean up the mess, she sighed.

He strode out the side door, revealing the wonderful pool Bishop and Laura had built on to the house. The cascading waterfall trickled down stair stepped stones and flowed into the water, glowing blue from the pool lights. She, herself, had strung white lights all along the area, and she noticed a bulb, flickering like a torch, had been added to one of the poolside lamps.

Sven settled into one of the lounge chairs, balancing the laptop on his lap. The light behind him created a silhouette, but he touched the flashlight on his phone and his face came into clear view. "Now, we're alone. I miss you something terrible, Connie. It just wasn't Thanksgiving without you here."

She smiled. "Did you eat at the house?"

He shook his head. "I came over for dessert. Darbi and Dusty make the best pies. They should go into business."

"I agree. For a horsewoman and a social worker, their baking is amazing."

"How was your day in the lovely city of Okinawa?"

Connie adjusted her position in her chair, settling back for the conversation. "It was okay. The food was great. We had a huge buffet with the soldiers. I so enjoy talking to them and hearing their stories. We had a kinship today as we all missed our families."

"I bet."

She sat for a moment, staring into those sea-blue eyes. Her heart warmed at the comfort his gaze invoked in her. She could tell him anything, he'd listen, offer sage advice, and love her unconditionally. Why then did she have thoughts of Logan, and, God forgive her, Trevor? Those men weren't half the man Sven was, yet she struggled with settling for him. *Am I nuts?*

"Are you okay, Connie? Your face looks weird. What's wrong?"

She laughed. "Not exactly what a woman wants to hear. My face looks weird?"

"Yeah. Sort of like you just smelled horse apples or something. I'm worried about you."

She sighed. "I guess I'm just homesick." She hoped that would cover her gaff. *I really need to keep better control of my facial expressions.*

"I'm sure you are. You've never been away from home this long, ever. When you make up your mind to do something, boy, you really go whole hog. Let's not travel to foreign countries for a vacation, oh no…let's sign a yearlong contract with the USO."

Did he mean to be funny? No, he's frowning. If the fact she was gone irritated him, wait until she told him about her offer from Trevor. *That will go over like a rattlesnake in the horse stall.*

"Um…what's up with you?"

His lids lowered over his eyes for a second then he stared straight at the camera. "I'm sorry. I just miss you, is all. Those few days in New York were amazing. It made me realize how much I want you in my life, and you being gone makes me a little crankier than I thought it would."

"I'll say," she commented. She took a deep breath. *Might as well rip off the Band-Aid.* "Then you might just get a bit crankier when I tell you this."

He sat back in the chair. His image rocked on the laptop while he settled it more comfortably. "What is it?"

"It's actually pretty amazing. Trevor Thornton approached me tonight and asked me to go to on tour with him. He has a spring tour coming up, and he wants me to come to Nashville and get ready for it. He said he even has a few songs which would suit my voice perfectly. I could record them solo." Her excitement grew as she told Sven about the opportunity. Never mind the country singer was a bit smarmy, she could handle him. This was the type of break she'd wanted all her life.

"Imagine, a real recording contract. And a tour. What do you think?"

She waited. Let him absorb the news. The roll of emotions crossing his face didn't comfort her one bit. Surprise morphed quickly into worry, then to all-out frustration.

"What about the USO? You can't just break your contract with them. They could sue you."

Leave it Sven to bring up the legalities first. No "that's too long, Connie." Or "sounds like an awesome opportunity, but what about us?"

She frowned. "He says his lawyers can get me out of it. This is the chance of a lifetime, Sven. He's Trevor Thornton for heaven's sake. He's the hottest country singer on the circuit. If I hook my name to his on an album, I'll be set for life."

"What else would you have to hook up?"

The expression on his face screamed jealousy. In a way, she was flattered, but it also annoyed her. When had the most confident man she'd ever known become so insecure?

"Not funny, Sven. You know me better."

"I do, but I don't know him at all. I hope you're being very careful over there. I'm worried about your safety. You're a young beautiful woman."

"Who can take care of herself, as I've reminded you before." Irritation built within her blood. She struggled to keep it off her face, but she didn't think she succeeded.

"I'm not trying to tick you off, Connie. I love you. I just want you to be safe."

There it was. The "L" word again. Could she say the same? She decided it would be best to change the subject.

"Are you still coming to England for Christmas?" She huffed out a little breath.

"Do you still want me to?"

She rolled her eyes. "Of course I do, you idiot. I'll send you the location information with some hotels and stuff later on today."

"Okay. That'd be good. I guess I just fly into London?"

"Yep, then Wrynn told me you can take the train from there. Should be pretty easy. I can arrange for Logan to pick you up at the train station once you get here."

"Who's Logan?"

"One of the security guys."

"What about Manny?"

"Or Manny, sheesh. Picky much?"

He smiled, but it didn't quite reach his eyes. "I just know Manny and liked him."

"He may be busy with setting up the tour, but I'll ask him. Logan's a great guy. You'll like him, too."

"You seem to be meeting a lot of great guys."

The sad puppy look on his face moved her, but she had to remain realistic. Her feelings for him grew deeper each time she saw him, but this romantic relationship between them was still new to her. He may have loved her for years, but his confession in October had taken her by surprise. Plus, she'd been bombarded by two other men all in a short amount of time. She needed to set something straight with him, even if it meant ruining their friendship.

She smiled into the camera. "Sven, there are a lot of nice men in the world, you the best among them. I know this is all new and still a bit overwhelming for both of us, but you said you supported my dreams. You didn't want to get in the way. If you've changed your mind, and can't deal with me becoming a singer then maybe we should just remain friends. I don't want to keep you from finding someone you may love and have a wonderful life with while you're waiting for me to come home, or you're having to jet all over the place to see me. It's not fair to you."

His eyes widened in alarm. "Connie, don't say that. Not yet. I truly do love you, and I do support your dreams, it's just harder than I thought it would be. Everywhere I go in Brooksville, I see reminders of you. I want to hold you, be near you." He paused, glanced down, and sighed. "I also know it's too soon to expect you love me, too, but I'm hopeful."

She laughed when he glanced up at her, a pitiful expression in his ice-blue eyes. She did love him, more than she realized, but she wasn't sure she could commit to the same feelings he had for her. At least, not yet. "You're a wonderful man, Sven. I've always loved you. You know it."

"I know, but not the way I need you to."

She winked. "You don't know for sure. This is still very new for us. We agreed to take it slow."

He sighed, ran a palm down his face. "I know, I know. I'm sorry. Listen, it's great news about Trevor. Really, it is. I still worry he's a bit of an opportunist. Be sure you get whatever his plans for you are in writing. Let me see them before you sign anything. I hear Nashville is pretty in the spring." He offered her a weak smile.

Her heart swelled. If he kept this up, she would love him exactly the way he wanted her, too. She knew how hard those words were for him. "Sven, you're the best. I don't even know if it's going to work out at all. He may be just blowing smoke. He might have even been drunk for all I know, but he seemed serious. I'll tell you more as details develop. Try not to worry. I'm not as naïve as everyone thinks. You don't broker deals for horse sperm if you're an idiot."

He laughed out loud. "You've got a point there. I love you, Connie. Happy Thanksgiving. I'll talk to you very soon. Take care of yourself."

"Happy Thanksgiving, Sven. I can't wait to see you at Christmas."

"Me, too. Bye."

She blew him a kiss and pressed the End button on her laptop.

Chapter Nineteen

Sven closed the laptop and sat staring into the glow of the pool. The slurping of the pool bot occasionally interrupting the buzz of the night insects. Mentally, he slapped himself on the forehead for the way he'd acted while talking to Connie.

The last thing she needs is a stupid jealous boyfriend. If I can even claim the title.

The slider opened from the family room, and Darbi stepped onto the patio. She strolled out to the pool and saw him seated in the lounge chair.

"Everythin' okay?"

He smiled up at her. "Of course. Have a seat."

"I hate American football. Just don't see the point."

He laughed, loving her Irish accent, the soft lilt of it.

"Pretty much a tradition around here on Thanksgiving."

"So I gather. Ya missin' Connie?"

He nodded. "Is it that obvious?"

"You've been struttin' round with a bit of a scowl for a few days now." She tapped her finger on his chin. "Still there."

Sven sighed. "I'm sorry. I hope I'm not ruining your first Thanksgiving. I thought I'd adjust better to Connie not being here, but I'm not handling it very well, I'm afraid."

"And ya think I didn't act like an eejit a time or two with Bishop? The whole romance thing takes a bit of gettin' used to."

"I'll say." He stared off across the pool. The pale blue of the lights reflecting out of the water didn't soothe him as he supposed they were designed to do.

Darbi remained quiet for a few minutes then whispered, "Things not working out like you'd hoped?"

Sven glanced at her. She truly was a lovely woman, flaming red hair, emerald eyes and all. Bishop was a lucky man.

"I fear I just made a fool of myself when I talked to her. She shared some fantastic news, or at least I think it could be fantastic for her, and I reacted like a jealous idiot."

"What's the news?"

"Trevor Thornton has invited her to go on tour with him in the spring. And she said he has some songs she could record solo."

"Oh, my gosh, what fantastic news. But she didn't sign a yearlong contract with the USO?"

"She did. But he says his lawyers could get her out of it. I'm not sure it's true, so I asked her to send me anything she receives before she signs it."

"Good thought."

Sven could feel her staring at him in the dim glow of the pool lights. He glanced over at her and raised one eyebrow.

"You want me to ask it of ya?"

"Ask what?"

"What made ya feel like an eejit? Sounds like good advice."

"I got mad about the offer, Darbi." He hauled himself out of the chaise lounge and began to pace. "I don't want her to work with the guy. She's pretty, young, a fantastic singer…I mean, who wouldn't want her to sing with or for them? But it just all seems to be happening too fast. The guy's famous, he's good looking…"

"Ya just don't want him to steal her away from ya?"

He sucked in a breath. He had to admire the way the Irishwoman could get straight to the heart of things. He'd seen her do it more than a time or two with Bishop and the triplets.

He stopped pacing and glanced at her sympathetic expression. "Yeah. This relationship, if you can even call it one, is still so new. I told her when I was in New York I didn't want to stand in her way, but…" He ran a hand through his hair.

"Now ya sorta do."

He huffed out a laugh. "Yeah. Now I sorta do." He sat on the edge of the chaise. "It's been so much harder than I thought, Darbi. I lay in bed at night thinking about all the men she'll meet, Trevor in particular. He's rich, can offer her all she's ever dreamed of. What can I offer her? I'm a small town lawyer, barely holding together a small practice."

"A small practice which has grown quite a bit, from what I hear tell. You've got the account of one of the largest horse breeders in the world. I'd say that alone makes ya a force to be reckoned with, so it does."

She placed a hand on his shoulder. "I think what you're sufferin' from is an attack of self-conscious thinkin'. You're doubtin' yourself, and it's perfectly understandable, but you can't discount all you've meant to Connie over the years. Steadfastness counts more to a woman than ya might imagine."

"It does?"

"Who does she call when she's got excitin' news? She didn't call us yet. She told you first. Haven't ya always been there for her over the years? From what she's told me, she's leaned on ya quite a bit." Darbi sat cross-legged on the other chaise. She leaned toward him.

"From what she's told me, she's quite smitten with ya."

Sven's heart swelled. "You're just saying that so I'll settle down."

"Aye, but it is the truth. I heard it from herself. She said she couldn't believe how lucky she was to have such a man as yourself interested in her romantically. She just wishes you'd have told her sooner."

"She might not have gone if I had."

"Aye. True enough, but the choice has been made now and you're just going to have to find a way to cope. You'll see her at Christmas, am I right?"

He nodded.

"Try to keep a cap on your jealousy till then. Perhaps you'll know more about her offer. Ya know the old sayin'…If ya love somethin' set it free. If it comes back, it's yours."

"Easier said than done, Darbi."

She rose. "I know, Sven. I know. But there's truth to it. If I know Connie half as well as I think I do, she'll make the right choice. She's young, and a bit naïve as am I, but she's no eejit. Give her some room to make up her mind. Ya might be surprised with what she does."

She bent down and kissed him on the top of the head. "Those dishes aren't goin' to wash themselves. Ya comin' back in?"

"In a minute. Thanks, Darbi. I really appreciate the chat."

"Anytime a'tall."

When the slider banged shut, he scooted back against the lounge chair. Letting Connie go when he felt like he'd just found her wouldn't be an easy thing to do. But he had made a promise. He'd have to believe the love in his heart for her would be enough to sustain them both until she made up her mind what she planned to do. And could he live with her choice? Only time would tell.

Chapter Twenty

Connie stared out at the gray dawn sky over the Army base in Germany. It was a week before Christmas, and the tour had taken a few days downtime to get the group ready to travel to England. Excitement filled her as time grew closer for her to see Sven. She'd spoken to him a few more times since Thanksgiving, and to her relief, he seemed to have the jealousy under control. He'd been positive about her opportunity with Trevor, and the USO tour itself. Almost too positive. Had he begun to have second thoughts about furthering their relationship? Maybe she'd scared him when she'd told him about Trevor's offer and how much it meant to her. Maybe he'd decided they should only remain friends.

She glanced around the sparsely decorated room. The performers had been placed in empty officer's quarters and she had a room to herself in one of the four bedroom houses on base. The room held a simple double bed, with institutional white sheets and duvet. The pillows were a bit hard, but the bed itself gave her a good night's rest. The oak furniture had no ornate designs, just plain and boxy. The dresser and armoire held no fancy handles, just practical pewter in a straight line. A small glass and wood desk stood against the opposite wall from the bed. The egg-shell walls held only a few generic prints of landscapes in black frames, and avocado curtains hung from the blindless windows.

She reminded herself not to marry a military officer, because he'd go broke paying for decorations. She needed to surround herself with color. Darbi's fall leaf decorations throughout Champions Gate sprang to mind, and she laughed. Her new sister-in-law was perfect.

When her thoughts returned to Sven, doubt coursed through her. She hated long-distance relationships because you couldn't tell one's true feelings through a video screen. It was difficult to know when Sven harbored ill feelings anyway, because as an attorney he'd learned to hide his emotions. He still told her he loved her before they hung up, but she feared something might be off.

Isn't this what I wanted? Not to be crowded? Time to figure out how I truly felt about him? I'll be glad to see him next week. Then I can look into those beautiful blue eyes and know for sure. The fact I'm worried about it means I love him, too, right?

She'd be stupid not to, yet whenever she spent time with Logan, or Trevor as well, other emotions stirred within her about both men.

Logan kept her safe. Sure, he had issues, but what man didn't? Being a fixer at heart, Connie wanted to help him get better. End his nightmares and ease his suffering to help him better cope in the everyday world.

She'd seen a few displays of anger from him which worried her. A few soldiers had gotten a bit too aggressive with her in a receiving line after one of the shows in Italy. She shuddered remembering the look of…she wasn't sure how to describe it…savagery, maybe? The look of savagery in his eyes when he'd shoved them away from her. One had even stumbled and fallen. She remembered placing a hand on his rock-hard forearm, trying to tell him it didn't matter, they were just being friendly. And when he'd turned to glare at her, she'd shivered at the pure animal-like gleam of his expression. She'd taken a step back. Would he ever turn that raw anger on her? Or had he with any other woman?

Wrynn had come up to him afterward, having witnessed the activity from across the room. She'd whispered something in his ear, and he calmed down and walked away. Connie felt like she had watched a scene from *The Avengers* movie where the Black Widow calms down the Hulk.

Logan had come to her later to apologize, but he still wouldn't confess any more about what had caused his PTSD. She wasn't used to men not confiding in her. She and Sven could talk about anything. Perhaps Logan's past remained too painful.

Then there was Trevor. She wasn't at all sure what to make of the country singer. He appeared highly interested in her, but she wasn't sure he contained the genuineness she'd hoped for. Still, she wasn't above a little opportunistic flirting. He just seemed so intense sometimes. Like when he got angry if she avoided him or didn't respond to his advances. One thing she didn't like in a man was ego and pride when it came to the way he perceived women should react to him. His celebrity had definitely gone to his head.

A loud banging on her bedroom door interrupted her musings. She glanced at her watch. Not even seven a.m. Who was it?

"Connie! Open this door."

She drew her brows together. *Angel? What the…?* She opened the door, and the buxom blonde shoved past her into the room. She wore a pair of tight jeans, and, despite the frigid temperatures in Germany, a tight black tank top that shoved her ample breasts up and almost out of the tiny garment. Her curly blonde hair hung in stiff straggly ringlets to her shoulders still full of hairspray from the day before. The expression on her face, murderous.

Connie whiffed an odor of sour alcohol. *Is this woman going to attack me? If looks could kill, I'd already be dead. Wow.* She held up both hands palms out, backing away a step.

"Angel, what's going on? Are you alright?"

"No, I'm not alright, you slut," Angel growled between clenched teeth.

Connie took a step toward the bedside table to be closer to her phone. She didn't want to take her eyes off Angel for one second. She ignored the foul name. "What's happened? You're obviously upset."

Tears began to leak down her opponent's reddened face. "Oh you think? Trevor fired me about an hour ago. He told me you'd be taking my place in the band, recording duets with him after this stupid tour. When did you sleep with him, you whore?"

Anger rolled through Connie. She may have flirted harmlessly with Trevor, but she didn't deserve the evil names Angel flung at her. She stiffened her spine, and stuck out her chin. "Now you hold on just a minute. I've never slept with Trevor, nor would I to get anything from him. I have no idea what he's told you, but I haven't agreed to anything with him. He made me an offer which I'm thinking about, but *never* in a million years did I think he'd fire you."

"That's not the way he put it to me. He said I was old and tired. My voice too smoky for where he wants to go in the future. He bragged you're the next great sensation. 'Sorry, babe, you've got to go.'" More tears poured down her cheeks. "I've been with him since his first recording contract. I even introduced him to my cousin who became his agent."

Sniffing, Angel swiped a hand across her nose. Connie took a chance and handed her a tissue.

"Come here and sit down." She led the distraught woman to the bed. Angel sank onto it, gripping the tissue.

"I don't know what I'm going to do now. When word gets around Trevor Thornton fired me because I'm too old and my voice is worn out, I'll never find work. I'll have to go back to a bar band in Nashville. God, that's awful."

Shock rippled through Connie. How could Trevor treat a woman who'd been with him for over ten years this way? She seemed to doubt his character more and more with each passing day. *I'm not sure breaking into the music industry is worth this. Maybe Sven is right.*

She sat next to Angel. "I'm so sorry. I have no idea why he did this to you, but I assure you I was no part of it. I can try to talk to him if you'd like?"

Angel shook her head, miserable. She reached into her pocket and pulled out a boarding pass. "He booked a flight for me for this morning. I have to be at the airport in two hours. One thing you'll discover about Trevor is he means what he says. Not much gets in his way once he's decided on something. And he's decided on you."

Angel's shoulders shook as a fresh bout of tears began.

Connie didn't want to be part of the reason for this woman's misery. Angel had a phenomenal voice, and everything Trevor told her was not true.

"You said your cousin is his agent, right? Maybe he can find you work. Don't listen to what Trevor says about your voice. Look at Reba or Trisha or any of those women. They're older than you and still performing. Perhaps you can even break out with your own solo album. The fact you sang with Trevor has to carry some weight with another artist or record label."

Angel used the tail end of the tank top to wipe her eyes and nose. Connie tried not to grimace and reached for the tissue box.

"You're so naïve. Such a babe in the music woods. Trevor is king in the country music world. All he has to do is say I'm no good and everyone will believe him. I'm done."

"Why would he do something so cruel? I understand he fired you, but why besmirch your reputation. He has no reason."

Angel snorted out a laugh. She glanced at Connie with bloodshot eyes. "Little girl, you are in for a ride. If I were you, I'd pack your bags and scuttle on home to that horse farm of yours. You're so not ready for the big time. Trevor will eat you for breakfast and spit out your bones when he's done. And believe me, someone will come along who's cuter, sexier, and perkier than you are." She raked Connie with a glance. "Hard to believe, but when it happens?" She slashed her hand across her throat. "You're yesterday's news."

Angel rose. "I suppose I owe you an apology even though you're the reason I'm being fired. Your face was so full of innocent shock when I accused you of sleeping with him to get what you want, so I can't be angry with you."

"Thanks," Connie said, surprised Angel had forgiven her so easily.

"This isn't the first time he's passed me over for a pretty little thing, but he's never fired me before. You sing like my name, Connie. You've got a real gift." She stopped at the door, wiping another tear from her eye. "Don't let Trevor Thornton or this industry ruin you. It's not all bright lights and cheering fans. There's a deep dark side to this business. Being famous comes with a high price tag. Especially if your star is hooked to Trevor Thornton's wagon. He'll expect things from you. Take care, little bird."

Angel opened the door, stepped through, and closed it behind her.

Connie flopped back on the bed, blowing out a breath. Her heart hammered from the confrontation. Could Trevor really be so cruel? Maybe, in her anger, Angel had exaggerated. It bore thinking about though. *The fact he thinks I've already said yes to his offer is disturbing. I'll need to set him straight on that right away. He may be the best country singer around, but he's not going to force Connie Champion to do anything she doesn't want to do.*

Chapter Twenty-One

Holding a mug, Quinton stood on the porch of his house on the Champions Gate property. He'd just finished lunch and needed to get back to his afternoon chores, but he'd taken a few minutes to enjoy his coffee.

He surveyed his three acres with pride. He didn't have the grand mansion Bishop built for his family, but Quinton didn't need all that space. His three-bedroom ranch suited him just fine. He had a view of the barns and the pastureland beyond. Subtle, rolling sandy hills stretched out as far as he could see.

Some days, he still couldn't believe his good fortune. To be a part of Champions Gate, Bishop's childhood dream, was a gift for this poor Brooksville farm boy. Who would have thought a two-bit horse trainer could end up with all this?

He glanced up at the blue cloudless December sky. *It's a little hot for the week before Christmas. Not so humid though. Dusty loves days like this.*

His thought of the little woman surprised him. Lately, she just popped into his brain with no warning. He missed her. Since they'd gone riding on Thanksgiving morning, he hadn't seen hide nor hair of her. He'd called a few times to see if she'd wanted to grab dinner in town, but she never returned his calls. He shrugged. *Must be busy is all.*

He didn't understand women. To him, they remained a total mystery.

A young girl's voice along with the Irish lilt of Darbi floated to him on the afternoon breeze. Scarlet walked with her soon-to-be stepmother down the path from the mansion to the barn. They held hands, and Darbi said something that made Scarlet laugh.

Quinton sighed then sipped from his mug. *I envy Bishop. I'd like to have a family someday. I'm not gettin' any younger. Daddy always told me being shy would cost me. I guess he was right.*

Just as Quinton was about to turn and go into the house, a car roared down the driveway to the barns. Dusty's Jeep rounded the bend nearly on two wheels. The vehicle shuddered to a stop in front of the barn. She departed and slammed the door, hard.

"Now what's got her dander up?" he wondered, hoping she wasn't looking for him. There'd been a time or two when he'd seen her red-headed temper.

He ran through the last few days in his mind. He hadn't seen her, so she couldn't be mad at him. Unless that was the reason for her tantrum. After placing his coffee cup on the railing, he strode down the steps and headed for the barn. It wasn't more than a five-minute walk, but just as he reached the barn door, Dusty flew past him on her quarter horse, Sweet Mountain Laurel. Bits of gravel and dirt struck him from the horse's hooves.

What the…?

"Dusty!"

She ignored him and tore out of the barnyard and headed toward one of the trails to the north pastures.

One of the grooms stood open-mouthed. "I ain't never seen anyone saddle a horse so fast. She's gonna kill herself, the horse, or both."

Quinton nodded. "Something's sure got her in a snit. I better go see what's goin' on. You got a horse saddled around here?"

The groom pointed to a glossy black Arabian. "I was going to put Midnight's Pride through his paces this morning."

Quinton vaulted into the saddle. "I'll take care of it. You see if Devil's Temper is of a mind for a ride this morning."

The groom visibly swallowed. "Um…okay."

Quinton laughed as he tapped Midnight's sides. No one wanted to fool with the Devil. Honestly, he was the worst tempered Arabian Quinton had ever dealt with. He made a mental note to have the vet, Chris, take a look at him to see if there might be an underlying cause for his bad manners.

Worry tensed his muscles. *What in the world is up with Dusty? I've never seen her charge out on her horse in such a manner.*

His mind ran through recent conversations with her. Truthfully, he realized, he hadn't seen much of her at all lately. That in and of itself was curious. She always came by the stables at least two or three times a week either to ride or watch him train. Then she stopped in more than once on the weekends, but he hadn't seen her but twice in the last…what…month?

He'd missed her. Her bright smile, the way the evening sun reflected off the red highlights in her auburn hair and made her freckles glow, the twinkle in her bottle-green eyes. He remembered their last encounter on Thanksgiving. They'd enjoyed a nice morning ride, then something changed. Darned if he could figure out what he'd said or done, but the change in her behavior confused him.

Dusty had been around as long as he could remember. From the time she was barely out of grade school, she'd started tagging along with Bishop, Sven, and him. She could outride both Bishop and Sven. He was the only one she couldn't beat in a race, but he had his doubts today. She'd torn out of the barn like Satan himself chased her.

It seemed Dusty had always been a part of their lives…of his life. His heart burned with the desire to figure out what had upset her, surprised at how concerned he was. Dusty could take care of herself.

Living in foster care most of her life had made her tough. A little too tough if he had to be honest. But it made her the fantastic social worker she was today. *I wonder if it's something to do with Mia or some other case she's working on.*

Concerned, he kicked the stallion's sides and increased his pace. He caught up with her at the pond. She strode round and round in wide circles, cooling down Sweet Mountain Laurel who'd worked up a bit of a lather. Dusty spotted him as he rode into the glade and began shaking her head.

"Go away Quinton. I want to be alone."

Ignoring her, he rode his horse up to the wrought-iron bench facing the pond and dismounted. He ground tied the horse and pulled a towel from his saddle bag. Since he enjoyed a hard ride, he always kept a spare.

"Here." He offered it to her. "Wipe down your mount."

She glared at him, tears streaming from reddening eyes. She snatched the towel from him and turned to her horse. As Dusty began to swipe the animal's flanks a little more aggressively than necessary, the mustang swung its head around and nickered. Clearly, Laurel wasn't fond of her treatment this afternoon.

Quinton didn't speak again but placed a large palm on her shoulder and held out his other hand for the towel.

Keeping his tone soft, he said, "Go sit down, Dusty. I'll do this."

She didn't argue but slapped the towel in his hand then continued to pace in circles near the pond. Quinton could not imagine what had her so worked up. She'd been so scarce around the farm lately he prayed it wasn't something he'd done. At times, he admitted to himself, he could be a bit clueless when it came to women and their moods.

He nearly jumped out of his skin when Dusty faced the pond, fists clenched at her sides, and ripped loose with a scream which competed with any burglar alarm he'd ever heard. Laurel reared, and he grabbed for the reins to keep her from bolting. The stallion he'd ridden snapped its head up so fast, he nearly loosened his reins fastened to a scrub palm.

"What the hell?" Quinton quickly tied Dusty's horse to the bench. The toweling off could wait. He ran to his lifelong friend and attempted to pull her into his arms.

"Dusty, what's wrong?"

She fought him, pounding on his chest with her fists. "Let me go, Quinton. I swear, I'll clobber your face."

He knew she wouldn't, or at least he hoped not, but he could take it if she swung at him. How much power could her petite form pack? But when he squeezed her tighter, she pulled back her arm and slugged him square on the jaw. Thank God she hadn't had much leverage or he believed she'd have knocked him back a step.

"Ow. Cut it out." He held her tightly with one arm and rubbed his jaw with his other hand. "I know it's not me you're mad at, so I'm going to let that pass, but I want to know what's going on."

She stared at him with wide eyes, like she couldn't believe she'd just punched him. The heat in those emerald orbs dissipated suddenly, replaced by tears and a soul-wrenching sadness.

"I'm sorry," she muttered. "But I did warn you. Please let me go."

"Not until you tell me what has you so upset. I've never seen you like this, Dust. What's going on?"

Adrenalin ebbing, she sagged against him. Quinton reached down behind her knees and swept her up into his arms. He walked to the bench and sat down, holding her on his lap. She tucked her head into his shoulder and sobbed.

He could not imagine what could have invoked such a violent rage in this normally emotionally stable woman. It had to be bad. So, he just held her while the storm raged within her, rocking her slowly in his arms. She'd tell him when she got good and ready.

After several minutes, Dusty grew so still Quinton thought she might have fallen asleep. He didn't move on the bench, even though his arm grew a bit numb. She needed someone, and he would be her harbor. His heart swelled with an emotion he'd never really attributed to Dusty.

He tucked his nose into her auburn hair, breathing in the citrusy scent of her shampoo. Her soft body warm against him felt good in his arms. He adjusted his position slightly to draw her a little closer. She stirred, glancing up at him with red-rimmed eyes and swollen cheeks.

"I'm sorry," she muttered.

Drawing back from her, he said, "It's okay, baby. Tell me what's got you in such a state. I've never seen you like this before."

A deep soul-cleansing sigh escaped her, and her shoulders shuddered. She slipped off his lap but didn't move away from him. He wrapped an arm around her shoulders and stared out at the afternoon sun sparkling off the still pond and waited.

"Something horrible happened today," she began.

No kidding. He didn't say anything, just waited for her to get it out on her own.

Another sigh. "I don't know if I ever told you about this case, but, about a year ago, I took a little two-year-old boy away from his abusive parents. They were burning him with cigarettes, beating him, and neglecting him. Keeping him in a dog kennel while they left the house to go down to Tampa and visit the casino. Hours, they'd leave this poor kid, no food, no water. It was the worst case of abuse I'd ever seen."

"Did the parents go to jail?"

"For some reason known only to Judge Harvey Wilkerson, they charged the parents with a third degree felony of child endangerment. They served a year in county jail. Toby has been in foster care and thriving with the family who has him. He's gained weight, enjoyed playing with his foster siblings, and was getting ready to start a little pre-school program."

Quinton stomach roiled. Dusty spoke of the boy in past tense. *Oh, boy. This can't be good.*

"The parents got out of jail last week. I went before Judge Harvey Wilkerson when I found out and all but begged him not to give Toby back to them. He told me the parents had been through intense counseling, knew the error of their ways, and were reformed. The best place for a child is with his natural mother."

Dusty rose from the bench and paced in front of him. "The son of a..." She paused wrangling in her rage. "The honorable Judge Wilkerson granted custody back to the parents. I just found out this afternoon the parents killed Toby. Choked the child to death for wetting his bed."

She faced the pond and screamed in rage again. Quinton, sick with rage of his own, went to her. He held her as her shoulders shook with another round of sobs.

"I couldn't stop it, Quin. I couldn't make the judge see how dangerous this situation was for that poor little boy. Why didn't he listen to me? What kind of man puts a child right back into the hands of his abusers? Reformed? It's bull…crap. These parents wanted to murder their baby from the day he was born. And Judge Wilkerson handed him right to them."

"Wow." Lame, he knew, but it was all he could think of to say without launching into a rage of his own.

"I failed that child, Quinton. I've never failed any kid before, and I've been doing this a long time. But I failed Toby." Her voice choked with tears.

Quinton would not allow this. He placed both hands on her shoulders and turned her to face him. "This is not on you, Dusty. You did your job. This is on the judge. What kind of ignoramus puts a child in such danger? He has no place on the bench."

Her green eyes blazed when she looked up at him. "That's what I told the Florida Bar Association today."

He sucked in a breath. "You turned him in?"

She nodded, her chin nearly slapping against her chest with the force of the gesture. "I did. He has no place on the bench. With the report I gave him, no person with any intelligence at all would have granted custody back to those parents. My report was stellar. I'd crossed all my T's and dotted all my I's. I had reports from counselors who had met with them while they were in prison. I had all the medical records from before they were sentenced. It was my most compelling case ever. He just didn't care. Wilkerson was too busy to read them.

"At the hearing, the mother was good. Convincing. But I knew better. I even asked to enter chambers before he made his decision."

"Did he grant it?"

"He did. I explained to him all I'd learned about these people. They were Class A manipulators. He barely gave me the time of day. Kept glancing at his watch, rolling his eyes. Finally, he looked at me and said, 'Are you done, Miss Carmichael?' I swear, Quinton, I just stared at him." She threw up her arms and sank into the dirt.

He knelt beside her. "Come on, let's sit on the bench."

She shook her head, fresh tears flowing down her cheeks. "I couldn't stop him. And a week later, the poor little boy is dead."

Rage filled Quinton Gates. Nothing made him angrier than abusing children or animals. He fought the urge to gallop back to the ranch, get in his truck, and go beat the snot out of that Judge.

"What will the Bar Association do?"

"Probably nothing," she fumed. "His brother is the sitting chairman."

Quinton winced.

"Exactly. All I've probably done is ruin my reputation with him, making my job ten times more difficult."

"They won't even look into it?"

She sighed. "Oh, they'll look into it, and find something wrong with my report, or come up with some cockamamie excuse saying Judge Wilkerson couldn't possibly have known the parents would kill the boy."

"Maybe if you trust the system, they'll do what's right."

She stared at him, a look of clear disbelief on her face.

He frowned. "What?"

"Are you kidding me right now?"

What had he said? *I swear I can't ever get anything right with this woman any more.*

"Trust the system? Like I trusted it to take care of me all those years ago? I battle this"—she ground her teeth—"system every day. It's full of power-hungry bureaucrats who only want to make a name for themselves in politics. They only care about themselves, not innocent children or the people who care for them. Toby's foster family is wracked with grief. They even testified at the hearing. This system sucks. And you want me to trust it?"

At a loss for words, Quinton stammered, "I-I only meant maybe they'll do the right thing and suspend him. It's a pretty compelling case. The point is you did everything you could. Don't take this boy's death on your shoulders, Dusty. It's his parents and this judge who are to blame."

She rose, dusted off her jeans. "I've got to go."

"Wait," he said, rising with her. "Don't go. Come back to the house with me. Have dinner. I'll break open a bottle of your wine you like so much."

Dusty stared at him then shook her head. "I don't think so. I just need to be alone for a while. Please don't come around for a few days."

Stung, he took a step back. The punch to the face didn't hurt as much as those words had. Whenever she'd been in crisis before, he'd always been able to comfort her. Why not now? What had he done wrong? He watched her back as she strode away toward her horse.

"Dusty, wait. Did I say something wrong?"

She paused but didn't turn around. "No, Quinton. You just are who you are."

She grabbed Laurel's reins and vaulted into the saddle. She rode away as he stared after her, open-mouthed.

What the devil had she meant by that?

Chapter Twenty-Two

Connie didn't get a chance to confront Trevor about Angel before the troupe had to board the plane for England. She'd tried a few times, but he'd been behind closed doors with his agent. He'd popped out of his room once, when she'd knocked, but waved her away, saying he'd catch up with her soon.

He's avoiding me. Probably a good thing, Mr. Donkey Butt, because I've got a few things I'd like to say to you. I'll not be party to throwing Angel out like she is an old newspaper. Why can't a band have two female singers? Who wrote that rule? Poor woman.

Connie lugged her duffel onto the plane and plopped into a seat next to a window. She didn't want company. Her mind still reeled from her confrontation with Angel, and it left her confused and disheartened. All these years she'd dreamed of a singing career and never imagined it could be so cut-throat. Maybe Sven had a point when he'd warned her to be careful.

Never thinking of herself as naïve, this trip had been eye opening. She looked forward to seeing Sven in England, hoping it would ground her to her roots. Grateful for her foundation, she offered up a prayer asking for guidance. It meant more than anything to her to sing, but at what cost?

She leaned against the window, her forehead touching the cool glass.

"Penny for your thoughts." Logan eased into the seat beside her.

She kept her gaze on the tarmac. "I doubt they're worth so much."

He punched her shoulder lightly. "Aw come on. What's wrong?"

Not sure she should tell him, she shrugged.

"Okay. Fine. If you don't want to talk about it. Oh…by the way….Manny talked to your boyfriend, and he's going to rent a car at the airport and drive out to the base."

She sat up straighter. "Why? He doesn't know his way around England and with this weather…" She gestured at the falling snow outside the window.

He laughed. "You look so surprised. Isn't he a big boy? I'm sure he's got a GPS on his cell phone. Besides, it's a straight shot here from the airport. Kind of hard to get lost."

She furrowed her brow. "I know, but..."

Logan reached for her hand. "He'll be fine. But while we're on the subject of your boyfriend, can I ask you a question?"

Connie looked down at their clasped hands. His palm was so warm against hers. She let go, but it comforted her to have someone who cared be physically close.

"You can ask me anything you want, Logan. But it doesn't mean I'll answer."

Laughter rumbled in his chest again. "Fair enough."

He shifted so he faced her. "How serious is it between you and this guy? Really?"

She met his intense gaze and sighed. *Why does this have to happen to me now? Why do I have to have three men interested in me all at the same time? Back in Brooksville, men wouldn't give me the time of day. Now I can't beat them off with a stick. What do I want? Who do I want? It doesn't seem fair to keep Logan hanging when I know I either want Sven or a singing career. What future would it give us?*

"Earth to Connie." Logan waved a hand in front of her face.

She blinked. "I'm sorry. I wanted to give this some thought before I answered you."

"I don't think I like where this is going."

"I haven't even said anything yet."

"You didn't have to. It was a long pause."

"A lot of new things are happening to me all at once. I left home for the first time ever to travel all the way around the world. I have a famous country singer interested in my voice and he wants to offer me a place in his band."

Logan snorted. "His band is not the only place he wants to offer you."

She slapped at his arm. "Stop. I'm not so easy. I want a singing career, but I'm not going to sleep with anyone to get it. I'm just not built that way."

The doors slammed shut on the plane, and all the other passengers took their seats. She spotted Trevor seated a few rows up, still head to head with his agent. *Are they talking about me?*

She buckled her seatbelt. Within in minutes, the pilot announced they were clear for takeoff. She swallowed as the plane rolled down the runway, engines revving."

Logan reached for her hand again. "You were saying?"

"I don't know how to answer your question, Logan."

"How about honestly?"

She sighed. "Okay. You asked for it." She took a deep breath, let it out. "I find you extremely attractive. You're exotic, have been a soldier, and always have my best interest at heart. What's not to like?"

He frowned. "I hear a 'but' in there somewhere."

"But…"

"Ah, see, I knew it."

Connie smiled. "This tour has been a whirlwind. I don't know if I'm coming or going. I'm excited about seeing Sven in England. I've known him for almost my entire life. There's comfort in it. He knows me. We've got a lot in common."

"How does he feel about you singing with Trevor?"

"I don't know. I don't think he's crazy about the idea. He's worried I don't know what I'm getting into."

"On that point, your boyfriend and I agree."

"Don't you start on me, too. I've wanted to be a singer since I was old enough to hold a microphone. It's who I am, and if Trevor can open the door for me, then I'd be stupid not to walk through it."

Logan released her hand and leaned back in his chair as the plane climbed into the sky. He closed his eyes.

"Are you okay?" Connie placed a hand on his arm.

He turned his head to face her. "I'm okay. I just don't like the takeoff and landing part."

"Me either. Do you need something? Should I call somebody?"

He shook his head. "I'll be okay in a minute. Then I'll tell you what I think about your decision to sing with Trevor."

She used the time for the plane to reach cruising altitude to think. *How honest should I be with Logan. If things don't work out with Sven the way I want them to, I'd be free to pursue a relationship with someone else, but do I want it to be Logan? He's hot, sure, but is he ready for a relationship? Has he made enough progress divorcing himself from his past so he can focus on having a woman in his life?*

Shame filled her. She wanted to help Logan through his troubles, but she wasn't sure she was the right woman to do so effectively. She remembered how Wrynn took charge when they'd found Logan having a nightmare. She'd known exactly what to do. Connie hadn't had a clue. Her first instinct had been to wake him up, and she could have been seriously hurt if she'd followed those instincts. Logan was a complicated man. Her life was about to be blessed with its own complications, and she wasn't sure she could handle any more.

"Okay." Logan captured her attention by tapping her arm. "I know it's none of my business."

Connie hated sentences starting with those words. It always ticked her off, but she raised her eyebrows in question.

"I've seen celebrities like Trevor before. He has an enormous ego, and while he can turn on the charm, he doesn't care about anyone but himself. He wants what he wants and doesn't care about what he must do to get it."

Angel's voice echoed in her mind. She'd used those same words.

"I'm concerned about his motivations where you're concerned. I don't believe he has your best interest at heart…only his. He knows how much money your voice could make him, plus he's looking for a new lover. I heard he sent Angel home this morning."

Connie sucked in a breath. "What is it with you people? First Angel accuses me of sleeping with Trevor and now you—

"Hold on," he interrupted, grabbing her arm. She twisted it away from him. "I didn't say you wanted to. I said *he* wants to. You can see it all over his face."

"Maybe everyone thinks I want to be his new squeeze so I can get a recording contract, right? Is that what everyone on this tour thinks of me?" She struggled with her seat belt.

"Whoa, wait a minute. Don't leave. I didn't mean to make you angry. What I'm trying to say is I'm worried about you. He'll make a move regardless of what you want. I've seen his type before. I know you aren't that type of person. You're a lady. And believe me, you don't see many of those in the entertainment business."

She glared at him, hurt filling her entire being. She wasn't angry with Logan, but the thought everyone might think she was capable of sleeping her way to the top devastated her. Her breath came in short pants as she struggled to get her emotions under control. When she'd succeeded, she captured Logan's gaze with her own.

"I appreciate your concern for me, Logan. I really do. But you don't know me very well. At all really. We've been on this tour for what, a month at most?"

He nodded, an embarrassed expression forming on his face. Blood seeped up his neck into his cheeks.

"I grew up with all boys. I was the only girl around for miles. Big strapping farm boys came over to play with my brother and Quinton. I held my own against all of them. Many a day they went home with a sore groin because of my fast moves. I've taken self-defense classes, and I can shoot the eye out of a squirrel from 50 yards, not that I enjoy doing so, but I can. I have a permit to carry a concealed weapon, and I won't hesitate to use it if I feel threatened."

He stared at her wide-eyed.

"I'm not some little doe-eyed girl who needs protection, although I appreciate the thought. I'm sure I can handle Trevor Thornton. He's been a complete gentleman, by the way."

Logan rolled his eyes. "How much time have you had alone with him?"

Okay, she had to admit, not much. And when she had, she'd felt a bit queasy about Trevor's intentions toward her. And the fact he'd fired Angel made it worse.

"Enough to know I can handle whatever he wants to throw at me." She swiveled in the tight plane seat to fully face him. "I want this shot, Logan. It's my time. I feel it with all my being. I wish I could describe how singing makes me feel."

He smiled, reached for her hand. "You don't have to. Your face glows with it." He tapped his phone in his breast pocket. "Remember? I'm the one who listens to you every night to fall asleep."

She relaxed and leaned against the seat. "I'm glad it helps you. I have no idea what triggers your nightmares, but I'm sorry for it."

He glanced away.

She hoped he might tell her about his experiences as a soldier. She wanted to understand what drove the horrific flashbacks and nightmares he suffered. Perhaps she could help. When he glanced at her, he wore a determined expression.

"Don't try to change the subject. Originally, I started out asking about Sven, and you haven't answered the question yet. How does he feel about these dreams of yours? Is he ready to follow you as you traipse across the country with the hottest country singer in the world?"

"None of your business." He wanted the truth, she'd give him the truth. "I'm not comfortable talking about this with you, Logan. Sven and I are trying to build something which may or may not be long lasting, and me discussing it with you doesn't feel right. I'm sorry."

Disappointment flooded his features, but he maintained a controlled tone. "Fair enough. I just wanted to take a moment to tell you how I feel about you."

Oh crap. I'm not ready for this.

"Logan, I—

"Let me say this while I've got the courage. I know we haven't known each other long, as you pointed out so eloquently. I also know I'm not a prize and have problems I'm dealing with on a daily basis." He paused.

She'd been staring at his chest, and she let her gaze drift to his soft chestnut-brown eyes. The intensity of his expression caught her breath.

"But I'm falling for you, Connie. I can't help it. I know you're not totally available, but I wanted you to know how I feel."

She blushed. Try as she might, she couldn't summon the same feelings toward him, but she didn't have the heart to shut him down completely. Probably wrong, but she didn't want to hurt him. For all his strength, he seemed so fragile.

She sighed. "I'm flattered, Logan."

He held up a hand. "Let me stop you before the 'but.' I'm not going to push you. I wanted you to know how I felt. I know it may not be fair with how you feel about Sven, but I didn't have much to lose." He unbuckled his seat belt. "I'm going to check on things. See how everyone is doing. I'll see you once we land."

He rose and walked toward the back of the plane. She turned to watch him go. *The man's got guts, I'll give him that.*

She rotated in her seat to stare out the window. White puffy clouds drifted by in an azure sky. She compared them to her life. All seems dreamy until the storm rolls in. *I wonder when my thunder begins.*

Chapter Twenty-Three

Connie paced her stark room in the barracks of the Royal Air Force Lakenheath Base. After Logan walked away from her on the plane, she'd read the brochure Wrynn had handed the troupe members about the location. Supposedly, the most populated base in England, it had been run by the United States since the 1950s.

The snowy weather outside had seeped its way into her mood. Even the thought of Sven arriving in a few hours couldn't lighten her heart. She worried about him driving himself. She didn't know how to drive in bad weather, and she doubted Sven had ever done so.

Her mind whirled with Logan's declaration of love for her, along with his harsh accusation of Trevor only wanting to take advantage of her in more ways than one.

I won't believe it. She prowled the small room, touching each piece of pressboard furniture as she went. The room was hardly bigger than her bedroom at home. The efficient Brits had crammed two twin beds, two dressers, and two desks into the tiny space, leaving her little room to roam. She stared through gray levered blinds covering the small window at a patch of snow-covered ground in between four barracks buildings.

She shook her head. *I'm smart enough to know when I'm being taken advantage of, and I don't feel that from Trevor. Do I? He's only trying to help me out because I'm good.*

She strolled to the small mirror mounted above one of the dressers. She'd swept her hair into a pony tail and put on a pair of warm pink sweats and a matching pink-and-gray sweatshirt. She glanced at the digital clock over her shoulder. The numbers were backwards in the reflection from the mirror, but she had about two hours before Sven arrived.

You're a good singer, Connie Champion. She pointed a finger at her reflection. *Some have said I'm the best they've ever heard. An angel.* She glanced toward the ceiling.

"Dear God, I don't know what to do. I want to honor you with this wonderful gift, but I'm also attracted to the glitz and glamor of it all. I like the feeling I get when people respond to my voice. I want to use it for Your glory. Guide me in what I should do about Trevor's offer. Bring Sven here safely, and help me know my own heart."

The door to the room opened, and Wrynn stepped in. "Who are you talking to?"

Connie smiled and pointed upward. "The Man Upstairs. Just trying to get some guidance."

Wrynn laughed. "I've never been much of a believer in a higher power, but if it gives you some comfort, I'm glad. Send one up on my behalf, would you? If Stan and I pull off this show, it will be a miracle."

"Why, what's wrong?" Connie left the mirror and plopped on the edge of one of the twin beds.

"Practically everything. The lieutenant I've been coordinating with is not the most intelligent man. He's confused all the times for the shows, and the space we were supposed to use for the stage is still full of storage. And I'm not talking boxes, I'm talking heavy equipment. The kind they use to maintain the runways."

"Oh, boy."

"Yeah…oh, boy is right. They also messed up the room accommodations and had Trevor rooming with one of the band members. He wasn't happy, let me tell you, so I had to shuffle everyone in the men's barracks around. Sheesh, what a day."

Wrynn flopped on the bed, her breath escaping in a whoosh. She placed an arm over her forehead.

"Is it all settled now?" Connie shifted to pull her legs up onto the bed.

"Yes, finally." Wrynn rolled over and braced her head on her palm. "So, what has you so wound up you have to ask the Almighty for help? I saw you talking to Logan on the plane. You didn't seem very happy with the conversation."

Connie blew air through her lips, sounding like one of her horses. "I wasn't. He all but accused Trevor of wanting to take advantage of me. Logan doesn't believe Trevor's offer of joining his band is in my best interest. He thinks the man only wants me for the money I'll make him."

"And the sex." Wrynn sat up.

"Oh, come on." Connie sprang off the bed, exasperated. "Not you, too. What is wrong with you people?"

"Connie, wait. Don't get mad. I've seen the way Trevor watches you. Like he could eat you up with a spoon, and then lick the bowl. And why not? Look at you. You're gorgeous, you sing like an—

"An angel, I know." Connie rolled her eyes. "I may not be too experienced with the ways of the world, but I know when a man wants me for sex, and I don't get that vibe from Trevor."

Why had she just lied to her friend? Of course, she'd known Trevor admired more than her voice. She'd had to ward off his advances more than once since the tour began,

193

but she had to believe his offer to record with her meant more than a roll in the hay.

"You don't?" Wrynn's expression held doubt. "I don't want to say you're blind, Connie, but…you're blind. He fired Angel for crying out loud. He wants you all to himself.

"Oh, I'm sure he's fed you all kinds of BS about what a great singer you are, and how the two of you will make beautiful music together, blah, blah, blah. But I know a letch when I see one. Just be really careful around him."

Connie faced her friend, hands on her hips. The sincerity in Wrynn's eyes, the firm set of her mouth—Connie had no reason to believe Wrynn wasn't expressing the truth as she saw it. Now, if they'd been talking about Logan, Connie doubted the expression would have held the same sincerity. The fact her friend mentioned them sitting together on the plane held hidden meaning.

I've got eyes, Miss Wrynn. I know you're developing feelings for Logan. What if you knew what he'd told me on our plane ride?

She turned away from the tour coordinator's gaze, shocked by her uncharitable feelings. She needed Sven. Wanted to sit down and discuss all this with him. He was her rock, her foundation in this terrible tempest she now found herself in.

All I wanted when I started this stupid tour was a shot at singing professionally. Who knew it came with so many strings?

Connie's phone rang. She sprang for it, snatching it from the nightstand. Trevor's face appeared under the red-and-green phones on the screen.

"Oh Lord, now what?" She slid her finger across the screen, putting him on speaker.

"Hi, Trevor."

"Hey, Connie. I know you've been wanting to catch up with me. Want to come down to my room? I've got some snacks and drinks in here. We can talk uninterrupted for as long as you need."

Connie caught Wrynn shaking head. "Don't do it," she mouthed.

Anger sprouted in her veins. She had a few things to straighten out with this man, and now was as good a time as any.

"I only have an hour, Trevor. I've got to get ready meet Sven."

He chuckled. "Oh, yeah. The boyfriend?"

"Right," she replied, her tone firm.

He snickered again. "Okay, don't get your dander up. Come on down for an hour. It should be plenty of time to talk about what's on your mind."

He gave her the location of his room then disconnected.

"Don't go alone." Wrynn rose from the bed. "Let me go with you."

"I'll be fine." Connie's voice held more sharpness than she intended. She held up her phone. "I'll have this in my back pocket. I'll call you if things get weird, okay."

Wrynn rolled her eyes. "Don't say I didn't warn you."

Chapter Twenty-Four

Sven tossed his suitcase into the *boot* of the car he'd rented. He patted his pocket for his cell phone and got into the driver's seat. He offered up a prayer he wouldn't kill someone on his way to the air base. He'd never driven on the opposite side of the road before, and his stomach roiled a little at the prospect.

He could have used a car service or taken the train, but he wanted to have the freedom to drive Connie away from the base and see a little of the English countryside before they flew home for the wedding.

He punched in the address of the base on his phone, and put it in the cup holder of the small SUV. Snow fell, covering the road—another daunting prospect. He'd rarely seen snow much less driven in the stuff.

He adjusted the rearview mirror. "You're an idiot, Sven Christenson."

Putting the car in gear, he rolled out of the lot and onto the street. Thankfully, the wet snow wasn't sticking to the roads…yet. As he drove from Gatwick to the Lakenheath base, he prayed the temperature hovered about the same.

Taking his time, he made his way to the highway that would take him to the base. *This isn't so bad. I'm managing to turn and stay in the correct lane. I might actually get the hang of this.*

He glanced up at the dreary cloud-laden sky. He imagined what the small village near the base would look like all decorated for Christmas. He'd done some research and already had a few restaurants in mind he wanted to take Connie to before they headed back to the airport. Three days wasn't much time, and she had to perform two shows, so they wouldn't get to see much. He made a mental note to bring her back. Maybe on their honeymoon.

He nearly hit the brakes on the highway. His eyebrows shot up at the thought. They'd barely begun this relationship and, already, he wanted to put a ring on her finger.

Yep. I'm certain of how I feel about her. But not as certain of how she feels about me. She's been surrounded by people giving her new exciting experiences. I'm sure Brooksville seems boring by comparison.

He glanced in the rearview mirror again. The road was relatively deserted. Tomorrow was Christmas Eve. In the United States, the highways would be packed with cars going to visit family. Perhaps the English had already gotten where they were going.

His brothers hadn't been pleased he wouldn't be home for the holiday. Like Connie, this would be the first one he'd missed. His oldest brother, Hans, and wife, Megan, always laid out quite the spread. Sven enjoyed indulging his many nieces and nephews with gifts. They'd still get them this year, he just wouldn't get to enjoy their happy faces when they opened them on Christmas morning.

A pang of regret shot through him as he remembered his conversation when he'd told Hans his plans while they stood in the kitchen of the old family homestead.

"You're crazy, little brother. Why fly halfway around the world when she'll be home for the wedding in a week?"

"Because she asked me to. I'm sure her first Christmas away from Bishop, Darbi, and the girls will be rough on her. She's struggled more with homesickness than she thought."

"Maybe so, but is it worth being away from all of us for Christmas? What's going on with you? You always thought of Connie as a little sister. What changed?"

Sven sighed. "I don't know how it happened, but, right before she left, it hit me how I've always felt about her. I just didn't know how to put it into words. Plus Bishop intimidates me."

Hans laughed. "Yeah, me, too." He wrapped an arm around Sven's shoulders. "If you love her, don't let her get away, man. If I hadn't pursued Megan relentlessly, she might have settled for a lesser man."

"Hah," Megan called from the screened back porch. "I heard you."

Hans hugged his brother. "Connie's a wonderful girl. I still don't see why you need to fly to England for Christmas, but it's up to you."

"You sound so much like Dad."

Hans nodded sagely. "I do, don't I?"

Sven smiled at the remembrance. His brothers loved him and wanted the best for him. Being the one in the middle of five, having two older brothers and two younger, gave him the best of both worlds. The younger brothers had gone off in pursuit of careers other than farming, but Sven and Hans had stayed behind. They'd divided up the homestead into four additional plats giving each brother land for a home when they chose to use it.

Sven loved his corner. His small farm gave him time to work his hands in the earth, take care of his animals, and still have time to tend to the legal needs of Brooksville. He wondered, as he drove through the gates of the military base, if his new-found love for Connie would force him to give any of it up.

He'd already had a thought on the topic, but he wasn't ready to share it with Connie just yet. He'd see how this trip went and then make his decision before she returned after the wedding. If he went through with it, the change for him would be astronomical. And not just for him. Champions Gate could suffer as well. He had a lot to contemplate.

Chapter Twenty-Five

Connie knocked on the door to Trevor's room. He answered in nothing but a pair of loose fitting gray sweat pants with a towel in his hand. Water droplets from his shower-fresh hair slithered down his chest. She swallowed, trying hard not to stare at his tan muscles.

Who keeps a tan this far into winter? Has to be fake. She sighed. *Really looks good though.* She stepped through the doorway.

"Sorry, Connie. After I called you, I caught a whiff of myself and you're going to thank me."

"Thank you."

He laughed, rubbing his hair with the towel. "Let me get a shirt and comb my hair." He stepped to the dresser and ruffled through a black duffel.

While he dressed, she glanced around. The room appeared as sparse as hers. A single twin bed stood by the small window, covered with white sheets and a thin cotton bed spread of light blue. Low light from the dreary snowy day filtered into the room through the levered blinds. She chose to sit in the small desk chair across from the bed and watched as he leaned down to see his reflection in the tiny dresser mirror.

"Guess people in the military aren't too vain." He chucked, and ran a comb through his full blond hair. He pulled on a plain, black T-shirt then sat on the edge of the bed, his knees bumping hers.

"Now, what did you want to see me about?"

Connie squared her shoulders and gave him her sternest expression. The one she used when she was about to discipline the triplets. He leaned away from her.

"I want to talk about you letting Angel go. Why did you do it, Trevor? She's a fantastic singer, and she's been with you for years."

"You're better." A simple statement of fact. His tone flat, he held her gaze.

She ignored the compliment. "Surely, your band can support two female singers. I happen to think Angel and I together could make a great duet team."

"Connie, baby." He leaned forward and placed both palms on her knees. "Why are you worried about an old fart like Angel. She's served her time, past her prime and all. Look at you…" He turned her face toward the small mirror, placed his cheek next to hers.

She jerked her face out of his grasp. "It was cruel, Trevor. I haven't even agreed to sign to sing with you yet, and you let her go."

He straightened. "Oh, you'll sign with me. I'm the best shot you'll ever get at the big time, and you know it. You've got a voice no one can top right now. Stick with me, and I'll sail you straight to the top of the charts."

Connie knew it was a true statement. Anyone who hitched their wagon to him would end up at the top. But at what cost? Angel certainly seemed to have paid the price.

"I'm not so sure I'm ready for that kind of commitment. I think I'll finish out this tour, and then, if you still have room in the band, we can talk."

His expression darkened, his dark-blond brows forming into a deep V. "What are you talking about? I've already worked with my agent to set up bookings at the recording studio for us. It doesn't come cheap. He's also started setting up photo shoots for marketing."

She rose and stepped to the window, looking out at the snowy day. *Hurry up, Sven. I need you.*

"I never told you for sure I'd tour with you. You've made a terrible assumption if you've gone so far down the path. You should have confirmed with me first and not assumed I'd just fall at your feet because you're Trevor Thornton. How naïve do you think I am?"

His expression answered her question. His scowl turned his normally handsome features quite ugly. Then, as soon as it was there, it disappeared behind one of his million-watt smiles.

"Connie." He patted the bed. "Come here."

Reluctantly, she sat.

"You can't be all that upset about Angel. You hardly knew her. Let me tell you everything I've got planned. You'll be so excited you'll forget all about it."

He listed dates and places she'd only dreamed of traveling to. For a moment, she got caught up in the magic, picturing herself on stage with him, all those screaming fans. She had no doubt after they released a few records and performed a few concerts, she'd rocket to stardom. Her life would never be the same again. And it bothered her.

Her signing the USO contract had been a giant leap from her family, and the only safety net she'd ever known. Listening to all Trevor threw at her caused her heart and her head to pound.

"It all sounds wonderful, but I'm still not sure. My boyfriend will be here soon, and I want to discuss it with him first."

Trevor draped an arm over her shoulders. "Connie, baby, listen to me. You're a grown woman. You don't need anyone's permission to live your life." He traced two fingers down her cheek. "You're a beautiful, passionate female, who knows what she wants to do. You don't need some albatross of a boyfriend around your neck."

Her stomach fluttered at his touch. She scooted over, putting as much distance between them as his arm around her would allow.

"He's an attorney. I wouldn't sign anything without him looking everything over, so I don't see the harm in you waiting until I talk to him about it."

He leaned in close. "Baby, I promise you this will be the ride of your life."

His embrace tightened, and his lips crushed hers before she could pull away. She put both hands on his chest, shoved, but he wouldn't yield. He pushed at her lips with his tongue, trying to deepen the kiss.

She twisted sideways, breaking the contact. "Trevor, stop."

He leaned a few inches away. "Connie, I'm so attracted to you. When you sing like you do on stage, it just does something to me. Don't you feel it, too? We could make such beautiful music together. With your looks and my fame, we'd be unstoppable. Come on, be my girl, huh?"

"I have a boyfriend, Trevor."

"Aw, honey. I'm sure it's not serious, right? You can blow him off. I know he can't offer you what I can."

His face came in close for another kiss, and Connie shoved him hard. He tumbled off the bed and flopped onto his butt on the floor.

She rose.

He sprang to his feet. "Hey, what do you think you're doing?"

"I'm leaving."

"Not yet you're not." He took a few steps toward her. "We've got a few things to take care of first."

She backed toward the door. He followed, pinning her body against the wooden frame with his hands on either side of her head.

"Don't be like this, Connie. I really like you. I want you. Just stay with me tonight and see if you aren't as happy about this as I am."

"I'm not going to be your lover, Trevor. If this contract comes with it as a *perk,* then I'll pass."

She watched his expression change. Her heart skipped a beat, and a chill fluttered up her spine. His normally cheery blue eyes grew dark. His cheeks flushed, and his brows drew down into a deep V. His mouth hardened into a thin line.

"It's not wise to say no to me, girl."

"Maybe not, but I'm saying it. Now move so I can get out of this room."

"Make me."

His challenge reminded her of all the rough-and-tumble boys she'd dealt with growing up with Bishop and his best friend Quinton. There were times when she'd had to defend herself against their unwanted advances a time or two. She sighed. *Okay, buddy. You asked for it.*

She shot her knee up into his crotch...hard. When he doubled over, she shoved his shoulders, resisting the urge to bring her knee up again and knock out a few teeth. He stumbled backward several steps.

"You bitch," he shouted.

"Don't try that again, Mr. Thornton. Of course, I wont be stupid enough to give you the chance."

She spun, reaching for the door handle, but before she could pull it open, he snatched a handful of her hair, yanking her backward. The strength of his grip surprised her. This guy wasn't fooling around. If she didn't think fast, she'd be in some serious trouble. So, she did what any woman worth her salt would do. She opened her mouth and let loose a window-rattling scream.

Trevor pulled her against him, her back to his chest. She wished she had her heels on instead of tennis shoes, but she screamed again and stomped on his instep. He yelped but didn't let her go.

He started to move her toward the bed. She struggled to break free ,but his grip was strong. She did the last defensive move she could think of. Leaning her head forward as far as it would go, she reared back butting him in the face.

Pain shot through her skull, but there was a satisfying crack. She screamed again, and he released her, both hands flying up to his bloody nose.

The door flew open, slamming against the wall. Logan stood in the doorway, looking as dark and menacing as she'd ever seen him.

He shoved past her.

"The bitch hit me in the nose," Trevor whined.

"She's not the only one, you bastard." Logan reared back and connected his fist to Trevor's jaw. The man spun and landed on the floor. Logan pounced. He sat heavily on Trevor's chest and began to pound his face and body with his fists.

"Logan, stop. I'm okay." Connie, knowing how bad this could get, stepped up behind him. She tried to grab his arm. "Logan, please stop. You're going to kill him."

She reached for his arm again, and in his rage, he threw back his elbow, catching Connie in the chest so hard, it knocked her backward. When she hit the floor, her breath blew out in a whoosh.

She couldn't draw in air. Her brain wouldn't register through the pain her lungs needed to fill. Edges of blackness crept in on her vision.

"What the hell is going on here?"

Sven? Oh thank God.

She tried to say his name, but her mouth wouldn't work.

Sven bounded into the room and locked Logan into a full Nelson, dragging him off Trevor.

"Stop fighting me, man."

Wrynn charged into the room. "What the—"

She ran to Connie and shouted to Sven. "He's got PTSD, be careful. He's strong as a bull."

Sven nodded and tightened his hold around Logan's shoulders and the back of his neck. "Take it easy, buddy. It's okay. You got him. He's down."

Wrynn stood in front of Logan. "Hey, it's okay. Come on back. Look." She pointed at Connie, but kept her voice soothing and calm. "You hurt her. Stop this now. Trevor is down. You took care of it."

By then three or four more people stepped into the room. Connie's lungs began to work, and she sucked in a breath. Pain shot across her breast bone. She slapped a palm to her chest. *This is definitely going to leave a mark.*

She glanced at Trevor. *Speaking of marks. Oh God. How are we going to explain this to Stan?*

Denny, Trevor's right hand ran to him. "Call 911," he shouted.

Trevor glared at Logan. "I'm going to sue you to within an inch of your life. You're finished, do you hear me?"

"It was worth it," Logan growled.

Wrynn spoke to Denny who was stepping out the door. "Hold on."

"But he needs medical attention." The man protested, pointing to Trevor's face.

"I'll get him medical attention, but before this all gets out of hand, let's think this through." Wrynn turned to face Trevor. "Do you want the scandal of you getting your butt kicked while trying to assault a woman on this tour?"

"I didn't try to—"

"Yes, you did." Connie's tone was slightly hysterical. "I'm the one who should press charges."

Wrynn spun around to her friend. "Do you want to?"

Connie took a full assessment of Trevor's face. Pride shot through her. He looked far from okay. She wouldn't be amazed if more than his nose was broken. It had already begun to enlarge, and two purple bruises were forming under his eyes. More large contusions bloomed on the side of each jaw where Logan had pounded his face more than once.

Logan still struggled against Sven's hold. "She was screaming when I came in. He attacked her. You should press charges, Connie."

Sven shot a look at Connie. "How'd you end up on the floor?"

"I was trying to pull Logan off Trevor," she wheezed. "He elbowed me in the chest." When she saw the sheer shock on Logan's face, she struggled to sit up. "But I'm okay."

Wrynn knelt and helped her up. "Did Trevor attack you, Connie?"

"Yes, but I had the situation under control."

"The hell you did," Logan growled. "I'm sorry I hurt you, but he's been trying to corner you since he arrived. What were you thinking coming in here alone? Are you nuts?"

"Hey," Sven interrupted. "That's my girl you're yelling at." He jerked Logan by tightening his hold.

"Let me go." Logan struggled against him again.

"I'm not going to have to put you down, am I?"

Connie stared at Sven. *Where did he learn that hold? Logan's strong as a bull, yet he's holding him like he's a toddler.*

"I'm fine. Let me go."

Wrynn nodded at Sven. "I think it's under control now."

Sven loosened his hold, releasing Logan. He stepped back a few steps, but stood on the balls of his feet ready to spring into action again if necessary.

Logan shook his shoulders and rolled his head around. He glanced at Sven. "Man, you've got some grip. Former military?"

Sven shook his head. "The middle of five brothers."

Denny helped his boss to the bed. "I'll have you arrested." Denny glowered at Logan.

Trevor put a hand on Denny's arm, his expression growing sheepish. "Nah you won't. Wrynn's right. Let's not blow this into more than it was. I guess I deserved it. Listen, man, just go get me some ice."

"You need to go to a hospital. I'm sure your nose is broken."

"Yeah, I'm sure it is, too. Just call Derek. He'll handle it."

Denny nodded. "You sure?"

"Yeah."

Wrynn walked to the door. "Everyone go on back to your rooms. Nothing more to see here." She shooed people out the door and closed it, leaving only Logan, Sven, Trevor, and her in the room.

"Connie, do you want to tell us what happened?"

Oh boy. How do I handle this one? I've already said he attacked me. But I really don't want to press charges. He looks like he might have learned his lesson. With me, anyway.

"He must have attacked you." Logan faced her, bloody fists on his hips. "I heard you screaming. That's why I rushed in the way I did."

Connie sighed. "Let's just call it a misunderstanding. Right Trevor?"

Trevor glared at her, drawing his brows down, then he winced. "Um, you broke my nose."

Sven's expression betrayed his surprise. "You broke his nose?"

Connie tried to hide the satisfaction which swelled in her, but nodded.

"You deserved it. I'm willing to let this go, and if you can finish the tour, I'll still sing with you. But I'm not interested in anything further." She pointed at his face. "I think I made it clear enough."

"Trevor, do you want to press charges against Logan?" Wrynn held up a hand when Logan started to protest.

"No. Let me just get to a doctor, and I'll let you know if I can perform tomorrow or not." He worked his jaw from side to side, grimacing as he did so. *My agent can spin this somehow. I've lived through worse scandals.*

"Very well, then." Wrynn took a few steps toward Trevor. "You're a very lucky man, Trevor Thornton. I'd get down on your knees and appreciate the chance you've been given here. I'll talk to Stan and help you come up with a way to cover up this disaster, if you can continue the tour. I'll send up the staff medic. No need to involve your man, unless you just want to."

Trevor shook his head. "Fine."

"I'd say we've all had a very long evening." She opened the door and ushered everyone but Trevor out. Denny was coming up the hall.

Sven wrapped an arm around Connie's shoulders. "Are you okay?"

She rubbed her chest but nodded. "A bit shaken up, but, overall, I'm okay." She glanced at him. "You're my hero, you know that?"

He held her close and kissed the top of her head. "Glad to be of assistance, my lady."

She snorted then moaned. When her limbs began to tremble, she leaned into Sven for support.

As they started to move down the hall, Logan touched her shoulder from behind. She stopped and turned to face him.

"I'm really sorry I decked you back there. I was in a rage about what he tried to do to you."

Connie hugged him, surprising them both. "Thank you."

Logan gazed at her a moment then faced Sven. "You've got a very special lady here. I still think you should have him thrown in jail."

"I know. Thank you for intervening."

"Yeah, well, I'll probably lose my job."

Wrynn took his arm. "I'll explain it to Stan. And once I do, I'm sure you'll get a medal." She glanced at the Trevor's door.

Connie heard Wrynn mutter something sounding like, "Jackass".

"Did you get a room at the hotel?" Wrynn asked Sven.

"I'm not sure how close it is to the base, but I have a reservation at the Riverside House."

"It's not far, but I'll find you a room here," Wyrnn said. "Can you cancel your reservation?"

211

"I suppose."

"Good." Connie and Wrynn spoke simultaneously.

Sven squeezed her close.

She glanced up at him. "If you even once say I told you so…"

"Are you kidding? And end up looking like Trevor? No way."

Chapter Twenty-Six

Christmas Eve dawned with the sun unable to force its way through the sky's ashen coat of clouds. Connie stood at the small window of the room assigned to Sven. She hummed a bit to test her vocal chords. A bit raspy, but she'd make it through the show tomorrow. She winced as she tenderly pressed at the spot on her breastbone where Logan's elbow had connected. She hoped the purple swollen knot hadn't spread any farther up her chest, or it would surely show above the neckline of her costume. Perhaps one of the acrobats could help her with their thick makeup.

She wondered how Trevor faired with all his injuries. Many emotions paraded through her heart and mind, but guilt wasn't one of them. Shock and dismay ranked at the top of the list. What she'd thought was a sure ticket to her dreams was now smashed like a crystal vase on a tile floor.

How could I have been so naïve and gullible? I knew Trevor was flirting, but to outright try to attack me to get what he wanted? I'm not a bit sorry I broke his nose. The creep.

She turned and glanced at the sleeping Sven. They'd lain awake all night, fully clothed as he held her while she cried. By the time they'd made it to his room, the adrenalin of her ordeal had worn off, and she'd crashed in his arms. The full ramifications of what she'd experienced bore down on her.

She smiled thinking of how loving Sven had been toward her. He plied her with tissues, went to the bathroom to get a cold cloth to wipe her face, then cuddled her as she droned on and on about her mistakes. Finally, when she'd wrung herself dry of words, he'd been supportive.

"Connie, this isn't the end of your singing career. Finish this USO tour, and then you can send demo tapes to Nashville. This disaster with Trevor will hurt him more than it will hurt you. I have no idea how he can go on with the show, so you'll be the main attraction."

He tipped her chin up to face him. "I'm sure word has already traveled about you singing duets with him. Everything is going to be fine."

Connie turned toward the window, stared out onto the foot or so of freshly fallen snow. "My first white Christmas," she muttered.

"Hey? Are you okay?" Sven's voice crackled with the dregs of sleep.

"Yes, I'm just looking at the snow. I can't believe it's Christmas Eve."

"Did you sleep at all?" Sven sat up. His light-blue button-down shirt was barely wrinkled. His jeans still held their pressed crease.

"How do you do it?"

His eyebrows rose. "Do what?"

"Spend the entire night attending my pity party and look like you just walked off the pages of GQ magazine?"

She stepped to the small mirror over the dresser. "Oh Lord, it's going to take a dump truck of makeup to repair this mess." She pointed to her face then stared at him through the reflection in the mirror. "You amaze me. Never a hair out of place, always looking fresh as a daisy? You make me sick."

He laughed and rose to gather her in his arms. "Just a natural-born talent, I guess."

He rested his chin on her head and they gazed at each other in the glass. "You've never looked more beautiful to me than you do right now."

Tears stung her eyes. *How does he know the right things to say? What a guy. My hero.*

She closed her lids and tilted her head against his chest. "I'm sorry you didn't get any sleep last night."

He rotated her so she faced him. "Hey, stop it. I can't believe what you went through. I'm sorry you had to endure that." He traced two fingers down the side of her cheek. "I love you, Connie Champion." He leaned in, pressed his lips to hers.

The kiss held all the tenderness and compassion she needed now. She relaxed and let herself experience the warmth of his body, the pressure of his mouth on hers, and her heart swelled. *I belong here. Like this, in his arms. We're a good fit. But can I say I love him back?*

Sven didn't seem to expect anything. He lifted his head and drew her in close, saying nothing. She pressed her cheek against his chest, listening to the strong beat of his heart.

"Sven, thank you."

"For what?"

"For not saying I told you so. Maybe Bishop was right. I just wasn't cut out for this. I'm not ready for all the sleaziness of this business. I probably never should have left home. I miss you, Bishop, Darbi, and the triplets. This has been a fabulous experience, but I think after the tour, I'm just going to come home."

He stepped back, and she glanced up at him, trying to read his expression. Troubled was the word which sprang into her mind.

"That's what you'd like, isn't it? You haven't been very enthusiastic about me embarking on this singing adventure."

He sighed. "Let's not talk about this now. Give yourself time to get over last night. I'm sure every person in the music business isn't like Trevor Thornton. You were far too generous with him. He deserved to be arrested for what he did. He sexually assaulted you."

Connie stepped away from Sven's embrace and strode to the window again. She glanced out, blowing her breath on the glass. She drew a heart and put her and his initials inside. He laughed.

"Now I understand the expression, pure as the driven snow. I bet if the sun comes out today, this will be beautiful."

"I'll take you to Norway sometime," he said, coming up behind her. This is nothing compared to the beauty there."

"I bet." She turned to face him. "I think we handled the situation the best way. Maybe his broken nose will teach him to think twice before he tries something with another woman."

Sven laughed heartily. "I bet he's never had that happen before. You kicked his butt."

She smiled. "Oh, I don't know. If Logan hadn't barged in when he did..." She shuddered.

Sven hugged her close. "Hey, it's over now. Logan is a fierce protector of yours. I've never seen such intense anger on anyone's face. He might have crushed Trevor's skull if I hadn't come when I did. That bruise you're sporting looks pretty painful."

She touched her chest. "It smarts, but I'll live. I feel so bad for Logan. Living with PTSD isn't easy. Did you know he plays a recording of my singing every night to help him sleep?"

Sven's expression darkened. "How many men do I have to fight off for your attentions?"

She lightly slapped his chest. "Oh stop." She wiggled her eyebrows and pointed to the bed. "I spent the night with you, didn't I?"

He grinned. "Not exactly what I'd call it, but you made your point."

Connie hugged him tightly then stepped away. She glanced at the digital clock on the small pine nightstand by the bed. It read 7:00 a.m.

"I have rehearsal in an hour. I better go see what I can do with this face of mine. You'll be okay until I come back to get you for breakfast?"

He nodded. "Yep. I'll get a shower and freshen up some, too."

"Yeah, like you need to." She shook her head as she moved to the door. "Unbelievable. I've seen you dirty and sweaty working on your barn, and you still look like you just stepped out of the shower. I wish I had your talent."

"It's the Norse god in me. I just blink and ta-dah."

She laughed and pulled open the door. "I'll see you in a bit."

Kelly Abell

Chapter Twenty-Seven

When Connie got back to her room, Wrynn had already gone. She breathed a sigh of relief at not having to go through the entire night's events with her. She gathered her things and went to the bathroom to take her shower.

Standing under the warm water, she allowed herself to relive the attack one last time. Goose pimples rose on her skin despite the hot spray when she remembered how close she came to being assaulted.

Thank you, Bishop for teaching me those moves. I'll be forever grateful. Now, I've got to put this behind me. These soldiers need all I can give them for Christmas. Lord, help me bring it to them.

She finished her shower, dried off, and slipped her sweats back on. She applied light makeup and twisted her wet hair into a messy bun. When she returned to the room, Wrynn was back.

"Hey, how are you this morning? I was worried."

"I'm fine. I really don't want to go through it all again if you don't mind."

Her friend hugged her. "Of course, you don't. Hustle up if you want to eat before rehearsal. We've got a table set up in the mess hall. You know where that is? Oh, and wear some boots. It snowed last night."

Connie smiled, relieved Wrynn understood how she felt. "I know. It's my first white Christmas."

"No way."

"Yep. Doesn't snow much in Florida."

Wrynn laughed. She grabbed a clipboard full of papers. "I guess not. See you soon."

Connie went to her suitcase and grabbed some jeans and a sweatshirt. She had just stripped out of her sweats when her phone chimed out the theme to the Lion King.

She grabbed it off the bed and glanced at the screen knowing she'd see Darbi's smiling face.

"Hey, almost sister. What're ya doing? Isn't it late there?"

"Connie, I can't go through with it." Her voice rang with panic, her Irish accent heavy.

"What? You mean the wedding?" Shock caused her knees to buckle, and she sat on the bed.

"Of course, the weddin', ya eejit. This is all wrong."

"Have you had some kind of fight? What's brought on all this panic all of a sudden? You still love him, right?"

"Oh, and I do. More than life itself. It's just I don't believe he's gettin' the best end of the bargain. What if my da gets here and gives him a puck in the gob?"

Connie shook her head at Darbi's use of Irish slang. "A what in the what?"

"Oh, sorry. Um…a sock in the jaw. They're arch rivals for cryin' out loud. I can't bring these two families together. It's nuts. The house'll be overrun with bairns. What in the world was I thinkin'?"

Darbi had gotten overwhelmed. Like every bride does, but, in this case, the wedding was being held at the ranch, which meant she had to host her large Irish family—three sisters and three brothers along with her father. The children ranged in age from twenty to ten.

"Listen, you're getting the pre-wedding jitters, that's all. I'll be home in a few days, and I'll help you. Put the triplets to work with the younger ones. They love kids. You'd be surprised what a help they can be."

"Oh, for sure, they are."

"As far as your father goes, I thought he and my brother put it behind them when Bishop agreed to help him out. Has something changed?"

"No, nothin's changed. It's just they've never met and one sued the other. I just don't know, Connie. Oh lord, why didn't we just go to the courthouse and get married? Instead of havin' all these shenanigans."

"I'm calling Dusty. You need a spa day. Something to help you relax. You hired the wedding planner I recommended, right? She'll take care of all the details. All you have to worry about is getting your family settled in. It will be great having them all there."

"When ya come home and find a frog or snake in your bed, ya won't be so accomodatin'."

Connie laughed. She couldn't wait. She'd needed this phone call more than Darbi did.

"You took care of your brothers and sisters for years. They think of you as a second mother. They'll behave. Listen, I'll call you later. Everything is going to be fine. Take several deep breaths and get some sleep. Just promise me you won't jump on the first horse you come to and ride away."

"By God it's temptin'."

"I know, Darbi. I love you. It's going to be fine. Where's Bishop?"

"He's at the barn. We've got a mare foalin'. I should probably be down there, so I came into the bedroom to change, and I saw my dress hangin' on the door, and I started thinkin', and…and…then I couldn't breathe."

"Good. You need something else to focus on. Put on your birthing clothes and go help Bishop. Focus on the horse. Bishop loves you, Darbi. I've never seen him like this. Not even with Laura. Oh he loved her, but there's something even more special between the two of you. I envy you the life you'll have with him and the triplets."

"Are things bad with Sven, then?"

"Oh no, I didn't mean that. Actually, I'll have a long story to tell you when I get home. Things with Nashville aren't turning out like I'd hoped."

"What? Oh no, what's wrong?"

Connie glanced at the clock. "I need to run to rehearsal, and you need to go birth a horse. I love you, sis. I'll see you soon."

Darbi blew out a breath. "Okay. Thanks for listenin'. See ya in a few days."

Connie pressed the button to end the call, and laughed. Poor Darbi. It sounded like the pre-wedding jitters had just about consumed her. She called Dusty as she ran out the door and arranged an intervention.

She met Sven for breakfast, and after they wolfed down a quick meal, they walked over to the hangar where the concert would be.

It always amazed Connie how fast the crew could get the stage together and have everything ready for the show. Sven stood at the foot of the stage next to Trevor's agent. The men shook hands, and the action seemed friendly enough.

Roger Cornell was an amiable man, short and round, with thinning dark hair. Sven dwarfed him in size. Roger had to look up at him, but the smaller man didn't seem intimidated.

They took seats next to each other. Connie had only spoken with him a few times, but she liked him. How he could manage to work with a man like Trevor baffled her. Again, it struck her how often money ruled people's decisions. She didn't want it to rule hers. Disappointment flooded her as she fully realized her shot at Nashville was done. Sighing heavily, she took her place with the other dancers.

Woodenly, she performed the show until it came time for her first solo. Squaring her shoulders, she approached the microphone. She'd give this all she had, even if it was just the rehearsal. She vowed to crank it up a notch at the actual performance tomorrow. These people deserved a *wonderful* Christmas with all the sacrifices they made. She wouldn't let them down.

As the music began, Connie said a short prayer and started to sing "O Holy Night." She allowed the words to uplift her soul, and, despite the pain in her chest, she filled her diaphragm with air and reached new heights in tone and clarity.

She glanced down at Sven, who stared at her in awe. Her heart swelled with warmth and what…love? Yes, that was what it was. Love for her hero and lifelong friend.

She caught sight of Logan leaning against the wall of the large building. His eyes were closed, and he wore a dreamy smile on his face. Connie loved him, too, but in a much different way. He was her protector and a very good friend, but she knew now which man she needed in her life.

She hadn't spotted Trevor yet, but she didn't really care to see him. As she'd told him last night, she'd be professional and sing with him for the duration of the tour, but no more. Her last note ended a bit choked with emotion over what all had happened over the last twenty-four hours.

Everyone in the hangar stood and applauded. She grinned. *This is why I do what I do. I just hope I can keep doing it forever.*

"Ho, Ho, Ho." The voice boomed through the speakers.

Connie and the rest of the stage performers spun to face stage right. Dressed in a full Santa suit, Trevor stiffly made his way on stage.

Her jaw dropped. What a brilliant idea. She looked around for Wrynn and found her standing at the foot of the stage, grinning broadly. Connie gave her a thumbs-up. Her friend had brilliantly come up with a way for the man to perform despite his injuries. She could tell by his awkward movements he probably didn't feel like doing it, to which she drew an immense amount of satisfaction deep in her being, but he'd not let his fans down. In a way, she had to admire him for his dedication.

He approached her. "Ready to rehearse our song?"

She nodded, not sure of how she wanted to respond.

"I think you're making a mistake not sticking with me." He muttered those words under his breath away from the microphone.

It took all Connie had not to knee him in the groin again. She'd hoped for an apology at the very least, but this sounded more like a threat.

She found her voice. "You may be a country music star, but as a man you're pathetic. One day, your fans will see it and you'll be very much alone. I hope you can live with yourself when it happens."

"You'll never be a star in Nashville if I have anything to say about it."

Connie drew from all the courage she could muster. "A decision which is not up to you. It's up to God who I believe holds more power over this universe than even you, Trevor

Thornton. Do your worst if you must, but I'll win in the end, whatever it looks like."

He took a step backward. Clearly, he wasn't used to people speaking to him in such a manner, but Connie didn't care. Her words were true, and, she chose to believe in them.

Chapter Twenty-Eight

Rehearsal wound down a little before noon. Connie approached Sven and hugged him.

"You were amazing as always."

She grinned. "You're sweet. Want to eat some lunch? I'm starving."

He tucked her hand under his arm. "I thought I'd take you into the village of Lakenheath for the afternoon. I hear on good authority it is a quaint village, not to be missed."

She jumped up and down. "Ooh, how fun. Let's go back to the barracks so I can change."

They strolled through the snow, Connie stopping to form a snow ball and throw it at him. Before long a few other cast members had joined them and a full blow battle emerged. She had never had so much fun. Sven's handsome smile reached from ear to ear as he plowed some of the other men with the sloshy mush. With the ladies, he took it easy, but she didn't. She smacked him upside the head with a supersized ball. He came after her. She ran but slipped in the snow and fell. He couldn't stop his momentum and landed on top of her with a grunt.

She laughed. "Are you okay?"

"You bet. You?"

"Never better." She reached up and brushed a strand of hair from his forehead.

He leaned in and claimed her lips in the sweetest kiss she'd ever experienced.

"Get a room," one of the cast members shouted.

Laughing, they helped each other up and continued to the barracks arm in arm.

Connie needed a romp in the snow. Her mood lifted considerably, but her future still nagged at her. What would she do now that Trevor would block all her attempts in Nashville? She believed in her words, but the path had yet to be revealed to her. *Oh well, I'll worry about it another day. It's Christmas, and I get to see a real English village.*

After a quick change of clothes, Sven drove her to Lakenheath. A village of less than five thousand, Connie immediately fell for the charm. Quaint houses, some centuries old lined the streets, all dressed up for the holidays with holly wreaths, strung lights, and other festive decorations. She and Sven parked the car on High Street near. St. Mary's the Virgin church. He had done some research on the old chapel and wanted to show it to her.

The old stone building stood proudly in the church yard with ancient gravestones all around. Connie sucked in a breath as she stood before a building older than anything she'd ever seen.

"Can you imagine what this must have been like in medieval times?"

Sven wrapped an arm around her as they stared at the beautiful snow-covered church and graveyard. "It's pretty amazing, alright. Want to go inside?"

"Oh, can we?"

"Let's try. It's Christmas Eve after all. Maybe they're having a service later."

"That would be awesome."

They strolled hand-in-hand to the heavy wooden doors. Sven tried one and it opened with a creak. Reverently, they stepped into the sanctuary. High, wood-beamed arched ceilings rose overhead and they faced a white stone altar which held six candles. A breathtaking stained glass window featuring the crucifixion of Christ dominated the back wall.

Connie sucked in a quiet breath. "This is amazing."

"Isn't it?"

She stepped slowly toward the altar. "This would be a fantastic place to get married." When she realized what she'd said, she slapped a hand to her mouth. "I was thinking of Bishop and Darbi." She rushed on, heat warming her cheeks. "Darbi called this morning before I went to breakfast. She's having doubts."

"Really? About Bishop?"

"No, I'm sure she loves my brother, but she's getting overwhelmed with the wedding preparations and her family descending on the ranch."

Sven chuckled. "Quite a brood, I understand."

Connie agreed. "I thought raising triplets was hard. Darbi had nine of them on her hands."

"No wonder she ran for the United States."

Connie smiled then waved an arm at the vastness of the chapel. "This is so beautiful. Thanks for bringing me here."

Sven wrapped her in a hug. "I noticed they do have a Christmas Eve service at five. Let's go find somewhere to eat, walk the shops then come back."

"Oh, Sven, how absolutely wonderful."

They exited the church and strolled through the graveyard a bit marveling at the dates on the tombstones. Connie couldn't believe how old things were. It humbled her to know how many people had passed before her on these grounds.

They found a charming pub called The Brewers Tap and enjoyed a lunch of traditional English fare and a few pints of Guinness. They spent the afternoon browsing through the quaint shops and Connie was even tempted by the tattoo parlor, but Sven talked her out of it.

By four o'clock, they made their way back to the church. A bit early for the service, they found a stone bench on the church property and sat to absorb the scenery. Sven shifted on the bench to face Connie.

"I have a little something for you," he said.

"A present?" Excitement filled her, then she remembered she'd bought nothing for him. "Oh, Sven, I'm sorry. I've been so absorbed, I haven't had time to shop."

He laughed. "It's fine, Connie. Just being here with you and hearing you sing is present enough."

"Oh go on….and on."

Grinning, he reached into his pocket and pulled out a small box.

Connie sucked in a breath. "Oh God, Sven, it's not…"

"Wait a minute. I haven't even shown it to you yet. But I do have something I want to say. I regret I've waited so long to tell you how much I love you. Things might have been different if I had, so in a way, maybe it's for the best. I wasn't crazy about you going away, and even less crazy about the news you gave me about the opportunity with Trevor."

"Well, it's over now." She fought the depression trying to worm its way into her heart.

"I know. And I also know how much it upsets you. But you'll finish the tour, and we will see what we see."

"You spent a lot of time talking to Trevor's agent, Roger. What were you talking about?"

Sven rattled the box in his hand. "A conversation for a different day. Right now…" He knelt before her.

"You are the brightest person who has ever entered my life. I do not expect an answer right now, but I wanted to present you with this on Christmas Eve in a very special holy place. I want it to be a symbol of my eternal love for you, and you can say yes when you're ready and not before. I know you have a bright future before you, Connie Champion, and I'd like to be a part of it. Will you consider becoming my wife?"

Her mind reeled with the proposal. He snapped open the box, and she peered inside. A stunning, two carat, square cut sapphire surrounded by diamonds set nestled in black velvet. It was the most beautiful ring she'd ever seen. She figured he hadn't chosen a diamond because of the obvious meaning. Her eyes stung with tears. Was she ready to say yes? Her mind roiled with thoughts about her future. If she married him, did it mean her singing career was over? What about the rest of the tour? Would he even support her being gone all the time? So many questions.

"My knee is freezing here. Will you at least accept the ring as a Christmas present and we can worry about what it means later?"

Speechless, all she could do was nod. It truly was a magnificent ring. She swiped at a tear and stuck out her hand. He slipped the sapphire on her left ring finger.

"I love you, Connie. Please think about being my wife. I know how much your singing means to you, so don't think I'll stand in your way."

"Oh, Sven." Guilt barraged her. She didn't know what to say to him. She so wanted to say yes, yet she wanted to see where this USO tour would take her. But when she imagined life without him or away from him, her heart sank.

"People are starting to go in." He rose and held out his hand. "Let's go."

She stood and wrapped her arms around his neck, kissing his lips. "Thank you."

He smiled. "I'm holding you to that answer some day."
"And you'll have it. I promise."
She hoped with all her heart she could say yes.

Chapter Twenty-Nine

Sven watched Connie stare out the window of the British Airways jet flying them home to Florida. He'd no doubt she was excited to be going home, but at the moment, the forlorn expression on her face worried him. He never liked to see her unhappy, and the incident in England had more than rattled her cage.

He privately thanked Logan just before the Christmas performance for landing blows on Trevor Thornton he'd wanted to land himself. He blew out a breath, a little ashamed at the relief flowing through him. He hadn't wanted Connie to travel with the lecherous singer, but having a singing career meant the world to her.

A whirlwind of emotions churned through his system which he imagined rivaled Connie's feelings. He glanced down at the gorgeous sapphire ring he'd given her for Christmas, then his gaze drifted up to her face. The frown lines creasing her features disappointed him.

I didn't expect her to say yes, but, watching her now, I wonder if she has regrets about accepting the ring? She called me her hero, so that means she loves me just a little, doesn't it?

He placed a hand over hers. "Hey, beautiful. You okay?"

She turned her face toward him and smiled. Her hazel eyes were more emerald than amber as her expression lightened.

"I'm fine, I guess. I can't wait to see everyone."

"But?"

She chuckled. "You know me too well, Svenster. I'm not sure that's a good thing."

He gave her a grin and squeezed her hand. "Of course it is, sweetheart. I can anticipate your every move."

"Oh boy." She twisted in her seat. "By the way, what were you and Roger talking about so much over the last few days. During rehearsal and even during the show I noticed your heads together. Thick as thieves you were."

Sven rubbed his hands together and twisted an imaginary moustache. "Oh, ho, my little one. It's our secret."

She laughed at his terrible French accent. "That was horrible."

He loved her smile, glad he could lighten her mood.

"Seriously though, what could you possibly have to say to the agent of that serpent of a singer?"

Sven sighed. "Fortunately, Roger is not the despicable man his client is. I bet he apologized at least fifty times for Trevor's actions. I get the feeling he does it a lot."

"Me, too. I'm still having trouble believing it happened. I'm so stupid." A tear welled in her right eye.

Immediately, he brushed it away with his finger, his heart swelling with love for this woman he'd known since childhood. She had not deserved what happened to her. No woman did, but especially his woman. He vowed to make it up to her.

"Hey," he said, wrapping an arm around her shoulders. "This was not your fault in any way."

She shook her head. "Logan tried to warn me. I had my own intuition I ignored. I guess I let my ego guide me. I thought I sing so well he was truly interested in me for my voice."

"And he was, but he thought he'd take advantage of your sweet gentle nature and claim you for his own. All he saw were dollar signs and his next conquest."

Her expression sagged, and tears slid down her cheeks. His heart broke. *You idiot. Now you just made her feel worse.*

"Hey, hey. Listen to me, Connie. You have the voice of—

"An angel, I know. I'm so tired of hearing the word. It apparently isn't getting me anywhere. I thought this was my shot, Sven. My dream. My way to share with the world the gift I've been given. Now, after the tour is over, so is everything else."

Should I share with her what Roger and I discussed? If it doesn't work out the way I've planned, she'll be even more crushed. He decided to wait.

"What I'm trying to say, sweetheart, is if a singing career is what you feel led to do with your life, then it will happen. I stood to the side during the Christmas concert last night and watched the faces of those soldiers and their families. Even the men were crying when you sang 'O Holy Night.' Some had their eyes closed and swayed to the sound of your voice. Enraptured is the word I would use. You have a power. God isn't going to let it go to waste."

Connie sniffed and wiped at her eyes with her palms. She dropped her head on his shoulder then twisted the ring on her finger. "You say the nicest things."

He waited, wanting her to add "I love you" to the statement, but she didn't. Hope remained eternal. He believed Connie loved him deep down, and when she was ready, she'd tell him. She just hadn't adjusted to their new relationship yet.

"You really are my hero."

"I'll settle for that...for now."

He wanted to talk more about an engagement but instinct told him to let her bring it up the next time. The last thing he wanted was to pressure or guilt her into saying something she didn't feel. He'd been through it with a few women and it never turned out well.

Within minutes, Connie dropped off to sleep, her head on his shoulder. He propped his head on hers and before he knew it the stewardess was announcing their arrival in Tampa.

Connie roused next to him and stretched. "We're here already? That went by quick."

He grabbed her hand. "Excited?"

She bounced in the seat. "Oh yes. I can't wait to see everyone. I've missed them all so much."

She glanced out the window then back at him.

"And Sven?"

"Hmmm?"

"Thank you for coming to both New York and England. I know it wasn't easy for you to get away. It really meant a lot to me."

He leaned over and captured her mouth with his. The kiss was warm and sweet. "I think you're learning, by now, I'd do anything for you."

She giggled. "I believe you would."

The plane landed, and the passengers disembarked. He and Connie climbed onto the tram which carried the passengers from the airline gates to baggage claim in the main terminal.

"I hope Darbi and Bishop are both here to meet us. Oh, and the triplets. I can't wait to see those delicious little morsels."

Sven laughed. They would all be there—he'd arranged it, knowing how much it would mean to her. He'd even rented a limo so they could all ride together in style. He looked forward to seeing her face.

The doors to the tram slid open, and Connie hopped out in front of him. She squealed before he even saw the family standing in the waiting area. By the time he turned the corner, she was in Bishop's arms, her legs wrapped around his waist. Very similar to the greeting he received in New York. His soul soared at her happiness.

Connie dropped her legs and reached for Darbi, grabbing her into a fierce hug, then she was mauled by Violet, Scarlet, and Ivory. The three girls nearly knocked her over. A fourth girl stood shyly beside Bishop.

"Wait, wait." Connie struggled to keep from falling to the floor. "Who's this?"

Violet jumped up and down. "This is Mia. She's staying with us for a while. She's going to have a baby."

Mia flushed scarlet. Connie held out a hand. "Don't mind our Violet. She's a bit outspoken. I'm very happy to meet you, Mia."

"Me, too," the girl replied in a soft, timid voice. "You're all the triplets talk about."

Connie smiled. "Well, don't believe everything you hear."

Mia rewarded Connie with a big smile.

Sven reached Bishop and gave him a hug. "Thanks for getting everyone together to be here."

"Hey, man, thanks for the limo. The girls were over the moon."

Sven laughed. "I bet. Merry Christmas."

"Merry Christmas. Darbi's laid out a spread back at the ranch. The girls have gifts for Connie and you."

"And we have an extra suitcase full ourselves. She went a little overboard in this small town near the base."

Bishop nodded. "I can only imagine."

Darbi hugged Sven and kissed his cheek. "Welcome home, weary traveler. I've got stew waitin'"

"Alright. Let's go get the bags. Hi, munchkins." Sven hugged and ruffled each triplet's hair, then gave Mia a warm hug. "Want to help me with the bags? I think there's something in it for ya."

The triplets squealed and dashed ahead to the escalator. Mia followed more slowly but equally as enthusiastic.

Connie held Darbi close for a moment. "How ya doin', champ? Calmer now?"

Darbi's eyes grew misty. "Yes. Thank ya for sending Dusty to the rescue. She's truly amazin'."

"Where are they?"

"The mare that just foaled isn't doing well. Quinton stayed behind to nurse her. Surprisingly enough, Dusty doesn't come around quite as much. I think she's tryin' to teach our Quinton a lesson."

"Oh boy. The man can be so thick. I feel sorry for her. She needs to find another man. Would bring him around quick enough."

Sven overheard Connie's statement and agreed with her. *It certainly worked for me. Knowing she could be snatched up by Logan, or God forbid, Trevor, I wanted the ring on her finger. Even if she's not ready to say yes yet.*

They gathered the luggage, and the limo driver helped them get it to the gleaming white stretch Lincoln in the parking garage.

"Wow, I feel like royalty," Connie quipped, as she slid onto the buttery leather seats. "Grab me a Coke out of the fridge there, will ya, Mia?"

Sven smiled, and he nearly burst with love for the woman offering this pregnant teen the same warmth and affection she'd shown the triplets. He imagined briefly what it might be like if all worked out and they had kids of their own. She'd be a terrific mother. But, doubt slid in, would she have time to be one if he carried out his plan?

The hour-long ride passed quickly as the family chatted and sang Christmas carols. Sven had reserved the driver for the following day as well to pick up Darbi's family from the airport. A sort of pre-wedding gift to the couple. As long as Darbi continued to feed him her wonderful Irish stew, he'd do anything for her. His stomach growled in anticipation.

The limo pulled up to the ranch house. Sven sucked in air. The place had even more decorations than when he'd left. Of course, he'd only seen it in the daylight, and now at full dark, he bet the astronauts on the space station could see this place. Twinkling white lights covered almost every surface of the house and the grounds. Several potted Scotch pine trees all decorated for Christmas had been placed along the driveway leading to the front door. He remembered how Darbi had gone all out with her autumn decorations. He could only imagine what the inside of the house must look like.

"The lights are amazing," Connie breathed. "I've never seen the ranch look more beautiful. Your wedding is going to be spectacular."

Darbi grinned. "I didn't go overboard?"

Connie laughed. "Well…I didn't say that, but, in this case, overboard is just what's needed. I'm starving. Let's get inside and eat."

Sven followed the family inside and he was right. Christmas exploded around every corner. Holly and pine boughs draped or hung from every flat surface. Some had shiny red ornaments placed in them, along with pine cones and sprigs of mistletoe. *I'll need to get Connie under one of those sprigs and soon.*

He peered into the living room where the enormous family tree had always stood, and he wasn't disappointed. A massive twelve-foot spruce crowded the corner on one side of the fireplace. Opened and wrapped gifts were piled around the base of the tree. He wheeled the suitcase they'd brought with the girls' presents in it to a spot near the tree. He couldn't wait to see their faces when they opened their gifts from England. Violet would be especially impressed with the royal family memorabilia Connie had purchased for her.

"Sven, you'd better get in here before it's all gone," Darbi yelled at him from the kitchen.

"Coming."

Excitement filled him as he anticipated the wedding in a few days. This wonderful home would be full of people, and happiness, just the way it was meant to be. He envied his friend Bishop's joy. Since he knew how he felt about Connie, he couldn't wait to make their relationship more permanent. *Slow down there, cowboy. The last thing you want to do is spook her. Things are going very well right now. Just enjoy the wedding, do your research, and maybe by then end of the week, you'll have the answers you need.*

He strolled into the kitchen. This room and the family room had not escaped Darbi's holiday embellishments. It would take him hours to view all the decorations she'd placed throughout the home.

The family sat around the large oak table, bowls and spoons at the ready. Darbi ladled out the stew and handed each person a fresh yeast roll. Sven marveled at the woman's talents.

As he sat and listened to all the happy chatter around him, he knew this was what he wanted for himself and

Connie. She glanced down the table at him. His whole body warmed at the sight of her smile. He wanted it all for her.

When he'd seen the enraptured faces at the USO concert, he'd known, deep within his soul, she'd been created to sing. Somehow, he had to provide something which worked for her, yet allowed them to have each other, too.

Chapter Thirty

On the third day after Christmas, Connie stretched in her bed, while yellow streaks of sunrise shone through the blinds, and a gentle winter breeze fluttered the billowy white curtains away from the open window. She remembered the night before when they'd opened presents for the second time this Christmas season. The triplets had all loved their gifts, and the delight on Mia's face to have received several presents of her own had warmed Connie's heart.

The sound of horses snuffling and whinnying in the corral by the barn drifted through the window. She'd missed those early morning conversations between the animals. Her body itched to go riding. She wasn't sure when she could fit it in with Darbi's family arriving today, but she'd sure try. Maybe when Sven got there this afternoon she could coax him onto a horse.

Someone knocked lightly on her door. She glanced at the clock. It was almost seven thirty. She hadn't slept this late in months. "Come in."

The door swung open, and Darbi stood on the threshold, two steaming mugs in her hands.

"Oh, thank God. Is that coffee?"

"Of course."

"Come in, come in." She shifted on the bed to make room for her future sister-in-law.

Darbi sat down and handed her the mug with the steaming caramel-colored liquid. "Tons of cream and sugar, just the way ya like it."

"You are a wonder. I couldn't find decent coffee anywhere. Those poor soldiers. Not having good java would be more torture to me than all the sand in the world. Although that's pretty bad."

"I can't imagine. I want to hear all about it. I needed some girl time before chaos reigns."

"What time do they all arrive?"

The flight gets in at eleven. Bishop and I will leave around nine thirty. It was so nice of Sven to get the limo. Da will be impressed."

Connie shifted on the bed to allow more room for her best friend in the world. "I'm sure he will."

"That Sven of yours…he is yours now, right?"

Connie's smile faltered.

"What? What is it?" Darbi leaned in, her face full of concern.

"It's fine. I want to show you something, but please don't say anything to anyone yet."

Darbi bounced on the bed. "It wouldn't be the giant sapphire ring you were a'wearin' last night, would it, now?"

Connie slapped her friend's arm playfully. "You eejit. You saw it."

"I'm sure men on the moon saw it. It's unbelievable. But what does it mean?"

"He asked me to be his wife, but he didn't want an answer from me right away."

Darbi squeaked in delight. "Oh, darlin' how wonderful. Why didn't you say yes? Is it because of the security guard ya told me about? Logan is it?"

Connie pulled her hand from under the covers and twisted the ring absently. She sighed. "No. I'm over him. He's a wonderful man and in love with me, or in love with my voice, I'm not sure he really knows. But he's not the one for me."

"The singer, then? He's a hottie."

Connie shuddered. She placed her coffee cup on the nightstand and grabbed both of Darbi's hands. She told her everything that happened with Trevor and watched the shock change to immense satisfaction on her face.

"Good girl. I'm so glad ya got in few good licks. He deserved worse. Sounds like your Logan and Sven finished him off for you, but are ya alright? Ya said, Logan hit you on accident?"

Connie smiled. "He did, and I really thought he was going to kill Trevor. He has so many triggers he can't yet control. He tries hard, but the only person he seems to respond to is Wrynn, the tour manager. She really understands him. Her brother has PTSD."

"How tough for him. Ya told me once he listens to your voice before he sleeps?"

"He does. I'm glad I can give him that at least."

A horse whinnied down by the barn. Connie glanced at the window. "Who's making all that racket?"

"Our new addition, Mia's Joy. A pretty little filly, but she's a noisy one, she is."

"Aw, I bet Mia was thrilled."

"She's a good girl, our Mia. Tough break for her, but I'll make sure she's okay."

Connie hugged Darbi. "I know you will."

"So, finish your story. Why won't you say yes to Sven if you're sure he's the one."

"He's not crazy about me being a singer. Before the Trevor incident I was going to Nashville to sing with the creep. Sven had a negative attitude the entire time."

"And rightly so, I don't wonder."

Connie nodded. "True, but just because that door is closed, it doesn't mean I don't still want the big contract." She shifted on the bed, leaning closer to Darbi. "You should see their eyes when I sing, Darbs. Sven used the word enraptured. You have no idea what it does for my soul. God has given me a gift I feel I must share with the world. I'm not sure Sven can handle it. He's pretty much a Florida home boy. He's not up for jetting all over the place, following a singing wife. If I don't get a recording contract, which is likely now that I've punched the hottest country singer in the world in the nuts, I still want to travel with some kind of group. Maybe I'll stay with the USO. It's a pretty decent gig."

"I don't imagine the pay is all that and a bag of crisps."

Connie laughed. "No, but there's room and board and decent food. I've made some good friends."

"Like Logan?" Darbi wiggled her eyebrows.

"Oh you." Connie pushed at her friend's shoulder. "I've already told you I'm not interested in him romantically. I'd like to see him get with Wrynn. Maybe it will be my mission when I go back."

"So you're definitely goin' back, then?"

"I have to. I've signed a contract."

"Have you told Sven?" Darbi shifted on the bed, smoothing the sheets with one hand.

"I'm sure he has to know I can't welch on my contract. I want to talk to him about a lot of stuff while we're here, but hey, the focus should be you and your wedding. Two days from now you walk down the aisle to my brother. Did you ever believe it would turn out like this?"

Darbi shook her head. "Not in a million. I'm still feeling guilty about the deception."

Connie punched her friend on the shoulder. "Get over it. He has. You're the best thing that's happened to him in a long time. Maybe forever."

A light blush crept into Darbi's cheeks. "Oh go on now. He loved Laura very much, and he sees her in the triplets every time he looks at them."

"Does it bother you?"

"Honestly? I try not to think on it. We've got something different, Bishop and me. I don't dwell on the past, and he doesn't either."

"Good. Now, I want to see your dress."

Connie put her mug on the nightstand and threw back the covers. Darbi jumped up and led her by the hand to her own room.

Hanging over the door to her bathroom was a beige garment tote, filled with a bulky wedding gown. Connie hopped from foot to foot waiting for Darbi to unzip the bag.

What seemed like tons of silk, lace, and crinoline popped out through the opening. Connie sucked in air.

The sleeveless gown was the color of a good rosé wine with a dainty sweetheart neckline lined with pearls. The bodice was smooth blush silk, then the gown flared into a rose-colored ballroom skirt overlaid with most elegant white lace, and pearl and crystal bead work Connie had ever seen.

"Oh my," she breathed. Approaching the dress, she ran the fabric through her fingers. "This is amazing. I love the blush color, don't you?"

"Dusty found it for me in a magazine then we went to a place called Patricia's Boutique, and she ordered it for me.

You don't think the blush is too much? Shouldn't it be white?"

The look of pure anxiety on Darbi's face made Connie laugh. "A little too late to worry now, isn't it?"

The bride-to-be wrung her hands together. "To be sure, it is, but I wanted to know what you honestly think."

Connie put both hands on Darbi's shoulders. "It's perfect. The blush compliments your flaming hair. You'd have looked too washed-out in plain white. Bishop's going to drop his jaw when he sees you."

Darbi's face turned scarlet. "Oh I hope so." She began stuffing the dress back in the bag.

"What are the girls wearing?"

"Oh their dresses are darlin'. They're tea-length and cranberry in color. They look beautiful in them. Now, come along, and I'll show you yours."

"Oh goodie! I've been dying to see it."

Darbi led her to a spare bedroom where she opened the closet door with a flourish. "Ta-dah!"

On the rod hung a beautiful silk ball gown the color of a ripe Georgia peach. It, too, was sleeveless with the sweetheart neckline. Connie reached out to touch the soft slick fabric. "This is wonderful."

"Dusty thought the color would make you stand out as the maid of honor."

A wave of guilt washed through Connie. She'd been gone this entire time while Dusty had pulled Darbi through almost every bride crisis. "Don't you want Dusty to be the maid of honor?"

"We talked about it and both agree. You should do it. Bishop is your brother, and if it weren't for you, we'd never have met. I owe ya."

"I know, but—

"Swallow the buts. You're the maid of honor. Dusty will wear cranberry like the girls. She's totally fine with it all."

Connie hugged her best friend. "You are so wonderful. I can't believe I got so lucky to finally have a sister like you."

Darbi glanced at the clock. "Oh, you've got to scoot. I've got to get ready to go meet Da and the brood."

"Want me to come along?"

"I do, yes, but there'll barely be enough room in the limo for my clan plus Bishop and me."

"I'll have everything ready here when you get back. Maybe your brothers and sisters and all our crew can go riding later today. I'll call Pig in a Poke and have them cater some bar-b-que for dinner."

"That'd be wonderful. I was goin' to have Bishop and Quinton grill, but delivery sounds even better. Now shoo. See ya in a bit."

Connie left Darbi to grab more coffee and some breakfast in the kitchen. When she entered, the triplets sprang from their seats at the bar and ran to her. She staggered back a step as she wrapped them in a hug.

"Good morning. I've missed you all so much."

"We've missed you, too, Aunt Connie." Violet buried her face in Connie's pajamas, squeezing her tight. "I'm glad you're home."

She traced a finger down each girl's cheek. "I hope you all have been behaving for Darbi. No shenanigans?"

Ivory rolled her eyes. "With us, there's always shenanigans, but we've been good for the most part."

"No more fights at school?"

Scarlet laughed. "Nope. We took care of that little problem."

"Mmhmm. Well, you three stay out of trouble. Poor Darbi has enough on her mind."

"Come out and see the new filly," Scarlet urged. "She's so cute."

"A noisy little girl from what I heard this morning."

Scarlet laughed the giddy giggle of a ten-year-old. "She is."

"Did you help deliver her, too?"

Scarlet's chest puffed out. "I did. Dad's been really nice about letting me help more with the horses."

"How wonderful, honey." Connie hugged her niece. "Let me get some caffeine in my system and have a bowl of Cheerios, and I'll be good to go."

The triplets ran out to the barn ahead of her. She followed them to a stall just inside the door, near Bishop's office. A solid black, wobbly-legged Arabian filly nursed beneath her mother, whose coat was gray.

"We hope she'll turn gray like her mama," Scarlet told her, leaning on the gate.

"So this is Mia's Pride?"

"Yep. Mia was so happy we named a horse after her. Dad thinks she's going to be a wonderful racer. What do you think, Aunt Connie?"

Connie opened the gate and rubbed the mare's head first. The filly detached long enough to swing her pretty head around. Connie caught her around the neck and ran her hands over the colt's back and forelegs. She studied the arch of her neck then let her go back to her meal. She stepped out of the stall and closed the gate.

"Oh yeah," she told Scarlett. "You've got a winner there."

"Yay. I'll go tell Mia."

When the girls raced out of the barn, Connie turned to head back toward the house. She spotted Quinton walking over from his house to the barn. She waved and he changed direction to meet her.

"Hey, stranger."

Throwing her arms around him, she kissed him square on the mouth. His cheeks flushed red.

"Hey, yourself. I've missed you, you stupid lug."

"We've missed you, too. You doin' okay? They treatin' ya alright on the tour?"

"It's wonderful. I'm really glad to be home, and I'm so excited about the wedding, but it's a great gig. I've seen more countries than I ever thought possible. I want you and Dusty to come over and look at all my pictures."

He lowered his gaze to the ground and shuffled his feet. "Yeah, maybe."

Connie chucked a fist under his chin so he'd raise his head. "What's this maybe stuff. You and Dusty having problems?"

"We ain't a couple, Connie. To have problems, ya have to be a couple."

"Oh stop. She's been crazy about you since grade school. Are you that blind? You better snatch her up before someone else does."

Quinton shrugged.

"Quinton?"

He didn't respond.

"You do know Dusty's in love with you, don't you?"

The big man shuffled his feet again. "Nah. She don't love me. Who'd want a ranch hand when she could have any of those city lawyers or bankers."

Connie shook her head. "You really are thick, you know? Dusty doesn't want a man like that. She wants you. I better see you two dancing at the wedding, or I'm going to embarrass you to death."

"She ain't talkin' to me right now. I don't know what I did, but she ain't been around in weeks."

Connie studied her perplexed friend. She felt sorry for the poor stupid man. "Hey, maybe it isn't what you did, but what you didn't do that has her all worked up. Is she special to you Quin?"

The man removed his Stetson and ran a hand through his hair, then replaced the hat. "You know she is."

"Then you need to tell her. Show her you care and are ready to show your affection. I bet you'd be surprised what happens after."

"Yeah, maybe. I don't know. She's pretty mad."

"Buy her some flowers and take her out to a nice dinner. Maybe down to Tampa or something. Treat her real special. I bet it wouldn't take much to win her over."

Quinton shrugged again. "Maybe."

Connie slapped him on the arm. "You're hopeless. Sometimes, what you need most is right under your nose."

Practice what you preach, girl. Practice what you preach.

Chapter Thirty-One

New Year's Eve became a favorite in Connie's memory bank. Darbi's family from Ireland descended on Champions Gate in a whirlwind. The six Brennan children plus the triplets and Mia filled the house to the brim with noise and happy laughter. Connie had managed to get them all on horses, and she'd been surprised at the skill Darbi's brothers and sisters exhibited. They ran a few races on the practice track, making for a fun-filled competition between the two farms.

Darbi's fears about her father were totally unfounded. He and Bishop got along well and spent quite a bit of time closed-off, discussing farm business. They had to drag them out at the end of the day for the cookout and fireworks.

Twilight descended on the ranch as the entire group came together by the pond. Sven and Quinton had arranged a small fireworks show over the water at the special spot where Bishop and Darbi had declared their love for each other. Connie had made the recommendation to keep flaming items away from the house lawn which was all decorated for the wedding the next day.

She sat next to Darbi, both of them with beers in hand. They watched the men bicker over the best way to light the rockets while the children bounced around them wanting to help.

"We'll be lucky one of them doesn't blow their foot off," Darbi commented, pointing at the group with her beer.

Connie laughed. "Yep. We'll probably be in the ER with one of them before the night is over."

"Ack, I hope not. That would a day-spoiler, now wouldn't it?"

Dusty strolled up to the two women. "Want to take bets on who gets burned first?"

Darbi jumped up. "Dusty, you made it."

"Are you kidding? I wouldn't miss this for the world. Sorry I'm late."

Connie hugged her friend. "I've missed you. Why haven't you come around?"

"She's tryin' to teach our stupid lummox Quinton a lesson. One he won't be forgettin' if he's smart."

Dusty glanced at the group of men and frowned.

Connie wrapped her arm around the woman's shoulders. "I had a talk with him the other night. Give him time. He'll come around. It's sort of like Sven and me. Sometimes you just don't know what's right in front of you."

Dusty rolled her eyes. "I'll say. I don't know what else to do to make him notice me. Darbi recommended not being as easily accessible."

"Is it workin'?"

"He calls a little more often, but that's about it."

Darbi stamped her foot. "Eejit. He's dumber than a sack of stones."

Dusty giggled. "You won't get any argument from me there."

"Don't worry, Dusty. He'll come 'round. Maybe we need to find you another man to shake him up a bit."

"Ha. Not with the hours I'm working."

A sizzle filled the air then a rocket shot skyward. The group by the pond cheered. With a loud bang the firework exploded into a burst of color, the water reflecting the showering sparks.

A collection of ooh's and ah's rose from the crowd. There was a little more bickering from the men then the second rocket bolted skyward. When it exploded, a shower of red, white, and blue sparks rained down on the pond.

The evening's festivities continued until one of Darbi's brothers shouted, "It's almost midnight."

The entire gang gathered in a circle and held hands. Bishop stared at the glowing face of his watch to get the last ten seconds. He began the countdown and the rest of the group joined in.

At exactly midnight, shouts of "Happy New Year" filled the night. In the glow of the camp fire, hugs and kisses were exchanged. Over Sven's shoulder, Connie caught sight of Dusty and Quinton standing awkwardly next to each other. To her delight, Dusty jumped into the big man's arms and planted a kiss right on his mouth.

Connie cheered inwardly. *Atta girl. Go for it!*

Sven pulled Connie close and his lips met hers again for a second kiss. Warm tingles spread all over her body. She knew deep in her heart she'd never find another man like Sven. She just didn't know if he could hold on to the type of future she wanted. It was the one thing which kept her from saying yes to his proposal. She'd have to talk to him about it soon though, as her time with her family and him was drawing to a close. In a week, she'd have to return to New York and resume the USO tour. Her heart ached a little at the thought. She stood in Sven's arms and watched her happy family enjoying each other's company at the start of a brand new year. It didn't get much better than this.

Can I leave all this behind? Maybe I'm the one who has unrealistic expectations. Maybe I should just give up the whole singing dream and settle down.

No. Not yet. She'd made a commitment, and she'd fulfill it, then deal with whatever came next. She just hoped Sven would stay in for the long haul.

She glanced up at him. "You've been kind of scarce lately. I've missed you."

He kissed her head. "I know, honey. I'm sorry. All my lawyer stuff, you know."

She sighed. "I know. I'm glad you're here tonight."

"Oh I wouldn't have missed this for the world."

She laughed, knowing he referred to the display of testosterone prior to the fireworks show.

"It's going to be a beautiful wedding tomorrow."

"It is. I can't wait to see you in a beautiful fancy dress."

"Oh man, my dress is nothing compared to Darbi's. Bishop's eyes are going to pop right out of his head."

She smiled, watching her brother and soon-to-be sister-in-law swaying together as Darbi's father began "Auld Lang Syne" on his harmonica.

Connie filled the night with her beautiful voice, leading them in the traditional song. Everyone stared at her as she finished the last verse solo.

The entire family cheered when her final notes drifted away on the warm night breeze. Florida in January could be chilly, but tonight, the fire and the balmy weather made for a pleasant night. Even the mosquitos decided to take a break.

Her heart warmed at the praise her family heaped upon her. Giving joy with her voice meant the world to her. She couldn't give it up unless she had to. She frowned, hoping Sven would understand.

The group packed up and headed for the house. Tomorrow was a very special day.

Chapter Thirty-Two

The day of Darbi and Bishop's wedding dawned clear and bright. No clouds muddled the crystal-blue sky, and the weather man promised no rain.

Connie stared out her window down at the barn. The work never stopped with horses, no matter who was getting married. Her brows drew together as Sven's car motored up to the side of the barn. He got out and walked toward Bishop's office. She glanced at the clock. Just past seven.

"He's here kind of early. Wonder what's up?"

She didn't have any time to think about it, because her door flung open and the triplets along with Mia charged into her room.

"Come on, Aunt Connie." Violet grabbed her hand. "The makeup lady and hair lady are here. We're going to get all beautified."

Connie grinned down at her diva-prone niece. She was in her element. She glanced at Ivory and Scarlet, who both rolled their eyes.

"Torture," Ivory commented. "Pure torture."

Connie ruffled her hair. "Oh, come on. It'll be fun. How's Darbi holding up?"

"That's why we came to get you. She's a wreck."

"Oh boy. Send in the cavalry."

They galloped toward the hallway together.

Sven strolled into the barn, hoping to catch Bishop in his office. His timing probably wasn't the best with this news, but he didn't want to put it off any longer. If what he planned bore fruit, he needed all the time he could muster between now and the day Connie rejoined the USO tour.

He entered the barn through the back door, and immediately his nostrils were accosted with the smell of horse and leather. He loved the smell. Some days he wondered why he hadn't just joined his brothers in working the family farm, but he loved his work in law. So much so, that what he planned would come as a shock not only to Bishop but to the rest of Brooksville as well.

He spotted Bishop at his desk staring at the large monitor. Rapping on the door with his knuckles, he stepped into the office.

"Good morning, groom-to-be."

Bishop glanced up, an expression of surprise on his face. "What are you doing here so early?"

Sven took a seat across from Bishop. "I've got something I want to talk to you about. I hate to do it on the day of your wedding, but it couldn't wait."

"Who's suing me now?"

Sven laughed. "Nobody."

"Whew." Bishop stared at him. "What's up, then? You look so serious. My lawyer shouldn't be so serious on my wedding day."

"I think you know how I feel about Connie."

Bishop leaned back in his chair. "Well, if the face sucking by the campfire last night was any indication, I think I've figured it out."

Heat climbed from Sven's neck to his cheeks. He cleared his throat. "Yeah, well…"

"What's on your mind, Sven?"

"Did Connie tell you what happened in England right before we came home?"

Bishop nodded. "I wish you had killed the guy."

"Believe me, Logan Richards put a pretty good hurt on him. He'll probably think twice before he tries it again, but it did ruin Connie's chances at doing a record with him."

"Good. I never liked the idea anyway. She's too young and inexperienced to try something like that."

"I'm not sure I agree with you there, but I do have an idea."

Bishop's eyes narrowed. "What kind of idea?"

Sven took a deep breath. *Okay, here goes.*

"I've had numerous conversations with some people in Nashville over the past couple of days. I've done some research, and…" He figured Bishop wouldn't take this well, so he took a moment to gather the right words.

"And what?"

"I'm going to offer to be her agent. I recorded her performance on my phone at the Christmas show in England, and through Trevor's agent, Roger, I've found some record executives willing to listen to the demo. They love her, Bishop. I've got two labels fighting over her already. She doesn't need Trevor Thornton to do this. With me representing her, I'll make sure everything is on the up-and-up."

Bishop stared at him wide eyed and slack-jawed. It took a moment for his friend to find his voice. When he did, the volume nearly lifted the barn rafters. "Are you nuts? Who's going to represent Champion's Gate? I can't function with you traipsing all over the country with my sister, who, by the way, should just stay home and give up this crazy notion of becoming a singer."

Sven waited for the storm to calm then leaned forward placing his elbows on his knees. "Listen to me, Bishop. Your sister has a God-given talent. I wish you could have seen the faces I saw in that crowd. When she sings, something in the air changes. Its magical. People forget their troubles for a while. She literally transports them to a better place."

Bishop's angry expression remained. "Maybe so, but she's too young, Sven. She doesn't have a clue how the world works beyond this ranch."

"She's a lot wiser than you give her credit for. You've taught her a great deal about business and how to deal with people. She has Stan eating out of her hand. She knows how to negotiate. But I agree, she needs someone to guide her. I can do it."

"Sven, seriously? I can't run this ranch without you. Can't you find someone else to do this?"

He shook his head. He understood Bishop's fears, but his mind was made up. "I've been working with Charlie Boyle and even considered making him a partner. He knows a lot about the horse business. He'd be an excellent lawyer for Champions Gate. It's not like we'd be on some remote deserted island. You can still call me, and we can Skype."

Bishop stared at him. Sven knew he'd landed quite a blow, so he just sat there and waited out the silence.

Finally, his best friend spoke. "She's really that good?"

Sven nodded. "She really is, man. I didn't need to do any convincing. Both labels are offering contracts. She'll be set for life if this all works out. Plus, I'll be with her to help keep her safe. I love her, Bishop. I want her to marry me, but I'm not going to rush her."

"Did you give her the honking sapphire?"

"Oh, you noticed it, huh?"

"Uh, yeah. Don't you think you could have asked me first?"

"You don't own her, friend. She's an independent woman who makes up her own mind. She hasn't even said yes, yet, and I don't want to push her. If it's meant to be, she'll come around. She thinks I don't want her to have a singing career, and at first I didn't. But then I saw what she can do to a crowd. It's amazing. She deserves her shot."

Bishop sighed. "I'm not happy about this. Losing you is going to hurt this farm."

"Oh, come on. You know all the right decisions to make. You have for years. I've only been a sounding board and the man who can draw up the legal papers."

"You've been a lot more than that, and you know it."

Sven smiled. He loved this man like a brother. "Thanks, but you know what I mean. Charlie is a good man. He'll do right by you."

"Looks like I don't have much choice."

"No, you don't, really."

Bishop rose and stuck out his hand.

Sven's eyebrows shot up in surprise. "What's this?"

"Welcome to the family, my brother."

"If she'll have me."

"She'd be nuts not to. Especially when she hears this news."

"I'll wait until after the wedding. This is your day, and you and Darbi deserve all the happiness life has to throw at you. I'm so happy for you, Bish."

Sven walked around the desk and grabbed his friend into a big bear hug.

"I'm not sure I'm ready to forgive you for this yet, but I wish you the best. If Connie agrees, you better take extra special good care of her."

"I will. You know it."

Bishop nodded. "I do know it, man."

"Now, let's go get you married."

Connie stood at the makeshift altar under the huge white tent on the lawn of Champions Gate. She gazed over the crowd. All their friends and most of the town of Brooksville sat in their chairs looking back up the aisle in anticipation of the bride.

Bishop beamed as he waited. He looked so handsome in his black tux, his sandy hair just touching the collar of his pristine white shirt. The cranberry bow tie slightly crooked at his neck. She itched to straighten it, but it was too late now.

Sven and Quinton stood beside him along with three additional groomsmen dressed in light gray. Their bow ties were the same cranberry color as Bishop's. She glanced down at the triplets who all but danced in place. Mia and Dusty stood behind them. All the girls and Dusty wore cranberry satin, and Connie as the maid of honor wore a lighter peach-colored gown.

Inside the tent was a bit stuffy, but the day was tailor made for a wedding. The sun shone bright, and a slight breeze stirred the limbs of all the potted Christmas trees lining the aisle Darbi would be come down.

The band began the wedding song, and the crowd rose. There was a slight bend in the path, and, suddenly, Darbi appeared, riding side saddle on the most beautiful Arabian mare Connie had ever seen. Her father led the horse by the bridle, and the entire crowd gasped as they came into full view.

"Where did the horse come from?" she whispered to Scarlett.

"Isn't she beautiful? Dad just bought her for Darbi. He wanted her to have her very own horse. She's called Princess Ebony."

Connie could understand why. The horse's midnight coat gleamed as it stepped up the aisle. Her eyes were brown and calm. The cocoa-colored mane and tail had been braided with white baby's breath and she wore a collar of woven white roses.

Darbi, in her blush-colored gown, looked like a queen. She smiled from ear to ear, her emerald eyes flashing with happiness. Her father held tight to the lead as he led them down to the altar.

The mare remained extremely calm in the face of the music and the murmuring of the crowd. Connie swiped a tear from her eye. What a creative and beautiful way for Darbi to present herself to her new husband.

She snuck a glance at Bishop, and, as she predicted, his mouth hung open in awe. Quinton elbowed him. He closed his mouth then grinned at his bride.

Darbi's father helped her slide out of the saddle, then stood facing the minister and the priest, still holding the horse's lead.

"Who gives this woman to be married to this man?"

Patrick Brennan stuck out his chest, lifted his chin and loudly proclaimed, "I do, sir."

He leaned over and placed a sweet kiss on Darbi's cheek then led the horse to the side of the crowd where a groomsman took her away.

Wow! I never would have dreamed of riding in on a horse. Connie had to fight to control a nervous giggle. Darbi glanced over at her and she gave her friend a quick thumbs up. Darbi grinned. Then her full attention turned to Bishop.

The ministers conducted the service and the couple said their vows. Connie stepped forward to take Darbi's bouquet as they exchanged their rings. Then, before the clergy pronounced them man and wife, Connie handed the bouquets to Scarlet and Violet and sang the wedding song Darbi had chosen. It just happened to be a new song by Trevor Thornton entitled "My One and Only."

As her angelic voice filled the afternoon, she caught a glimpse of Sven smiling broadly at her. Her heart filled with love for the man. She couldn't remember a time when he hadn't been there for her. It occurred to her at this moment she needed to tell him her heart belonged to him.

When she finished singing, a hush fell over the crowd. Many swiped at their eyes with tissues and handkerchiefs. She even heard Bishop sniff. She stepped back into her place and returned the microphone to the priest. He announced Mr. and Mrs. Bishop Champion, and the place erupted with cheers.

Darbi and Bishop walked down the aisle, acknowledging all their well-wishers, and then were followed by each bridesmaid and groomsman couple. The rest of the crowd headed off to another tent for cocktails while the bridal party took some pictures.

Connie couldn't wait to get her hands on the horse. "Oh, Bishop, she's amazing."

He stepped up and patted the mare on the neck. "Gentle as a lamb. When I saw her, I just knew she needed to belong to Darbi."

"Where did you get her?"

"Shiek Abdul shipped her over about a week ago."

"She's from Saudi Arabia?"

Bishop grinned. "Indeed."

"Wow."

Darbi joined them, stroking the horse's cheek. "She's a wonder she is. More gentle than a kitten, but she can run like the wind. I love her almost as much as I love this man." She stood on her toes and kissed her new husband.

Connie grinned. She couldn't be happier for her brother and now sister-in-law. Sven stepped up and wrapped an arm around her. He leaned down and kissed her cheek.

"You look amazing."

Heat rose in her cheeks. "You don't look so bad yourself."

"The song? Oh wow. I've never heard you sing more beautifully."

For some reason, those few words of praise meant more to her than anything else he could have said at that moment.

Darbi quickly agreed. "Oh, Connie. I was completely gobsmacked. You sing it better than that snake of a country singer. I refuse to even say his name. I'm sorry it was one of his songs, but ya sang it beautifully."

"I'm glad you liked it. You both deserve every happiness."

The photographer shouted at the wedding party to come together, and, for the next hour, Connie was consumed with modeling. She loved every minute of it. The photos were going to be gorgeous. She especially loved the one of

Bishop, Darbi, and the girls with Princess Ebony. She definitely wanted a copy.

"Here." Sven handed her his cell.

"Aw. You are the best man ever." She glanced at the photo he'd just snapped with his cell phone. Now she wouldn't have to wait for the wedding photographer to send Darbi the prints.

"Have I ever told you I think you're the most thoughtful man in the world?"

"No, but you can say it again."

She laughed. "You're the most thoughtful man in the world."

He swept her into his arms and kissed her.

After photos, the wedding party joined the rest of the guests for a full sit-down dinner complete with champagne toasts and dancing. The food, catered from a company all the way from Tampa, was fabulous. The DJ had the best personality and before long the entire group crowded the makeshift dance floor. They did every dance from the electric slide to the boot scootin' boogie.

Connie plopped into a chair and blew out a breath. "Oh man, I'm worn out."

Sven sat beside her, watching the couples still gyrating to the music. "I agree. Looks like some people are starting to say their goodbyes."

Connie twisted Sven's wrist to glance at his watch. "No wonder. Its nearly eleven. We've been at this all day."

"Yeah, but it's been great. We couldn't have ordered better weather. And Darbi and Bishop look so happy."

"I'm sure they're thrilled they finally get to share the master bedroom."

Sven laughed then reached for her hand. "Come on. I want to show you something."

He led her away from the festivities and around back to the barn and Bishop's office.

"Where are we going?" Curiosity filled her. "If you wanted to neck, we could have gone to the house."

He chuckled. "Oh, I'm planning on getting in a good bit of necking, but I wanted to show you something first."

"Okay." She followed him into Bishop's domain at the back of the barn.

"Sit down, please."

She drew her brows together as she sat in one of the wing back chairs across from Bishop's desk.

He reached for an envelope then sat in the chair opposite her. "I just couldn't wait to see what you thought of this." He opened the envelope and pulled out a stack of papers. "I've been doing a lot of thinking since I met you in England. I watched those soldiers and their families listen to you sing, and something just told me I had to do whatever I could to ensure more people could experience what you have to offer."

What the heck is he talking about?

"Remember when you asked me what Roger and I were discussing so much?"

She nodded, really curious now.

"I did some research, and I'd like to present a proposal to you." He handed her the document.

She read the first page and nearly dropped the paperwork. "What is this, Sven?"

"What does it look like?"

"It looks like a contract for you to be my agent, but I don't understand."

Sven reached for her hand. "I want to do this, Connie. You need someone to protect you and make sure you aren't taken advantage of ever again. I want to be that person. I want to travel with you, book your gigs, whatever the lingo is. I've already spoken to two record labels, and they both want to sign you."

She did drop the papers then. "What?" The word was more breath than spoken. She swallowed. "What did you say?"

"I recorded you at the Christmas show, and when we got back to the States, I used some of Roger's contacts and sent them your demo. Both Monumental Records and RCA want to sign you. Personally, I think your best bet is Monumental."

Connie stared at him. She couldn't believe her ears. When had he done this complete turnaround from not wanting her to have a music career to wanting to be her agent? She couldn't wrap her mind around it.

"But…what about Champions Gate? Bishop needs you here."

"I've already talked to him. I'll have Charlie work with him. I still have a phone. It's not like I can't do both, but he knows I'll be pretty absorbed in getting your career started."

She couldn't speak. What he offered her blew her mind. He was willing to sacrifice everything for her. Her heart exploded with love for this man. She never dreamed she could have her career and Sven, too.

"Why?" It was the only word she could manage.

He knelt before her. "Because I love you. Your gift is too amazing to not share it with the world. And I want you to have every advantage and not get screwed in the process. I know I don't know much about the music industry, but I can learn. We can learn together. I'm sure we'll make some mistakes along the way, but if you'll trust me, I'll make sure you reach the stars."

Tears spilled from her eyes. She knew at this moment what she wanted in life. For a man to sacrifice his own career to help her achieve her dreams, that was love.

"Sven, are you sure?"

"Positive."

He reached down and retrieved the contract from the floor. He spread it out on the desk then reached for a pen.

"Let's do this together, Connie."

"What about the USO tour?"

"You can finish it if you want. Both record companies said they would wait."

"Wrynn's going to crap a brick."

He laughed.

She took the pen in her trembling hand and signed. Then she put the pen on the desk, turned, and threw herself into his lap. "I love you."

He almost dumped her in the floor.

"What?"

She planted kisses all over his face. "I love you, I love you, I love you."

Sven gathered her as close as her gown would allow. "Look at me, Connie."

She held his gaze, her entire body vibrating with her overwhelming sense of how right he was for her.

"I need to know one thing."

She smiled, knowing his mind. "I fell in love with you years ago. I may not have known what the feeling was, but now I do. I didn't say so before now because I didn't know how I would make it work if you didn't want me to have a singing career. I have to do this, Sven. God wants me to do this. And—"

"I know. I also know He wants me to be a part of it. I love you, Connie." He reached down and grabbed her left hand in his. The sapphire winked in the dim light. "Be my wife."

"Yes, Sven. I'll be your wife."

Thank you for reading *A Champion's Hero*, Book Two in the Champions Gate series. Keep following the Champion clan as you learn the Dusty and Quinton, in *Gates of Honor*, Book Three; and if you missed the story of Darbi and Bishop check out *Winning A Champion's Heart*, Book One.

For an exciting pre-view of *Gates of Honor*, read on for Chapter One.

Authors thrive on reviews. Please take a moment to leave yours.

Kelly Abell

Gates of Honor

Book Three

Champions Gate

A Small Town Romance Series

Kelly Abell

Gates of Honor
Chapter One

Dusty Carmichael stretched out her slim legs, propping her sneaker-clad feet on the wooden coffee table. She pointed the remote at the huge wide-screen TV hanging above the stone fireplace in the den of Darbi and Bishop's home at Champions Gate Horse Ranch. A glance at the clock told her the movie she planned to watch was starting in five minutes. Just enough time to pop some popcorn.

As she ambled toward the kitchen, she glanced out the floor-to-ceiling windows in the family room, meeting her reflection against the dark of night. Her favorite pair of pajamas, long black T-shirt and black yoga pants, nearly blended with the gloom. The triplets and Mia had gone to bed around nine, still exhausted from all the shenanigans at their father's wedding to their former nanny.

It was a beautiful wedding. Having it on the ranch was the best idea ever. The grounds were so pretty, still decorated for Christmas. And Quinton looked so handsome… No! No! No!

Dusty opened the cabinet door, snatched the box of popcorn, then banged it shut. "I will not think of that man again tonight. Seeing him at the wedding and ignoring him was hard enough. I won't give him another moment's thought."

She tossed the popcorn bag into the microwave, slammed the door, then pushed the buttons on the timer. As often as she'd been in the Champion kitchen, she never failed to marvel at its vastness and beauty. For years, she sat at the bar, watching Connie Champion prepare meals for her brother's family. The white-tile backsplash behind the gourmet stove, the marble countertops swirled in gray, black, and white, and the stainless-steel appliances were as familiar to her as the tiny kitchen in her small bungalow closer to town.

Pushing thoughts of the stubborn cowboy and partner to Bishop aside, she forced herself to relax. Perhaps a glass of wine with her popcorn would help. She opened the fridge and grabbed an already open bottle left over from the wedding celebration. She poured herself a large glass, nearly to the brim. She doubted the beverage would be enough to force Quinton Gates from her mind, but she'd give it her best shot.

The timer dinged, and the aroma of buttered corn filled the kitchen. After finding a large plastic bowl in one of the cupboards, she dumped in the treat. Gathering her wine and the bowl to her chest like precious treasure, she shuffled back to the family room to settle in and watch her movie.

She sat on the couch and sighed, releasing months of pent-up of tension. Dusty, a social worker for Hernando County, had been at her wits' end to find a family for Mia when her former foster mother refused to have a girl in "the family way" in her house. She was so grateful Darbi had stepped up. Not only did Mia live with Bishop, Darbi, and the triplets, but she also had a job in the Champions Gate stables, helping out with riding classes. Mia loved the work.

Dusty had not been by recently to check on her, so being at the wedding had been a great chance to catch up with the girl. She appeared to be as normal and well-adjusted as any pregnant girl could be. She smiled thinking of the teen who was six months into an unexpected pregnancy but appeared happier than the day Dusty met her.

Not wanting to cloud her mind with any more worry, Dusty curled her legs under her on the couch, settled the bowl of popcorn in her lap, and set her wine glass close by on the end table next to the sofa. She focused her attention on the screen and was twenty minutes into her movie when a sudden tapping on the window startled her. The bowl of popcorn shot into the air and bounced on the couch sending kernels flying.

Stifling a curse, she jerked toward the window. Quinton grinned on the other side of the glass.

"I'm going to kick your butt," she yelled at the window, shaking her fist. "Go ahead and come in since you've scared me to death."

He is the last person I want to see tonight, but I should have expected he'd show up. As soon as Darbi and Bishop left this morning, I've been on edge looking for him, and now…here he is.

She stood, sweeping popcorn from the couch into the bowl then stooping to pick the pieces up off the floor. The back door opened and closed, and Quinton entered the kitchen, chuckling.

"I'm sorry. I didn't mean to scare you." He stood facing her, hands in his pockets, keys jingling.

She glared at him. "Oh, sure you didn't. You wouldn't be laughing if you hadn't done it on purpose."

He glanced at the television. "Ooh, *Pet Sematary*. I love that movie. No wonder you jumped a mile. Are the girls in bed?"

She nodded, marching into the kitchen to dump the popcorn in the trash and pop a fresh bowl. "Been in bed about an hour. They're exhausted. So am I, so I won't let you stay too long."

He stepped into the family room, cleaning up the last of the kernels. "I should have brought Scout. He'd have cleaned up all the popcorn for you."

She snorted then placed another packet into the microwave, pressed some buttons. "You might as well sit down."

He threw away the few kernels she'd missed and sat on the sofa. "Wow, some wedding, huh?"

Dusty smiled. As frustrated as she was with him, she had to agree it had been the most beautiful wedding she'd ever attended. "Darbi coming in on her horse was a stroke of genius. Whose idea was it?"

"I don't know. I thought it was yours."

"Nope. I found the dress, but the entrance was all Darbi, I guess." She retrieved the snack from the microwave and dumped it into the bowl. She smoothed down her T-shirt then clutched the bowl close.

I should have known he'd drop by. Thank God I'm wearing black and nothing see-through.

She sat on the opposite end of the couch, putting a few of the fluffy throw pillows between them.

"Whatcha doin' way over there?" He patted the cushion next to him. "I can't reach the popcorn."

"Who said I planned to share it with you?"

He pasted on a sad puppy expression, poking out his bottom lip. "Please?"

Crap, why does he have to look so cute? So much for my steel magnolia resistance.

She pushed the pillows onto the floor and scooted over next to him.

" Much better." He placed an arm around her shoulders.

She stiffened. The last thing she wanted was to get cozy. She still hadn't fully executed her plan to make him appreciate her more. Darbi had suggested she step away from Quinton since he didn't seem to recognize how much she loved him, nor did he appear to return her love. As many times as she'd hinted, he still treated her like a little sister. The thought made her blood boil.

"Dusty, what's wrong? You barely spoke to me at the wedding. You didn't even dance with me."

Tears stung the back of her eyes, and she blinked them away. She refused to let him see her cry. How dumb could he be?

"You haven't been around for weeks. Has work been so busy? I know you were upset about the little boy being killed. Did the county do anything to the judge?"

Okay, work is a safe enough topic. I can talk about it without smacking his face.

"Of course not. They did an investigation, even brought in the Bar Association, but he's back on the bench. And probably really pissed at me. I hope I don't need a ruling in my favor for a while…if he ever gets over this."

Quinton tightened his arm around her shoulders. "You did the right thing. I can't believe he wasn't at least suspended or something. He knew the mother and father weren't stable. Your reports would have spelled that out."

"Brother on the Board of the Bar, remember?"

Quinton sighed. "Oh yeah, you mentioned it."

"At least the sheriff believed me, and the parents are going to trial. I can get a little solace from that."

"I'm sorry, babe. I know you're torn up. I've never seen you so upset."

Dusty sniffed. "Their baby boy shouldn't have died. I hope they both serve life sentences for what they did."

Quinton reached out with a finger to lift her chin up, forcing her to look at him. She wanted to turn away, but his brown eyes held her gaze. She loved this man with all her soul, and the fact he couldn't see it devastated her.

He leaned in to kiss her...

"Dusty!" Mia's screech emanated from the bedrooms upstairs.

Dusty jumped to her feet, dropping the bowl of popcorn as she did so. She ran for the stairs, Quinton right behind her. She dashed down the hall and into Mia's room, flipping on the light as she did.

The teen sat in the middle of her bed, wearing a pair of Winnie the Pooh pajamas. The sheets were thrown back, and a small amount of blood stained her yellow pants and the bed.

"Something's wrong. My stomach hurts really bad, and I'm bleeding. Oh God, is the baby going to die?" Her voice was shrill, her blue eyes wide in distress.

"Quinton go call 911."

"Nah, it will take too long. Let's get her into my truck and run her to the hospital."

Would it be okay to move her? Dusty didn't know. But he had a point. They lived at least fifteen miles outside of the town proper. The time it would take the ambulance to get here and back to the hospital would take longer than if they just drove straight there.

"Go get your truck, I'll help Mia get downstairs."

Quinton tossed his keys at Dusty. "You go get the truck. I'll carry her down." He scooped up the girl, bed sheets and all, and started for the door.

By this time, the triplets had awoken and appeared in the hallway.

"We heard a scream. What's going on?" Ivory stood, blurry-eyed with her arms around her sisters—three wide-eyed, blonde ten-year-olds.

"Something's wrong with Mia. Grab your shoes, we're going to the hospital."

They moved like lightning, dashing back to their room, chattering along the way.

Dusty ran down the stairs, slid her feet into sandals, then opened the front door. She flew down the path, past the barns to Quinton's property. She opened the truck, dove into the driver's seat, and started the engine. Gravel spun from the wheels as she backed up to turn around. She spotted Scout barking on the porch. She rolled the window down and shouted for the dog to stay.

She drove to the driveway at the front of the house. Quinton was already standing there with Mia wrapped in his arms. The triplets stood with him, all eyes on their new friend.

Dusty shot a prayer skyward Mia wasn't losing this baby. It was horrible enough for the girl to be pregnant at this age, but who knew what the trauma of a miscarriage might do?

Scarlet opened the passenger door for Quinton, and he slid in with Mia. She shut the door then clambered into the back seat with Ivory and Violet.

Dusty roared down the driveway. Before she pulled out onto the road, she glanced at the teen. The dim light of the streetlamp revealed the fear in Mia's pale face.

"It's going to be okay."
Dusty prayed her words were true.

ABOUT THE AUTHOR

Kelly Abell is a romance author who writes characters with passion, power and purpose. Her aim is to write about gripping characters in tense situations that keep a reader turning the pages.

She also spends a great deal of time helping other writers through her Writing Tips on her website, teaching writing workshops in her local community, and as a member of the Florida Writer's Association.

She lives in Florida with her family.

Visit Kelly's website for the more information about her and her other titles
www.kellyabellbooks.com

Connect with Kelly on Facebook

Twitter @kellyabellbooks

CPSIA information can be obtained
at www.ICGtesting.com
Printed in the USA
BVHW080124090919
557876BV00014BA/1861/P